MW00618650

TYRANT

(KING BOOK TWO)

T.M. Frazier

Copyright © 2015 T.M. FRAZIER
Print Edition
ISBN: 978-1682304723
All rights reserved

This is a work of fiction. Names, characters, businesses, places, events and incidents are either the products of the author's imagination or used in a fictitious manner. Any resemblance to actual persons, living or dead, or actual events, is purely coincidental.

Acknowledgements

I want to thank my readers for being as excited to read more of King and Doe's story as I was to write it. Every message, every review, every single comment about how much you love them keeps me motivated to write more.

Thank you to Karla, for being your lovely charming self as always. (SARCASM)

Thanks to Vanessa and Manda at Prema Editing for taking me on at the last possible second and talking me off a bridge. You ladies have been a pleasure to work with and I look forward to tackling new projects with you.

Thank you to the agent that has taken me on and all the baggage that comes with me. You are so fantastic and I couldn't ask for anyone better to deal with my crazy. Kimberly Brower you are a literary agent MACHINE!

Thank you to all who have shared the love for King and Doe on social media; authors, bloggers, readers, friends, and family. I love all of you and appreciate everything you do for me and my books.

Thank you to everyone who has left a review for King, good or bad, on Amazon. Taking the time to leave a review means the world to an author.

Thank you to Jodi, you beautiful British twat, I love your face. Thanks to Aurora Rose Reynolds for being a great friend and support system. Thanks to Milasy and Lisa over at The Rock Stars of Romance for knowing how to represent a release right! Thanks to Aestas for speaking up when you find a book you love so others can love it too!

Thank you to Julie Vaden for your support. For being a

great beta-reader and for doing the work of an employee without a single one of the benefits. You are a rock star to me. Love you.

Thank you to my parents, Anne & Paul, for all that you do for me and for others. Every day I realize more and more how extremely lucky I am to have parents like you.

Thank you to my husband. I cannot express my gratitude to you enough. Some days I wonder why you love me so much. You make every single day an easy one to exist in. Thank you for taking good care of me, and not just with every day things so I can write, but for taking good care of my heart too. I know it will always be safe with you.

Thank you to baby Frazier. I've done nothing in this life to deserve you or your father, but I promise I will try each and every day to be worthy of you. Mommy loves you to the moon and back.

Dedication

For my Popop.
And for everyone who has to live each day
without the love of their lives by their side.

When the love of your life passes on,
the person may be gone,
but the love rages on.
−T.M. FRAZIER

Prologue

KING

THE AVERAGE TIME spent between incarcerations for a career criminal is six months.

I'd only been out three.

I'd expected to find Max in that car. Instead, cold metal clinked around my wrists, and the asshole pig had the audacity to laugh when he tightened the cuffs to the point of pain.

I didn't wince, though. I wouldn't give him the satisfaction. He pressed down on my head roughly and shoved me hard into the back of the old police cruiser. I landed on my side, and my cheek slammed against the sticky seat. It smelled like vomit and bad decisions. My hands tingled from the loss of blood flow.

The motherfucker was lucky I was in cuffs.

Three years. They already had me for three fucking years, and they were going to have me for a whole lot longer.

Kidnapping wasn't exactly rewarded with a light slap on the wrist, especially for someone whose record was as long as mine. I promised I was never going back, but keeping my promises is just another thing I was never very good at.

I was all out of fucks to give though. The system could have me. I belonged to them, but they didn't fucking own me. They would NEVER fucking own me.

She owned me.

Heart and black fucking soul.

I will walk to the fucking chow line with a shit-eating grin on my face wearing my scratchy orange jumpsuit every mother-fucking day. I will play cards with the worst of the worst and make nice with the guards who are willing to cut me some slack. At night, when I'm alone in my windowless cell with my dick in my hand, I will remember what it was like to have her in my bed; how her innocent wide eyes stared up at me as I moved inside her. The way she arched her back into me as I made her come over and over again.

I kept telling myself I didn't have anything to offer her, but that wasn't true.

I had love.

Pup. Doe. Ray. Whatever the fuck her name was. I loved her more than what was normal, rational, or sane, and I would gladly rot in fucking prison with a smile on my face if I knew my girl was going to be okay.

But I didn't know that. I couldn't know that.

I should have known that motherfucker was going to fucking cross me.

"The notorious Brantley King," the pig said with a smirk as he got into the front seat. The plastic-like leather squeaked against his belt as he closed his door and started the engine. "You'd think you'd have learned your lesson by now, boy."

He laughed and shook his head. It was obvious this guy was getting some sort of sick pleasure out of being the one to put me in cuffs.

"King," I corrected him defiantly. Nobody called me Brantley but her.

"Excuse me?" he asked, raising an eyebrow at me through the rearview mirror.

I sat up straight, meeting his gaze with mine, as if I were staring straight through to his pussy-ass soul. "They call me King, motherfucker."

The rage inside me grew to epic proportions. That's when I noticed the detective didn't turn onto the main road but instead drove straight onto the path through the woods.

This guy was no fucking cop. I spotted his gun; he'd set it on the dash. It was a Judge, not the kind of gun that was standard police-issue. This guy wasn't taking to me jail.

He was taking me to ground.

There was no time to waste.

My girls needed me.

More than that, I needed them.

The moron had cuffed me in front. That should've been my first indicator that something was off. A real cop would've never done that unless he was transporting a nonviolent criminal.

Which wasn't me.

Using the chain that connected my cuffs, I trapped the fake detective's neck against the headrest and yanked back with all my might until I felt like my biceps were going to explode.

His hands left the wheel and flailed about as he tried to connect with my head, but I dodged him by lowering myself behind the seat.

The car veered off the path and bounced from side to side as it ran over a patch of knee-high roots.

The pressure mounted behind my eyes as I tugged back on the cuffs, squeezing tighter and tighter. I didn't release my hold until the car came crashing to a stop and every inch of life had drained from his body.

The fake cop was right; I would never be anything more than the notorious Brantley King.

That was fine by me because the senator had a lesson to learn. You did not take what was mine and not expect to pay in blood, sweat, or pussy.

He took my girl. He wanted to take my life.

His payment would be in blood.

Chapter One

KING

REVENGE IS SWEET.

That's what they say anyway. But it wasn't until I crawled out of the wreckage, picking shards of glass from my skin, that I realized how true that saying really was.

I could practically taste the revenge on my tongue, I was salivating in anticipation of the moment I would be able to unstrap a belt from my arm and wrap it around the senator's fucking neck for crossing me.

It had only been minutes since I'd killed a man.

But it had been a long time since I'd taken pleasure in it.

Adrenaline like I'd never known, in an amount great enough to wake a corpse, coursed through my veins.

I was high on it.

I fed off of it.

It was like I'd pushed my nose into a bowl of blow and inhaled over and over until I felt like I was invincible.

A motherfucking god.

And until I fixed the fucking mess I'd made, I wasn't planning on coming down. I felt sorry for any motherfucker who had big enough balls to try and stand in my fucking way.

That was the moment I'd first heard it.

Him.

Preppy.

"Time to show those cock suckers they fucked with the wrong kid from the wrong side of the motherfucking trailer park." Preppy's voice was as clear to me in my head as if he stood beside me.

I was going fucking insane.

By the time I'd crawled out from the woods and made my way back to the house Bear was just getting off of his bike. When he saw me, he tossed his cigarette to the ground. He marched toward me with hard, angry steps; his forehead creased with lines, his fists clenched. The dry grass crunched under his heavy steps. "Listen, motherfucker, I didn't want it to come to blows, but the way you fucking handled that shit just ain't fucking right. She deserves better than that, better than this, better than to be fucking lied..." Bear stopped when he saw the mud and blood I was covered in. "What the fuck happened to you?"

I pushed past him, ignoring his question, running toward the house, taking the steps three at a time. I threw open the front door so hard, the screws from the top hinge shot out and clanked down onto the deck. "Pup!" I called out. A small part of me held out hope that somehow she had found a way to stay. But the second I entered the house I didn't have to search the rooms to know she was gone. I felt the emptiness. "Fuck!" I roared, picking up one of the kitchen chairs. I launched it across the room, where it skipped over the glass coffee table, cracking it down the center, punching a basketball-sized hole in the thin drywall as it came crashing to a halt.

Bear followed me into the house. "Are you going to tell me what happened or you gonna tear the fucking house up some more?" I moved passed him on my way to the garage. I needed my bike and some provisions.

The kind of provision that required bullets.

"Nothing a fucking body bag couldn't fix."

One handcuff was still locked on me, the other end was open and dangling from my wrist, the chain stained with the fake cop's blood. As soon as that fucker was dead and the car crashed against the tree I'd pulled myself over into the front seat. Thank fucking God the handcuff keys were still in that fuckers pocket. "I see that," Bear said. "Where the fuck is Doe?" There was a protective tone in his voice, which rubbed me the wrong fucking way, but I'd deal with that later.

After I got my girl back.

"The good senator fucked me over. There was no Max. And the last time I saw Pup, she was kicking and screaming as I was being carted away by a guy hired to take me out." The image of her struggling in the senator's grip made me see red. "Make a few calls," I clipped. "Find out where he might be taking her."

"Fuck," Bear said. Instead of pulling out his phone he bent over and rested his hands on his knees.

"What the fuck now?"

Bear pinched the bridge of his nose. "There was a reason why I came back here, man. Besides to kick your ass for fucking shit up with Doe. I'm thinking that before you solve this problem with a spray of bullets, you should probably know that it might not have been the senator who was trying to put you to ground," he said, standing up straight and leaning up against the wall where he lit a cigarette.

"What the fuck is that supposed to mean? He was the one who had the guy arrest me. Of course it was him."

Bear shook his head. "He's a problem, but he's not our only problem. Rage called not twenty minutes ago, and as you know, that fucker's got eyes and ears everywhere. Word is that the shit that went down with Isaac isn't over. Far fucking from it." He ran his hand through his hair and the ash from his cigarette fell to the carpet.

"I made that fucker's head explode myself. Looked pretty over to me," I argued.

"No, not Isaac. He's fucking worm food, but someone who's fucking pissed about Isaac not being able to continue selling his shit in Florida on account of him being dead. Someone who ain't afraid to kill entire families to get to the people who wronged him."

I stiffened, knowing exactly who he was talking about. "Eli."

"Yeah man," Bear confirmed. "And if I was a betting man I'd put my money on it being Eli wanting to take you out over daddy dearest."

Eli Mitchell was who Isaac had filtered his drug money up to. Well, he did until me, Preppy, and Bear ended him and most of his crew. With his thick rimmed black glasses and his short stature, no one would never think the guy was capable of half the shit he did on a daily basis.

When you wanted to scare a rabbit out of a hole you sent in a smoke bomb. Eli's version of a smoke bomb was killing anyone you've ever loved until you showed yourself and he could finally kill you too.

"The intel I'm getting says Eli's still in Miami, but he's making a move, and soon. The MC is on lockdown, afraid of the blowback. Pops is pissed as fucking hell."

"First Isaac and now fucking Eli," I said. "Can't catch a fucking break. Sometimes I feel like I would have been better off staying locked-up."

"I feel ya, man. Same here. This isn't just biker shit anymore. This is cartel shit. Bigger, badder...deader," Bear said. "And I can't put Grace on lockdown. I know she's more a mom to you than your cunt of a mother ever was, but Pop's ass is all sorts of chapped lately. He don't want no one in the MC bringing civilians into the club, especially during lockdown, but we need to find somewhere safe for her to stay for a while." Bear looked up at me and as he spoke, I realized what he was trying to tell me. "I ain't got anyone close enough to me that warrants killing, who isn't in the MC, but you sure as shit do."

Pup.

"Fuck!" I shouted, realizing I couldn't bring her home. I turned and punched the wall, making a dent clear through the drywall to the cement stucco on the outside of the house. Pain shot up the bones in my arm all the way to my shoulder, but pain was a better feeling than the feeling lying just underneath it. The feeling of failure. "It's my fault Prep's dead. Should have never let him start the Granny Growhouse shit. Should have…" I ran my hand over my hair. There was too much to list. Happiness, sadness, and regret filled every inch of space within the last few months of my life. There was so much I would go back and change. I thought all that was missing from my life was Max. But now it was Max, Pup…Preppy.

And no matter what I did, who I killed, Prep was never coming back.

"What's the plan, man?" Bear asked.

"We're going to get to him before he can get to us…tonight," I said, cracking my knuckles. The time for a pity party was over. I had more people to kill.

"Ballsy move, man."

"Maybe, but I have to find out where Pup is first. I may not be able to get her the fuck out of there, but I have to get to her. Tell her what's going on."

Bear nodded. "I can find out where she is. Get her a message to her," he offered.

I shook my head. "No, this message needs to be delivered personally. It's the only way she'll listen."

"I can understand that, 'cause if I were her, I'd want to chop your fucking balls off by now," Bear said. I flashed him a look to remind him he was stepping close to the edge of whatever patience I had left. "I'll find out where she is," Bear mumbled, pulling his phone from his pocket. He stubbed his cigarette out into the ashtray on the windowsill and lit another one. "All this shit, it's fucking ballsy, man. You got a head injury or something?"

I stepped onto the deck and leaned over the railing, breathing in the salty night air. "Yeah, as I matter of fact, I do. I suffer from the same condition Pup does."

"And what's that?" Bear asked, following me out and leaning up sideways against the railing.

"We both forgot who the fuck we were."

Bear dialed a few numbers; I could hear the ringing through the speaker as he held it up to his ear. "You remembering now?"

"Yeah, I'm remembering now."

"And who exactly are you?" Bear asked.

"I'm the fucking bad guy."

Chapter Two

DOE

S HOCK.
Mouth gaping. Can't find the words. Overwhelming. Stunned.

But *shock* was the word that best describes how I felt in that car.

I had a million questions and couldn't find my voice to ask a single one.

And I certainly couldn't bring myself to make nice with the two men who called themselves family. They were just strangers, who, when I wouldn't go with them willingly, brought out the big gun.

A little boy with blond curls and icy blue eyes that matched mine.

A little boy who'd called me Mommy.

My life since waking up without my memory has been a cluster-fuck of unbelievable events strung together in one monstrous knot. Every time I was stupid enough to think I could untangle it, the knot just wound tighter, until it consumed every ounce of available space around me, wrapping itself around the potential for anything good to result from my being alive.

Strangling it to death.

It was shitty of them to bring the boy. It was only because of him that I sat in stunned silence, unable to ask my usual million questions. Too afraid to scare him or say the wrong thing and traumatize him for life.

The silence in that Town Car was deafening; so quiet that I'm sure if you listened close enough, you could actually hear my state of shock. The sound of the tires spinning against the asphalt as we accelerated onto the highway was a welcome reprieve.

The man who claimed to be my father sat in the front passenger seat. Everything about him was stiff and hard as stone. His suit hadn't a single wrinkle or sweat stain, and despite the heat and humidity, he'd kept his suit jacket on. I was beginning to think that the suit was its own living, breathing entity. It was too damn perfect. I wouldn't have been surprised if there was a small wrinkled alien living in the sleeves, controlling the senator/suit being.

A phone vibrated in the front seat. "PRICE." The senator barked into the receiver. After a few seconds of mumbling into the phone, he reached overhead and pressed a button, closing the blacked out partition, separating the front seat from the back.

I sat in the back on one side of the bench seat, a small child's body length away from the boy who'd introduced himself as Tanner.

My boyfriend?

No *HER* boyfriend.

"You know…," Tanner said to me in a whisper, a mischievous look in his chestnut eyes. "…he's the very reason they stopped calling the thing you say when you answer the phone a 'greeting.'" I forced a small smile and Tanner went back to staring out the window.

For most of the hour-long ride, when I knew he wasn't looking, I stared at Tanner's profile and willed my broken brain to scroll through its lost Rolodex, hoping to locate the card that listed Tanner and what my feelings were for him.

Tanner was good-looking in that fresh-faced toothpaste commercial kind of way. But all I kept thinking when I looked at him was that he seemed...nice. And even though he was my age, he was still just a boy.

Which was one word I could never use to describe...him.

I couldn't bring myself to think about him just yet. I didn't want to. It was all too much to process. King's betrayal, his arrest. I couldn't process it. But when I looked over at Tanner again, I couldn't help but make a comparison. Where Tanner was clean skin and sunshine, tall and lean like his body was built by swimming laps in a pool, King was tanned and tattooed with a constant thunderstorm in his eyes. His muscular body looked as if it were built by wrestling with the devil himself.

When I wasn't staring at Tanner, I knew he was looking at me because I felt his stare burning a hole in my cheek. But every time I turned my head his way he averted his eyes and pretended to be interested in something out the window.

And then there was the little boy.

The fact that I could be a mother was completely ridiculous. Unbelievable at best.

But oddly enough, he was the only thing in that car I felt sure about.

My father, my boyfriend, my son. The Town Car was filled with my supposed family, and yet, with the exception of the little one, every fiber of my being was telling me my family was getting further and further away with every mile we drove.

KING.

Maybe it was all a lie. Every single bit of it. King had told me he loved me. Maybe that was a lie too. I didn't know what I could believe anymore.

Don't just be alive. Live. He'd told me.

So I lived.

And I loved.

The anger I'd been feeling toward King for lying to me had temporarily fallen away the second I saw the look of disappointment cross over his face when he realized Max wasn't in that car. And then when the detective put him in cuffs, all I felt was blinding rage.

I wanted to fight for him. I wanted to be the one to give him his daughter back. I wanted to give him everything in my power, but all I could do was watch the horrible scene that unfolded in front of me, paralyzed in the arms of the senator as they hauled King away. My insides felt like they were being squeezed to death as King was shoved into the detective's car and carted back to a windowless cell somewhere.

I meant it when I'd told the senator that King had saved me. And I didn't mean the times he'd saved me from Ed or even from Isaac.

I meant when he'd saved me from myself.

I never expected to fall in love with King. My captor, my tormentor, my lover, my friend, my world.

But I did.

The boy on my lap stirred, his little breaths warmed my skin through my shirt where his nose was pressed tightly against my stomach.

I had questions. So many questions that my head was ringing worse than when Nikki had shot me. I wanted to shout them out rapidly like rounds from a machine gun, but I didn't want to scare the chubby cheeked boy whose eyelashes touched his cheeks while he slept. I ran my fingers through his soft curly hair and he sighed with sleepy contentment.

"I can't believe it's you, Ray. I thought I would never see you again and here you are sitting next to me. Do you remember me yet? Or him? Or anything?" Tanner asked tentatively. My eyes darted up to meet the only thing I remembered from my past life; the beautiful chestnut colored eyes from my dream.

I shook my head. "Just your eyes. I dreamt about them. Once," I admitted.

"So you dreamt about me, huh?" Tanner wagged his eyebrows suggestively. He nudged my shoulder with his elbow and I shifted away from the unfamiliar contact. "Sorry," he said when he saw me stiffen. "Habit."

"It's okay," I offered, although I wasn't sure if it really was okay. "I need to ask you about him though."

Tanner looked lovingly down at the boy. "Ask away."

"I mean, how old is he? You said I'm eighteen. When did all this happen? How?"

"How?" Tanner laughed nervously. "Well, Ray, when a man and woman love each other…" He paused when he saw I wasn't smiling. "Sorry. I'm so used to joking around with you. You're kind of the only one who gets my jokes, or at least you used to." Tanner ran his hand through his curls and sighed. He pulled at the stitching on the leather seat.

The car pulled to a stop in front of a large three-story house, with bright pink stucco. Tall twisting columns lined the front porch which was full of pink plastic flamingos and garden gnomes in various sizes. The long driveway was cut into lines that mimicked fans and was also painted the same garish shade of pink. The lawn was littered with more plastic flamingos. Concrete fountains, at least thirty, all in different styles were scattered around the yard.

"This is me," Tanner said, opening the door. He picked the little boy off my lap and my heart constricted.

"Wait, where are you going?" I asked, suddenly feeling panicked.

"He's had a long day. He used to spend most nights at your place but he's been staying with me since you've been gone," Tanner said. And although I didn't remember the little boy I couldn't help but feel disappointed he wasn't coming with me. Tanner must have sensed my disappointment, because he added, "But I promise, I will come by soon. Go and get settled in, then we'll talk more."

The senator emerged from the passenger seat.

"Wait!" I called out. Tanner turned back around. "What's his name?" I pointed to the boy whose cheek was pressed up against Tanner's shoulder, and although he had been jostled around quite a bit, he remained sound asleep.

Tanner smiled. "Samuel."

My heart fell out of my chest.

Samuel.

Preppy's name was Samuel.

"But we call him Sammy," Tanner said.

"Tanner," the senator said dismissively. He took the seat next to me in the back. Instantly the contempt that had been temporarily put on the back burner for the sake of Sammy was back with a vengeance, and as we pulled back out onto the road, I launched my questions. "Why did you have King arrested?" I asked, unable to hide the bitterness in my voice. "He took me in. Gave me a place to stay. Before him, I was living on the streets, struggling to find protection, or food. My only friend was a homeless hooker who thought I was the pitiful one!"

The senator didn't flinch hearing my tale of woe, nor did he seem affected in any way, for that matter. Instead, he adjusted a cufflink and clicked away on his phone. "Brantley King is a felon, a con man, and a murderer," he stated, without looking up. "Whatever relationship you seem to think the two of you had was a farce. A barely legal one at that. I really was hoping that when he indicated that the two of you had been…intimate, that he was just baiting me, but I see now that he was indeed speaking the truth. That *man* came to me with the sole purpose of using you as a pawn to get what he wanted. Nothing more. He took advantage of you, a teenager, and tried to con me. Now he's going where he belongs, and getting what he deserves, and that is the last I want to hear about that, young lady."

"He just wanted his daughter back," I argued, crossing my arms over my chest. He might've thought he effectively ended the conversation but tough shit.

"We don't always get what we want," the senator said flatly. His words echoed in my brain as if I'd heard him say them before. "Besides, I don't know what kind of power he seemed to think a senator has. The most I could've done for him would've been to write him a letter of recommendation to the family court. Maybe make a call to Judge Fletcher if he's still on the bench over there."

"Then why did you make the deal!? Take me back," I demanded. "I don't even know you. Take me back!" I yelled reaching for the door, not caring that the car was back in motion and barreling down the road. I pushed on the handle and opened the door enough to see the blurring gravel road. The senator reached over and closed the door abruptly, clicking the lock shut.

"Ramie, don't be ridiculous. There is nothing for you to go back to. And besides, do you really want to leave your son?" he asked, raising an eyebrow.

Fuck.

"Tanner said you told people I was in Paris so you wouldn't be embarrassed by the fact that you had a runaway for a daughter. Don't you think that instead of inventing lies, your time would have been better spent looking for me?" I asked with my hand still on the door. "If you were me, would *you* want to stay knowing that?"

The senator sighed. "We did look for you, Ramie. But we didn't know about this memory business. We just thought when we hadn't found you that you didn't want to be found. And stop making this all about you. It isn't just you who this debacle affected, so think about that before you go around hurling your accusations at people."

"King didn't abduct me. I want you to drop the charges. I don't want him back in prison," I stated, crossing my arms over my chest.

The senator narrowed his eyes at me. "I tell you what, visit with the specialist I've contacted. Make a real effort to assimilate back into your old life. Try to remember some things before you go and throw everything away to be the first lady of…Logan's Beach." He said *Logan's Beach* like the entire place left a bad taste in his mouth. I opened my mouth to argue but he continued.

"Give it a month. A month of real effort toward your recovery. If after that time you still want to go back, I'll drop the charges against him and have my driver drop you back off at his house with a letter of recommendation to the family court judge, which he can use for custody of his daughter. That's the deal." He straightened his tie. "And the only one I'm offering."

"I don't exactly trust your deals. Look what you did to King," I spat.

"Ramie, he's a felon! He's got no voting rights for Christ's sake. He's a non-citizen as far as I'm concerned, and I don't make deals with criminals. You're my daughter." He finally looked up from his phone. "I would never make you a promise I didn't intend to keep."

I didn't trust him. Not one bit. He was a fucking politician after all. But what other choice did I have? He was right; there really was nothing to go back to. Then there was the nagging curiosity, which had never died down, reminding me that I really did want to find out who I really was. What my life was like before. "Okay," I agreed. "But I have more questions. About me, about my—" The senator's phone rang and once again he barked his greeting into the receiver, effectively putting an end to our conversation.

I'm not sure exactly what kind of relationship I'd had with my father, but I was beginning to feel that he wasn't the cheering on the T-ball team, helping with my math homework type.

Within a few minutes after we'd dropped off Tanner and Sammy, the senator announced, "Here we are." He placed his phone inside his jacket. Royal palm trees, which were at least twenty feet tall, lined both sides of the driveway. We came to a stop in the center of the U-shaped drive, right in front of a big southern style open porch with white railings.

I craned my neck up at the house. "You live *here?*"

"No, *we* live here," the senator corrected. "You, your mother, myself, Sammy, and the housekeeper, Nadine. And when I'm not here, I'm up in Tallahassee or D.C."

The senator leaned over me and opened the door. He motioned for me to get out of the car. I had to shield my eyes from the rays of the sun burning through the separated palm fronds.

The house wasn't as big or palatial as I would imagine a politician's home would be. It was on the small side, with immaculate white siding, accented with blue shutters. The rocking chair on the porch screamed old southern charm. An American flag waved beside the front door. Wind chimes hung from the trees, *tinging* and *tanging* hypnotically with every hint of breeze. "Home sweet home," the senator said dryly.

No. It might have been somewhere I'd lived, but it felt like anything but home.

It didn't even have stilts.

"Nadine will show you to your room," the senator said, nodding to the middle-aged woman with olive skin and dark brown hair pulled into a bun at the nape of her neck, as she emerged from the house. She wore black slacks and a white short-sleeved Polo shirt. "Nadine here has been filled in on your situation. She can answer any questions you might have." The senator looked satisfied with his introductions, as if he'd just introduced a new man on the job to his boss. "Do you remember Nadine at all, Ramie?"

"No, I don't remember *anyone*," I clipped.

The senator rolled his eyes. "I see your attitude hasn't suffered along with your memory. Nadine is...well, Nadine does it all. She's been with us since you were born. We will talk more soon." With a curt nod the senator popped back in the car. He rolled down the window. "Despite what you may be thinking, it *is* good to have you home, Ramie."

"You're leaving?" I asked. "Just like that?"

"I should be back in a few days. I have meetings. Your mother isn't around. She's at the spa...again. We'll talk soon." The car drove off.

"Mr. Fucking Personality," I mumbled. Nadine laughed out loud then clasped her hand over her mouth. She cleared her throat. "Well, he's right about one thing," she said with a slight southern accent, "that attitude of yours hasn't gone anywhere."

Nadine led us up the steps and opened the front door, stepping aside so I could enter. "So you know me well, I take it?"

"Girl, I've known you since you were in diapers. I know you *the best*," she said with a smile that made me believe her. "Now come on, let's get you something to eat and then I'll let you get settled in your room." I followed Nadine like a lost baby duck and I hated it. I hadn't felt so helpless since I'd lived on the streets and I'd promised myself I never would again. But there I was, following a stranger around an unfamiliar house because I had no other options.

No, I'd been *left* with no other options, I reminded myself. Sure, I could have called a cab and hightailed it out of there, but there was only one other place I could go.

And it was empty.

Even if King weren't on his way back to prison, would he even still want me there after being fully prepared to give me away?

Would *I* even want to be there after all that?

I wasn't prepared to think about that just yet.

Inside the house, the floors were all dark wood. The walls a light dove gray. It was tasteful but not overbearing. Comfortable yet modern.

I fucking hated it.

"Kind of simple for the house of a politician, no?" I questioned.

Nadine shut the door behind me while I stood in a small foyer, which doubled as a hallway, and took in my surroundings. "He's a rising politician," she explained. "He doesn't come from old money like a lot of the good ole boys in this state. He was a computer programmer. He's made it to where he is on his campaign promises, not his bank account," Nadine informed me. "And that's rare these days."

"You sound like you like him" I asked in surprise.

She shook her head. "It's not a matter of liking him or not liking him. He has his downfalls. We all do. But the man deserves credit where credit is due." She stepped out in front of me and again led the way. "Certainly his fathering techniques leave a lot to be desired, but when it comes to politics, no one can argue that the man hasn't achieved some remarkable things."

We came to a stop in the center of the house. The kitchen, dining room, and living area all shared one open space, with the kitchen at an angle in the far corner. The cabinets were tall and off-white. The countertops a shiny black. "Sit." Nadine nodded toward one of the high-backed barstools tucked under the raised counter. But I just stood there; the realization of what was really happening finally started to resonate. I'd wondered what the house I grew up in looked like, and I was finally there. However, I didn't feel any of the elation I'd imagined I would.

I was still in shock. Angry. Bitter. Confused as all hell.

But elated?

Nope.

Nadine pulled out ingredients from different cabinets and turned on the gas burner. "Sit, girl. I'll fix you something. You can ask me anything you want. I know how you are with questions." She grinned and wiped her hands on the apron she'd tied around her waist.

"Well, I guess that hasn't changed," I said, finally taking a seat. "I've been told I ask too many questions a lot over the last few months."

Nadine cracked an egg into a bowl. "But you have changed. I

can see it."

"And I guess that's a bad thing?" I sighed.

"No." She came over to me and rested her elbows on the other side of the counter. "Actually...I think I kind of like it."

"How am I different though?" I asked.

Nadine pursed her lips. "I'm not a hundred percent sure yet, but I'll tell you what, as soon as I do figure it out, I'll be sure to let you know." Reaching out, she tweaked the end of my nose. With a wink she turned back around to the burner where she started mixing ingredients together with a wooden spoon.

"It's not fair," I said, but it came off a lot whinier than I intended. "Everyone knows me, but everyone is a stranger to me. I'm practically a stranger to myself."

"Child, I hate to break this to you, but did your father somehow give you the impression that he's the warm and cuddly type?" Nadine pulled a ladle out of a drawer.

"No," I answered immediately.

"Well, in a way, the two of you have always been strangers. So, in that way, things are exactly as they were before," she announced with a smile.

I bit my bottom lip. "I don't know if that's a good thing or a bad thing."

Nadine shrugged.

"And my mother? Who goes to the spa when their missing kid is on the way home?" There was no hiding my bitterness, because I *was* bitter.

Nadine winced, like she'd been hoping I wouldn't ask about my mother. She kept her attention on whatever she was mixing up. "Spa is a code around here. It either means she's holed up at a hotel somewhere or she's drying out at a rehab or a desert retreat or whatever it is she does to clean out her abused liver."

She wiped her hand on the towel on her shoulder. "I mean. I just—"

I was already over hearing about my mother so I cut Nadine off when I felt like she was about to make an excuse for her behavior. "What are you making?" I asked, leaning forward on my elbows.

"Your favorite; breakfast for dinner!" My heart sputtered when she scooped up some batter and poured it onto the hot griddle. When she used a spatula to flip the contents of her pan over I saw Preppy, standing in her place, wearing his favorite red lacy apron.

"Pancakes," I whispered, my heart sputtering into an all-out seize. I felt suddenly light headed. Stars danced in front of my eyes. I braced myself on the counter so I wouldn't fall off the stool.

Nadine came over and set down a plate in front of me with three perfectly circular pancakes in the center, dripping with syrup. A square pad of butter swam around on top before completely melting and falling to the plate. The sweet smell assaulted my senses, dragging out every ounce of hurt and pain I felt the night I watched my friend die.

"You don't like pancakes anymore?" Nadine asked, misinterpreting my reaction.

I shook my head. "That's not it," I said, struggling to make the words come out of my mouth.

"Then what's the problem, baby girl?" Nadine asked, placing a concerned hand on my shoulder. I didn't answer.

I couldn't.

So when she pulled me into her soft chest and cradled my head, I didn't bother resisting her hold. I was so concerned about King in the weeks after Preppy's death that I never realized I hadn't properly grieved for my friend. I didn't realize I was crying until I felt my shoulders shaking. "Why the tears?"

"Because," I managed to spit out on a short exhale.

"Because, why?"

"Because…pancakes."

Chapter Three

DOE

NADINE HELD ME until I calmed down. She pushed away the plate as if it really was the pancakes that had been the source of my little episode.

We both agreed that what I needed was a good night's rest. Nadine led me up the stairs to a door at the end of the hallway.

My room.

Lacey white curtains, soft blue walls, and a poofy pink comforter. A small off white chandelier with electric candles hung above the bed, which was lined with stuffed animals. Looking around, I couldn't help but think of another small bedroom in another town not too far away. One with a flat mattress, the most comfortable faded blue blanket, and a broken fan blade from when Preppy's head connected with it after enthusiastically jumping up and down on the bed.

My heart did a little flip.

In this room—*my* room—a corkboard hung above a simple white desk. Pinned to the board were sketches drawn on pages torn from a notebook. I walked around the room slowly, running my hand over the slightly textured walls, the shiny fabric of the throw pillows on the little window seat, and finally, over the sketches themselves, which were mostly landscapes mixed with a few portraits. I recognized a few as Sammy and another as

Tanner. In the center of the board was one of the both of them together, sitting under a tree, smiling straight ahead, presumably at me.

"You love to draw. Your father about had a coronary when you said you wanted to go to art school," Nadine offered from the doorway. "All of this has got to be hard on you."

Yes, and for more reasons than you think.

I felt Nadine's eyes on me as I walked around the room, willing for something to jump out at me as familiar. "I know that look," she said.

"What look would that be?" I asked. Plucking a sketch from the board, I walked over to the bay window and held it up. The drawing of the view matched perfectly; right down to the window frame and the buttons on the cushions, as well as the expansive lawn and scattered oak trees, including the one partially obstructing the window. Nadine came into the room and sat down on the corner of the bed. I kept my back turned and continued comparing the drawing to the real version.

"Sadness. You are a beautiful girl, but sadness is not a good look on you." I turned around and caught the tail end of Nadine's sad smile.

I set down the sketch on the desk. "Honestly? I don't know what to think."

"This may sound odd, especially since you don't remember me, but I love you like you're one of my own babies. And no matter what your friends were doing, you were always your own person and had a good head on your shoulders. So I knew that when you disappeared out of thin air that you didn't run away like they said. And I certainly didn't buy the Paris crap. You just weren't...that kind of girl."

A blast of laughter escaped me. "Not that kind of girl? Apparently I'm the daughter of a senator, a teen mom, and was doing shady enough shit for my entire family to write me off as a runaway, so excuse my laughter, but I have no fucking clue what kind of girl I am." It all came out in one long breath leaving me feeling a pang of guilt the instant the harsh words left my mouth.

Nadine rose from the bed. "I'll let you get some rest," she said, smoothing down her pants with the palm of her hands and straightening her shirt.

"I'm sorry," I said softly as she reached the door.

"Me too," Nadine said, our apologies hanging in the air between us. Her once casual demeanor turning professional. Her smile, easy and genuine when I'd first arrived, was now tight and forced. "Your mama isn't feeling well these days. She will see you in a few days when your father gets back."

"Where is she?" I asked.

"In bed with a migraine," she said flatly.

"I've been gone for months and on the day I return my father is working and my mother is in bed with a headache?" I asked.

"Yes," Nadine confirmed, leaving the room and pulling the door closed. Before it clicked shut, she added, "All is back to normal."

I spent most of the night examining the sketches on the cork board. Looking through the closet at clothes that were my size but not my taste. Lots of matching skirt suits and long-sleeved shirts. Too conservative. Too expensive. Too...everything. I finally found a pair of sweatpants and a yellow tank top at the bottom of one of the drawers, and after I had a shower in the attached bathroom, I got dressed and searched through the desk for anything that might trigger a memory. I found a pink iPhone and tried turning it on, but the battery was dead. I plugged it into the wall charger on the nightstand.

I stopped when I glimpsed at my reflection in the full-length mirror. I lifted up my shirt and examined my flat belly. How on earth was there ever a baby in here? I ran my hands across my smooth skin and stuck out my stomach as far as I could to mimic a pregnant belly. It was weird to see myself all puffed out, especially since I was skin and bones before Preppy's cooking added some meat to my bones.

Preppy.

My knees buckled and I caught myself on the edge of the desk right before I hit the carpet. I still didn't want to believe he was gone. I keep thinking that I was going to see him come around a corner or hear him yell something that was going to make me laugh. But it wasn't just Preppy. In a way I felt like King had died too, because no matter what lay ahead for me, nothing would ever be the same. If the senator went back on his deal with me, like he had with King, the chances of King ever being a real part of my life again were almost nonexistent.

Suddenly feeling a level of tired I hadn't felt since sleeping on park benches, I moved to the bed, sweeping the plethora of stuffed animals onto the floor. Crawling up toward the pillows, I landed on my side. The mattress and comforter were plush and soft, but the bed felt empty.

It's because he's not here.

Only a few months ago I was just a girl without a home, a name, or a family.

Then I was Pup. A girl who lived in Logan's Beach with the family of her choosing and a home I loved.

Now I was Ramie Price, daughter to a senator, a mother. I was finally back where I'd come from. Where I belonged.

I was finally home.

Drifting off into a heavy sleep I wondered why this place which was supposed to be my home, felt like anything but.

Standing in the middle of the ice, I take a hesitant step toward the shore, the first echoing crack of the ice under my heavy boot is deafening. I have to take another step. I have to make it across before it's too late, but I can't move my legs. All I can do is stare in disbelief as the crack expands into millions more, and like jagged snakes, they race in every direction, sending the thin foundation of ice, and me, crashing into the freezing dark waters.

It's so cold.

I'm going to drown.

Deeper and deeper I sink into the dark water until two arms appear above me, hands extended out, calling for me to grab them so I could be saved. One arm was adorned with a gold wrist watch, the other was wrapped in a thick leather belt. I try to grab onto both of them, but I can't reach and they don't reach into the water any deeper.

It's then I realize that in order to be saved, I can only chose one.

I reach toward the belted arm and grab hold, but instead of being lifted out from the abyss and thrust back into the frigid air as I expected, the arm turns me around and pushes me down deeper and deeper until I have no choice but to inhale the murky water.

I fade into oblivion wondering if there really was a right choice, because I have a feeling that no matter which one I chose, they both would've pulled me under.

Chapter Four

DOE

*T*AP, TAP, TAP

I thought what I was hearing was still the ice cracking from my dream, but when it grew louder and more impatient I opened my eyes and realized that the sound was coming from my window.

When I opened my eyes I realized that the TV I'd left on for light had turned off sometime during the night and I was encased in darkness that made my fear spike to epic proportions.

And then I heard the distinct sound of the window slowly sliding open. I froze, having no clue where there might be something I could defend myself with and not wanting to bring any more attention to my location. The only thing I could do was clutch my comforter to my chest, and wait.

The unavoidable shadow slinked through the window, one long leg after the other. I spotted a snow globe on the desk and was about to make my move to grab it and launch it at the intruder when the shadow started toward my bed. Then to my surprise as the shadow moved closer to the bed, my panic receded.

There was only one person whose very presence could quiet my overwhelmingly loud fear of the dark.

King.

My anger toward him, which I'd been suppressing all day, was barely a thought in the back of my mind as I leapt out of bed. But just as I was about to jump into his arms, a cloud rolled away from the moon, the light beaming into my room like a spotlight, revealing my visitor's identity.

Tanner.

I stopped abruptly and when I realized I was still holding my arms open in the air, I lowered them and awkwardly held my wrist behind my back.

"What are you doing here?" I asked breathlessly.

"I told you I was coming to talk to you," Tanner answered. "And who did you think I was?"

I shook my head and waved my hand dismissively. "Oh, no one. You just surprised me is all, when you came through the window," I lied. "Who's with Sammy?"

Tanner gave me a look that said he wasn't buying my answer, but thankfully he moved on anyway. "My mom's watching him."

"Oh," I said, twisting around at my waist, while avoiding Tanner's gaze.

"I'm sorry I surprised you. And honestly, I didn't even think about coming through your front door instead of the window, because unless I had Sammy, this is just how I always came¬…" Tanner stopped and closed his eyes tightly. He shook his head and moved over to the bed. He shot me a tentative look and I nodded. Taking up only a small portion of the corner of the bed, he wasn't really sitting, more like bracing himself. "I keep forgetting that you don't remember any of this." He motioned between the two of us.

"You don't have to explain anything to me," I said.

But despite my protest, Tanner attempted to explain anyway.

"Your father… He's an ass, always has been. But you've probably figured that out already. He only mildly tolerates me because of my family's last name. My dad's a fourth generation Redmond Shoes C.E.O. and although the senator has been trying to convince you to get rid of me since we were in diapers, after we had Sammy, I think he finally came to terms with the fact that I wasn't going anywhere. But no matter how much he likes my name, I'm still the dude that knocked up his teenaged daughter. So even though we share a kid, I'm still climbing that damn tree and sneaking in your window like I've been doing since we learned how to climb trees, because your disapproving father likes to think he has control over everything that goes on in his house." Tanner flashed me a smile that glinted in the moonlight. "So, yeah, me being here, like this, is…frowned upon."

"Frowned upon?" I asked. The turn of phrase sounded out of place being spoken by someone my age.

"Your father's words, not mine," he admitted. "And you know what I mean, Ray. Don't be a smart ass," Tanner said playfully.

I sat down at the foot of the bed. "I have so much to ask you. My head has more questions than answers, but I don't have a clue where I should start," I admitted.

Tanner nudged my elbow with his. "Well, I have some questions of my own…if you don't mind," Tanner said. "So how about we trade off, one question at a time. But you have to promise to answer honestly. We've never lied to each other and I'm not about to start now."

"Okay," I agreed.

"You start," Tanner said. "What do you want to know first?"

There was one thing I needed to know first. "I want to know about us, about Samuel. Sammy. I was a bit in shock earlier to ask you too much about it."

Tanner clapped his hands onto his knees. "Then I shall start at the beginning," he said in some sort of strange accent. I raised an eyebrow, not sure how to react to his brand of humor. He looked down at the carpet and continued on, accent free. "You and I have been together since we were in diapers. If you take the short cut, it's only a five-minute walk between our houses. Our moms were close, well, before yours decided that vodka made a better friend than people do. We were in every class together growing up. We used to pretend to get married in our fort when we were little. Another one of our friends used to pretend to be the reverend. She even cut up one of her dad's Hugo Boss shirts to make her 'sacred robes' and got herself grounded for a week, and after her parents told ours, the three of us didn't see each other for the entire summer." Tanner laughed nervously. He rested his chin on the back of his hand and sighed. "It feels really weird to try to explain *us* to you."

"I can assure you that hearing it is probably weirder," I admitted.

Tanner struggled, stopping and starting again, but he took a deep breath and continued, "We were fifteen when Samuel…happened. We had originally planned to wait to have…to be…physical, until we graduated." He looked pained, as he tapped his sneaker on the floor. "But, then I got sick. Real sick." He turned to face me. "Leukemia."

I didn't know how to react under the circumstances so I gave him a small smile and said, "I'm so sorry."

He pressed his lips together then continued, "On the day they told me I might never see graduation, we moved up our plans. We were young and stupid, but we said our own made-up vows to each other right here in this room." Even though the story he was telling was pulling on my heart strings, I felt removed from it. Like it wasn't partly about me.

Tanner scratched his head and again looked through the open window. "I promised to always smash Cheetos into your sandwiches and you promised you wouldn't forget me when I was gone. And then we…," he trailed off awkwardly, but quickly recovered, "…and then we made Samuel." He smiled again, this time a large proud smile that told me he was genuinely happy with what we'd done.

And who we'd made.

"It's a night I'm really hoping you'll remember someday, because I may have been at death's doorstep, but it was the by far the best night of my life," Tanner finished. He folded his hands on his lap and with his chin to his chest he looked up at me, waiting for my response.

Unsure of what to say, I said the first thing that came to mind, "The Cheetos thing I still do," I admitted.

Tanner offered me a small smile and an even smaller laugh. The emotional weight of what seemed like the most important part of our history together, obviously weighed on him heavily. "Are you still sick?" I asked.

He shook his head. "No. Much to your father's dismay, I survived. Shortly after we found out you were pregnant I got accepted into an experimental treatment program in Colorado. By the time Sammy was born, I was back home and getting better every day. I still have to take some pills here and there, but the cancer is gone, and now they think I will live forever, like a vampire, or better yet, like a mutant," he said, crossing his eyes and sticking out his tongue.

I bit my lip, wondering if I should even attempt to ask him the question on the tip of my tongue. "Do you think I can see him? Sammy? Maybe spend some time with him?" I asked. "It could help me remember more," I added, hoping it would help Tanner say yes.

He waved his hand through the air as if my question was a ridiculous one. "Of course, Ray. You're his mom. You don't even have to ask." Tanner reached for my hand but just as it was about to clasp over mine, he hesitated, before withdrawing it completely and resting it on his knee.

"Now can I ask you a question?" Tanner asked.

"Yes, it's your turn," I said.

Tanner chewed on the tip of his thumbnail. "You and the guy with the tattoos. You were living with him, right? And then when we came to get you, you guys were arguing, like you two were…," Tanner trailed off.

I didn't want him to feel awkward so instead of forcing him to ask the difficult question, I volunteered the answer. "King. His name is Brantley King." Saying his name made me feel like I could breathe, yet, at the same time, knocked the wind from my lungs. But that was King; a contradiction in every single way.

Tanner leaned his elbows onto his thighs and dropped his face into his hands. "This is so fucking hard to ask you, Ray, but I feel like I just need to know. No, I *have* to know," he moaned. "Have you guys, I mean, did you…?"

I just wanted to get it over with. Rip it off like a Band-Aid. "Yes." After all, I'd promised him honesty, not delicacy.

"Oh my God. I think I'm going to be sick," Tanner blurted out, jumping up from the bed.

"You said you wanted me to be honest!" I exclaimed, jumping up as well. "And don't look at me like I cheated on you. I didn't even know there was a *you* to cheat on!"

Tanner shifted from foot to foot. "I know, I know what I

said. But I didn't expect your answer to break my heart!" Tanner whisper-shouted. "And I know it's not like you cheated on me because the Ray I know would never have had sex with some strange guy she'd just met." Tanner paced the room. He wasn't being purposely mean, he was just upset, but it was the judgmental tone in his voice that grated on my nerves and made me regret my promise of honesty.

"Newsflash buddy, I don't know you or the Ray you know. My name isn't even Ray, they called me Doe. As in Jane Doe. As in nobody knew who the fuck I was. So if you want to talk about being angry and who wronged who, then get in fucking line!" I shouted.

Tanner clutched his arms around his stomach as if I'd physically socked him in the gut. "I looked for you, you know. I spent days, weeks, months. I never gave up hope." His voice was so low I barely heard him. He shook his head. "But you're right, I really don't know you."

"This isn't getting us anywhere," I said. I fell back into the mattress and rolled over onto my stomach, shouting my frustrations into my comforter. When I rolled back over Tanner's jaw was on the floor.

"What?" I asked, looking down at my body to make sure I was properly clothed. Everything was in place. I stood up and checked again.

Nothing.

Tanner stammered. "It's you..your..shh..shoulder. Your..ba.ba..back. You have a...tattoo," he said in disbelief, barely able to finish his sentence.

"Okay? So?" I asked, crossing my arms over my chest and resting my palm on the place where King had marked me, feeling defensive and ready to snap.

Tanner paled. "Of his name. You have a huge tattoo on your back, of his name," he repeated. It wasn't so much a statement, but an accusation. I didn't feel like explaining to him that my tattoo wasn't anyone's name, but it was dark in my room, and the artwork was intricate, so it would've been easy to mistake it for something else. I took a deep breath and tried to remember that Tanner was going through something that was hard for me to understand, just as I was going through something that was hard for him to understand.

"I don't want to hurt you, Tanner. But I don't need to defend myself to you either."

"I don't know where we go from here. Where I go." He ran his hand over his open mouth and then his jaw. "You were with someone else."

"It's not like I wanted to want him. You know, I had this whole idea that I was going to preserve myself, keep myself clean or pure or something, for the person I was before I lost my memory. For this Ray person. But time passed, and King and I, we grew close. And after a while, I was so tired of fighting it. Tired of putting the life I could have on hold for a life I knew nothing about. So I let him in. I let him tattoo me. I let him...love me." The words brought back memories that caused tears to prickle in the back of my eyes. "I don't regret it though. Any of it. I won't. And it doesn't matter what you say, because you can't make me."

"Jesus Christ, Ray. He's like thirty, and you're just a teenager! On top of that, you're the only girl I've ever been with, and the last time we had sex was when we were fifteen! You're standing here telling me that you let him..." He took a step toward the window seat and bent over, leaning his hands against it for support. "You let him...touch you." He finished in a much calmer tone of voice than he'd started.

A lump formed in my throat. "Yes," I said, fighting back the tears. "Don't you dare judge me. I can be sympathetic to you because I know how it feels to be confused and overwhelmed, but that doesn't change the fact that I don't know you." I stared him down and held my ground. I was not about to let him or anyone tell me that what King and I had was somehow wrong.

Tanner threw his hands in the air. "Well, that makes two of us. The Ray I knew never once raised her voice, never yelled, never swore. You may look like her, but you're just an imposter." His words slapped me across the face. I could feel the sting as real as if he'd used his hand. "Maybe you shouldn't have come back after all." He said, the corner of his lip turned up in disgust.

"Leave," I demanded, stomping my foot on the ground and pointing toward the window he'd used to come in. "Now."

Tanner stepped up on the window seat and had one leg dangling off the ledge when he hesitated for a moment. Slowly he turned back toward me, watery eyes shimmering. "I'm sorry. I really am. I just…I still love you, Ray," Tanner said softly.

I was still in defense mode, but I realized that the only reason Tanner was lashing out at me was because he really was heartbroken. I couldn't let him leave without giving him something. "I can't tell you the same, but I know I felt something for you, before all this. It's the only reason I can think of that your eyes were the only thing I recognize in all this. That's got to mean something, right?" I offered. Tanner smiled a small sad smile that didn't reach his eyes. "I even sketched them once," I added, hoping that little bit of information might bring him some sort of comfort.

"Do you love him?" he asked with sadness in his voice. "Tell me the truth, Ray. I can handle it." I didn't believe that for one second. I searched my brain and my heart for the answer, one that despite all the bullshit, all the lies, all the misunderstanding, I'd never doubted.

"Yes," I answered simply.

Tanner cringed. He turned and leapt from the window onto a nearby tree branch. By the time I walked over to the ledge he was on the ground brushing leaves off of his pants. He looked back up to my window. "Even though he knew who you were but didn't tell you? Even though he used you in order to get his own daughter back? You still love him despite all that?" He whisper shouted his question.

I tried to explain my complicated feelings to him the best I could, "You can be pissed off and still love someone at the same time."

Tanner walked across the lawn but before he disappeared into the dark shadows, I heard him mutter, "I can relate."

Chapter Five

DOE

I SPENT THE next three days in my room, alone. Only getting out of bed for a quick shower and change of clothes. But I didn't sleep. I couldn't sleep, with the exception of a cat nap here and there when my body argued that it was tired, while the rest of me was on high alert.

It was past midnight when I awoke from such a nap and found myself in pitch blackness. The panic started to set in. I tried to take a deep breath but I couldn't pull in enough air. I fumbled for the remote, but when I found it and pressed every button on it, nothing happened. Willing myself to keep searching for a light source, I felt around on the wall beside the bed for a switch but couldn't find one. Finally, I ran over to the window and pushed back the curtains, hoping the light from the moon was enough to allow me to catch my breath for a second. No such luck. Storm clouds hung low in the air, rumbling across the sky, vibrating the floor underneath my feet. All I could think of was that I was going to die from sheer panic.

I crouched down onto the floor and wrapped my arms around my knees. My chest was so tight. The room spun around me, books on the shelf blended together in a line. It was then I finally realized something. Maybe my panic wasn't about being alone in the dark.

Maybe it was just about being alone.

The only person I felt any sort of connection with in this new/old life was Sammy, and I'd only seen him for a matter of minutes. And with the way Tanner and I had left things, I didn't know when I would be able to see Sammy again.

Maybe never.

I could've said the same thing about King.

Suddenly I felt like breathing the air in that house, in that room, was like inhaling poison. The more I breathed it in, the more I felt like I was going to die right then and there on the bedroom floor I didn't remember.

I was going to suffocate.

I had to get the fuck out.

I didn't bother with shoes. Still in the shorts and tank top I wore to bed, I stepped up onto the window seat and pushed open the window. I shuffled until my legs were dangling over the edge like Tanner had done. There was nothing but darkness beneath my feet. Holding onto the window frame with one arm, I stretched out the other and felt around for the tree branch I knew was there. The second my hand touched it a sense of familiarity encompassed me. The tree and I had long been acquaintances, I was sure of it. I may have not known where to look or what to hold onto, but my body knew. Without a single misstep, I managed to lower myself onto the tree branch and with a second nature type precision, I found a branch to grab and ridges for my footing, without much thought at all. At one point, without knowing exactly how far down the ground was beneath my feet, I felt the urge to jump.

So I did.

Sharp blades of thick grass stung the soles of my feet on impact. I crouched down to brace myself as I landed. When I stood up, a motion light buzzed to life, its soft hum breaking into the quiet of the night like a freight train barreling down the tracks at full speed. Tanner must have known where to step without turning the light on.

And then I ran.

Darting off across the yard, kicking up water, grass, and mud onto the backs of my calves, I sprinted as fast as I could make my short legs move.

The short iron fence around the property stopped at the line of bushes that defined the back yard. The natural foliage acting as its own kind of fence. I ran directly for a small tunnel like opening in the bushes, barely slowing down as I ducked down into it, maneuvering through like I'd done it a thousand times before. Leaves and thorns both licked and stung my elbows, pulling at my hair as I passed through, but I continued on until I emerged on the other side of the path onto a small beach.

The clouds took turns slowly passing over the moon; the light reflected off the still water looked as if someone were playing with a dimmer on a light switch. I followed the shore-line, the cool water lapping over my feet, the mushy sand pushed up between my toes with each step.

When I came across overgrown mangroves in my path that were growing from the 'fence' of the backyard out across the water several feet, I didn't give what I was about to do a second thought. I turned and waded into the dark water. It had felt only mildly cool on my feet when I was walking but as the water inched up higher and higher on my legs, it was downright cold.

When the water rose over my waist, I shivered.

I pushed through water, sinking into the soft earth, sending little waves crashing against the base of the trees. Something darted out into the water in front of me. At first I thought it was a snake, the way it slithered from side to side making an *S* shape in the water. I waded out further to avoid it, but when it slithered right by me, I realized that it wasn't a snake at all, but a large lizard. It hissed as it passed, like an angry driver giving me the finger.

Once I cleared the trees I sloshed back up to the shore on the other side. My shorts hung heavily off of my hips, clinging to my thighs.

I found myself in a small alcove with an old weathered dock that connected to an even older and more weathered pier. Tethered to the pier was a dilapidated houseboat that was decades over its expiration date. The tethering was entirely unnecessary as the boat was mostly on the beach, resting at an angle that told me it had probably been that way for a long time. As I approached the strong odor of mildew, mixed with the salt air, grew stronger and stronger. Much to my surprise I inhaled deeply and unlike the extreme sense of panic I'd experienced in the house, an eerie sense of calm washed over me.

I smiled. I knew this place. I loved this place.

I didn't know or understand the *hows* and *whys*, I just needed to be closer to it.

I stepped up onto the dock and it protested my intrusion, creaking and hissing as I made my way down the pier. As I got closer, I realized the boat was a good five feet away from the pier. I spotted a long piece of plywood and picked it up off of the dock, sending ants scurrying all around it. I quickly set it down across the gap, creating a makeshift bridge.

I carefully crossed over it, hopping down onto the cracked wooden deck of the boathouse, which was large, but for the most part empty, with the exception of three rusted folding chairs set in front of the sliding glass doors under the little overhang. A rusted can of Dr. Pepper sat in each of the cup holders. A pink flashlight with a My Little Pony sticker was propped up on one of the chairs. I picked it up and tried to click on the switch. Nothing. I gave it a vigorous shake and banged one end against the palm of my hand. Surprisingly enough, it came to life, shining directly into my eye, temporarily blinding me. I blinked and waited for my eyes to readjust. With my working flashlight to help light the way, I found the handle on the door and attempted to slide it open. It took quite a bit of force to get it to budge, as debris and mud caked the threshold.

Much like the deck, the cabin was empty, except for a few cabinets lining the far wall. Most of the doors were hanging off the hinges. All the shelves were missing. Three faded sleeping bags sat up against another wall. One purple, one pink, and one blue. All three were covered with mildew and frayed at the seams.

Every single inch of wall and ceiling space was covered with magazine pages and clippings. And when I looked closer, through the layer of grime that had coated the pictures over time, I could still make out the different teenage stars from boy bands or TV shows.

Teen magazines. Wall-to-wall teen magazines.

I closed my eyes again and inhaled, hoping to catch another hint of what triggered my recognition. This was a place I'd spent a lot of time. I was positive that one of those sleeping bags was mine and I was even more sure that I'd at least helped wallpaper the place with the magazine pages, because as I walked around, I found myself humming one of the tunes from one of the boy bands. That particular band seemed to have their own section of wall space dedicated completely to them.

I was so lost in my mission to remember more about that

place that I didn't hear the approaching footsteps.

A strong calloused hand covered my mouth from behind, muffling my scream of surprise; an arm wrapped around my waist, pulling me flush up against a very hard, very familiar body. "Miss me, Pup?" A deep voice vibrated against my neck. The light scent of cigarettes and soap, mixed with a bit of sweat, invaded my senses. My body instantly softened at the familiarity of his touch. My breath quickened. He released me just enough to spin me around to face him.

King.

I should've been happy to see him. Elated even. I'd been thinking about him almost nonstop since I last saw him days ago.

But my happiness was muted. By anger. A lot of anger.

I was fucking pissed.

And that feeling seemed to be mutual because I could only describe the way King's green eyes blazed into mine, as *furious.*

"What are you doing here? I thought—"

"No," King interrupted. "I know you're about to start your question and answer bullshit, which I normally think is fucking adorable, but right now, before I lose my fucking shit, you're going to have to answer one of my questions first." His voice sounded strained, raspy, like he was fighting to maintain control.

I tried to speak again, but he covered my mouth with his hand, pushing his thumb inside, silencing me with his makeshift gag. "Why the fuck was that little shit climbing in and out of your fucking window a few days ago?" He pulled his thumb from my mouth, and I regretted not biting down on it when I had the chance.

"How? Were you were watching me?"

King took his wet thumb and rubbed it over my lips, and I

instinctively leaned into his touch. "Not me. But I've got eyes on you." King's brows drew into a downward point. His grip around me tightened. "Answer me, Pup," he demanded, his fingers digging into my hips.

King wasn't someone who could be ignored.

His tongue darted out between his lips; he slid it along the seam. I tried not to stare and instead focus on the anger that had been building for days, but my body's reaction couldn't be contained. It was amazing how such a little thing like wetting his full lips with his talented tongue already had my nipples standing at attention, ready for his touch.

King growled against my neck, "If he so much as touched you, I will tear his fucking head from his body with my bare fucking hands." There was nothing about King's demeanor that said he could be exaggerating or joking. As soon as he'd said it, I knew he'd meant it.

I was about to answer him. To relieve him of the thought that Tanner might have touched me, when another emotion slammed into me headfirst.

Fury.

Why did I need to alleviate his suspicions, to put his mind at ease when I was the one who was wronged? I was the one who he pushed out the door. If he thought I could just pretend like that never happened, King had another fucking thing coming.

I placed my hands on his chest and shoved with all my might, gaining only a few inches of space between us. "You! How dare you! You have no fucking right to be angry with me right now!"

"Pup…," King started, his hard glare remained firm, a thick vein bulged in his neck under a brightly colored tattoo of Max's name.

I shook my head and tried to take another step back but he stepped forward with me. "No! Don't 'Pup' me. You knew who I was and you never told me! All that bullshit about me being 'yours' and you send me away the first chance you get!?" I threw my hands in the air.

"I didn't think I had another choice," King said. He attempted to press his forehead to mine, a gesture that would normally render me calm and compliant, but I wasn't ready for calm and compliant. I jerked my head back, avoiding the contact.

"No! You did have another choice. You could have fucking told me. You could have let me make that decision *with* you instead of making it for me!" I once again pushed on King's chest, this time gaining enough space between us to shimmy out from his grip. I left the cabin of the boat and climbed back onto the dock, walking briskly back the way I came. The humid night air hung heavily like damp laundry on the line. I waded back into the water, not as carefully as I had the first time around. The thunder cracked overhead. Lightning lit up the sky like fireworks exploding all around me. And because I was racing through the water and wasn't as cautious as I was the first time around, I lost my footing on every other step, sinking up to my ankles in the soft ground.

There was a loud splashing behind me. "Did you come here to apologize? Because it's too fucking late! You should have thought of that before you lied to me," I shouted over my shoulder. Before I even rounded the trees King grabbed me roughly by the wrist, spinning me around. Water whipped through the air as my hair skipped across the surface.

"Look at me," he growled, tilting my chin up to him.

"I can't," I said, pressing my eyes shut tightly.

"Look at me, Pup," he demanded again. "I'm not letting you go until you do."

"This isn't fair!" I shouted, struggling to free myself from his grip. "I don't want to look at you! I just want you to let me fucking go!" When I finally wrangled my hand from his grip, I raised it in the air. My palm was about to make contact with King's face, when he caught my wrist midair.

"Oh, Pup," he said and his deep voice rumbled with something sinister. He leaned down until his face was level with my own. I felt his cool breath across my cheek when he said, "You're going to pay for that." I looked up at him through my lashes just as he lifted me in the air by my waist and tossed me up into the air. I landed on my ass with a splash as I sunk underwater. I didn't even have a chance to come back up for air when strong arms grabbed me under my arms, hauling me back up into the night air.

I sputtered, spitting out water, wiping my eyes. The salt water burned my nostrils. "What the fuck!" I shouted.

King wiped my matted hair from my forehead. Again he tipped my chin up to him. "No look at me or you're going back in."

"Fuck you," I spat. King went to throw me again, but this time, I fought against him so strongly, he couldn't lift me up so instead he held me tight and dove into the water, dragging me under with him.

When he resurfaced with me still in his arms, in the shoulder deep water, he dug his fingers into my hips. "This shit was so much fucking easier when you were afraid of me."

I'm not afraid of you anymore, I'm only afraid of a life without you.

And he had gone and thrown it all away.

And this was about more than being angry with him.

I was hurt.

I decided to open my eyes and get it over with. I told myself that I wasn't going to feel anything. That I would look at him and still be able to walk away.

It's still a lie even if you're only telling it to yourself.

Slowly and begrudgingly, I opened my eyes and when they locked onto his, my breath hitched in my throat.

I told myself that it was the heat lightning flashing across the sky, charging the air around us. I told myself that it was because we were standing in the thick line of light that the full moon painted across the water that was making me want to reach out and touch the soft glow of his colorfully tattooed skin.

Because it most certainly wasn't the way I could practically see the flames dancing in King's burning gaze as it penetrated my fucking soul. It couldn't have been the way his hard lines of muscle rose and fell with his quick breaths, stretching the fabric of his already tight wife-beater across his chest.

Panting. He was panting.

We stood like that for what seemed like an eternity, daring the other to make the first move, frozen in the moment. I didn't feel one thing for him.

I felt everything.

Anger, confusion, love…lust, and it all swam around us in the water as we stared each other down.

The sky opened up. A thunder clap boomed so loud and deep, I felt it in my chest. The surface of the water rippled, and then came the rain, cold and relentless. Every drop sent the river water splashing back up at us, but it still wasn't enough to interrupt the staring contest that was so much more than just two sets of eyes staring at each other. It was a challenge. A warning.

A power struggle.

"You could have told me—" I started to argue again, fully prepared to keep up the fight. I needed it. It'd been too long since we had a true blow out, not since the night of the carnival and I craved the back and forth between us that needed to happen.

The night I gave him my heart.

"No," he barked. "I couldn't have told you." He raised his voice over mine, pulling me so close, that I could feel he was as affected by me as I was by him. He was hard, thick and ready against my thigh. And like the stupid girl I am, my knees trembled and started to buckle.

"Why?" I spat. It was hard to concentrate on our words when I knew what was going on just beneath the surface. The rain was pouring down so hard it muffled our voices as if we were talking underwater. "Why couldn't you?"

"Because I couldn't risk it! If you knew the truth, you would've... I just couldn't risk it," King said.

"Risk what? What couldn't you risk?" I prodded.

"Losing you!" he boomed. "I couldn't risk losing you!" King wrapped an arm around my waist and pressed his erection against the soft spot between my legs that was reacting to his every word, his every touch. A place that craved him almost as much as my heart did.

He cupped my ass and lifted me up, wrapping my legs around his waist. "There was one point I'd made the decision to tell you the truth. I owed you that much. But then all the shit went down with Isaac and Preppy, so when I made the deal with your father for Max, I thought I was doing you a favor by giving you your life back and getting you out of all the shit that came with being in mine."

I squeezed my thighs around his waist, rubbing myself against his hardness. I moaned. "But you weren't giving me my life back," I corrected. I placed my palms on his cheeks and held his face in my hands, searching for any sign in his eyes that what I felt for him might have been wrong, but instead what I found was a resounding need to fix what was broken between us. Tears formed in my eyes. "You were taking it away." King's lips parted. He ran his thumb across my lower lip, turning his head as he kissed his way up my arm.

"Goosebumps," King observed, running his fingertips across my already stimulated skin. I bit my lip and stifled another moan.

"It's just the heat," I lied.

"You've got that fucking right," King growled, bending my wrist behind my back, his lips came crashing down over mine. We were a tangling of lips, clanking of teeth, sloshing through the water to better line ourselves up with each other. It wasn't pretty.

It was need.

"I'm still fucking mad at you for letting me go," I said into his mouth, while our tongues did things other parts of me throbbed to do.

King stilled and held my face away from his, our chests heaving in unison, my erect nipples rubbing against his hot hard skin as we panted together. Our breaths mingled in the air. He ran his hand down the side of my face and cupped my cheek in his palm. "I didn't give you away, Pup. I released you."

I stilled. "You released me?" I couldn't hide the hurt in my voice. For some reason, releasing me sounded worse than letting me go.

King ran his tongue across the tip of my earlobe, holding me tightly against his warmth. Chills ran down my spine and into my very core and they had nothing to do with the temperature of the rain.

"I *tried* to release you, Pup. For Max. But there was a major problem with that plan, and no matter what happened, it would never have worked," King confessed.

"Why is that?" I asked, needing to know, but at the same time acutely aware of the pulsing between my legs. Relief and release was only a scrap or two of fabric away. Throbbing for me.

"The problem was…you never released me," King growled, crashing his lips to mine. He moaned into my mouth when I rubbed myself up against his straining erection. He pushed the fabric of my shorts aside and the second he parted my folds with his index finger, I shuddered. He plunged a long index finger inside of me, and for a second my eyes rolled back in my head until he withdrew it. I cried out in frustration, wiggling myself against him, needing him to make me feel anything other than empty.

King unwrapped my legs from around him and yanked my shorts down over my ass. I stepped out of them and he tossed them to the shore. Still holding onto me with one arm he undid his buckle and jeans. He pushed my underwear to the side. "Wrap your legs around me again." I did as he said, my clit rubbing up against his thick shaft. He lifted me up just enough to line himself up with me. "This is going to be quick and dirty, baby, but I need to feel you." He pressed me down onto him, filling me quickly. When he met my body's tight resistance he pushed harder, as if he were starving for me. The deeper he sank the louder he groaned.

"Fuck!" I said in a loud whisper. I needed him to move, but

the feeling of being so full was overwhelming.

"Yes, Pup. That's the fucking plan." He thrust inside of me fully in one long hard movement that left my thighs quaking.

"God damn it. Holy shit. You're so fucking tight," King swore. "I love this fucking pussy. My fucking pussy."

I held on to the back of his neck while he fucked me with a fury that told me just how much he meant it when he said he needed to feel me. And it was almost as much as I'd needed to feel him.

"Yes. Yes. Yours." I nodded furiously as he found his delicious rhythm, stroking my insides, creating a whirlpool of water around us. The pressure in my lower stomach intensified. Tighter and tighter I wound with each hard twist of his hips that left me more and more breathless. His strokes became longer, harder, faster.

"You feel so fucking good around my cock," he breathed. I was ready to finally acknowledge my complete lack of control over this larger than life connection we shared. I wasn't giving in to him. It was a fight I couldn't win.

It was a fight I didn't even want to fight.

"This. You. This is everything," King groaned. With a hand under each of my thighs he gripped me hard, ramming into me over and over again. Each time he filled me to the hilt, my muscles clenched around him. When he dragged himself from me, I clenched again, seeking him out, needing more. I sat up, with my cheek pressed up against his scruffy face, as the beautiful man I loved pounded into me relentlessly.

Unforgivingly.

I felt his frustration and his hate and his blind lust, and as overwhelming as it was, I took every single thing he could give me.

Without much warning I was exploding around him, trembling as I pulsed and pulsed. Just when I thought it was starting to die down, it racked my body all over again. His cock twitched inside me. His lips parted, his eyes never leaving mine as he thrust up into me one more time, pushing in as deep as he could, holding himself there as his muscles tensed, the chords in his neck strained as he followed me over the edge.

We remained in each other's arms as the rain assaulted us. The gentle pulsing of his cock still inside me made me want to start all over again. I slowly rolled my hips against him, relishing in the feeling of how he felt against my deliciously sore and sensitive body.

"Easy, Pup," King teased, resting his forehead on mine. And this time, I let him. And just like I expected, a calm washed over me as we both continued to breathe heavily. "Don't you see what you fucking do to me?"

"I can feel it," I said.

"Even fucking better," he said, lifting me up against his chest.

King gently drifted us around in the water, with me still attached to him in every way. "I'm still really mad at you," I managed to say. "I'm not cuffed to your bed anymore, but when you lied to me, you were still holding me captive, because you took away my options."

King's gaze hardened. "Yes. But ask me if I feel bad about it. About lying to you. About keeping you. There are a lot of things I would do differently, Pup, but that isn't one of them. If I had to do it a million times over again, I still would have kept you for myself. And if you tried to run again, I still would have chased you down and cuffed you to my bed." He held on to the back of my neck as he spoke, trapping my head, like he was making sure

I wouldn't turn away from him this time. "And when I finally gave in to whatever this thing is between us, and you let me inside you that first time, and I fucked you up against the house…I don't think you have to guess that I wouldn't change that either. Not a fucking second of it."

My breath quickened. Remembering the night of the carnival when we'd fought right up until the moment he was inside me, and then even our sex had been combative.

Deliciously combative.

"The only thing I'm sorry for is the how it all ended when you left. The shit with the senator. That's all on me. I was fucked up after prison, after Preppy. I thought it was the only way to get back the only blood I've got." King ran the back of his hand down the side of my face and leaned in closer. "It was a mistake, because this thing here, between us? It's not the kind of thing that can just go away." He brushed his lips against mine and I leaned forward, seeking more contact, but he held me in place by my shoulders.

"What?" I asked.

Hard lines appeared between his eyes. "I told you what you needed to hear. What I needed to tell you. Now you need to tell me what I need to know." King's tone grew harsher. "You got ten seconds to tell me why that fucking kid was in your room. You don't have to answer if you don't want."

"I don't?" I asked, suddenly feeling very confused.

King shook his head. "No, you don't. But just know that if you chose to go that route, I'm killing the little fucker regardless," King seethed.

"Jealous much?" I cocked an eyebrow at him. I was baiting him, but the fucker deserved every second of uninformed agony after what he'd put me through.

"Very," he admitted, much to my surprise. "So don't push me, little girl." His hands tightened on my shoulders, reminding me that King wasn't someone who liked to play games.

"He wanted to talk," I explained. "And then..."

"And then...what?" he said through his teeth.

I bit my lip. "He asked me if I loved him, and I told him the truth. He made it seem like I was breaking up with him."

"He didn't try to touch you?" King asked again, a shimmer of relief in his voice.

"Nooooooo!" I said, drawing out the word to drive my point into that thick skull of his.

King looked almost disappointed. "Kid gets to live after all," he said. "For today."

"You still haven't told me how you are even here," I said. "How did you get out so quickly? Did you post bail or something? I don't really know how that all works."

King sighed. "Always with the questions, Pup." He tucked my wet hair behind my ears in a move that was both soft and intimate. "I missed your annoying ass questions."

"I thought I might never see you again," I said, burying my face in his neck, willing the tears away that threatened to spill onto my cheeks.

"That was never going to fucking happen. Even if the senator hadn't crossed me. I will always find my way back to you, baby. Always." King traced his fingertips over my eyelids.

"What aren't you telling me?" I asked, sensing his hesitation.

"The detective that arrested me wasn't a detective and he wasn't taking me to jail. He was a contractor."

"I don't understand..."

"He was hired to take me out."

"Holy shit," I said, feeling foolish for fighting him like I had when he'd been so close to losing his life.

"Thank fuck I realized it before it was too late." The rain stopped instantly, like a faucet being turned off. Immediately, a mist started to rise from the water around us, cloaking us in white cloudy wetness.

"What did you do? How are you still alive if he was hired to kill you?" I hung on to him tighter, grateful that he was right in front of me. The question made me feel sick to my stomach to even ask.

King shrugged. "In my world it's kill or be killed, baby." He set his mouth in a hard line. "So I killed."

It should have bothered me that King had just admitted to killing someone but strangely enough it didn't.

I was glad.

Then it hit me. "Fuck, it was the senator wasn't it? He hired that guy to kill you!"

"That's what I'd thought at first. That maybe your father didn't view sending me back to prison as a permanent enough solution to keeping me away from you," King said. "But as it turns out we've got even bigger problems. There is this guy, Eli. He was Isaac's main supplier and he's not taking kindly to the idea of his gravy train running dry. And all signs of the reason for that happening, and Isaac ending up as worm food, point right back to me and Bear."

My eyes widened. "And he's coming for you." I whispered, my heart hammering in my chest.

King nodded. "Yeah, Bear's guy, Rage, his intel is as tight as it comes. When he says someone's gunning for you, you shut the fuck up and listen." He seemed to be thinking about how to phrase what he was going to say next. "This guy Eli? He's different. Worse than Isaac if you can believe it."

I felt my face pale as the blood rushed from it. "What are you going to do?"

King kissed me on the temple. "Same thing I did with the fake detective. Get to him before he gets to us."

"Why the hell are you even here when your life might still be in danger?"

"I had to come tell you myself," King said.

"But it's too risky. You shouldn't have come!" I tapped his chest with my closed fists.

King snarled. "You don't seem to get this shit yet, Pup, so I'm going to make it real fucking clear. You are *mine*. If I had it my way, I would have already tossed you over my shoulder, carried you to my bike, and been halfway home. But it's not safe there now. And as much as it fucking *kills* me, the safest place for you right now is probably right here." King looked like he couldn't believe what he was saying. "I won't have you in the crosshairs of that shit. Not again." He looked off into the distance, collecting his thoughts, calming himself down. He closed his eyes and took a deep breath.

"It wasn't your fault," I said. It was my turn to force him to look at me. "I don't blame you for any of it. I may have a shit memory, but I'm not a child. I can take care of myself. I can take responsibility for my own actions. I know that being with you comes with certain risks." I pressed a soft kiss to his jaw.

King pressed a soft kiss to the inside of my wrist. "Look, about what happened with Isaac, I know we never really talked about it after that shit went down with Preppy, but you need to know that I won't ever let something like that ever fucking happen—"

"Stop." I raised my hand to cut him off. "I refuse to be a victim, so don't fucking treat me like one. I escaped with my life, but only because of you. That is how I see it, and that is how I want you to see it. I will not be pitied, Brantley King, so don't you go pitying me and treating me like a victim, because I sure as shit don't feel like one."

"Where did I get this amazing strong girl from?" King asked, gazing into my eyes as if he were searching them for his answer.

"You got her from a party. She tried to whore herself out and failed miserably."

"Ray?" a voice called out.

"Shit, that's Nadine." When King shot me a confused look, I clarified, "The housekeeper."

"Fuck!" He pushed us in closer to the mangroves so we wouldn't be seen. "I got eyes on you here. You'll be safe, I promise."

"Yeah, you've said that. Who?"

King shook his head. "Doesn't matter. Just know they're on you." He pressed his lips to mine and softly sucked on my bottom lip. He pulled back. "I'll come back as soon as I can, but I don't know how long that's going to be. Whatever you do, don't try to reach me. Eli looks for shit like that. Feeds on coming after the people close to his target so it's easier to take them out. I can't have him coming after you. I won't have you in harm's way again." He kissed my forehead. "I can't."

"Ray, are you out here?" Nadine called out again, her voice was louder now. She was closer.

"Shit!" King hissed. "There is one more thing I need you to know." His lips hovered just above mine. "You need to know that I don't give a fuck if your memory returns while I'm gone, 'cause it doesn't change shit for us. But from this point out there is only one thing I need you to remember."

"What's that?"

"This." King gripped the back of my neck and pulled me into him, crashing his lips to mine in a kiss that had me trembling with both desire and fear.

An angry passion.

A possession.

And he was right. There was no way I would ever forget it. He pulled back reluctantly pausing to look into my eyes as we both caught our breaths. I touched my bottom lip, swollen from his kiss.

"There are so many things I still have to tell you. Things I can't even wrap my head around," I told him.

Things like having a son.

"We'll figure all this shit out. I promise. No matter what it is."

"But what if my situation here is more complicated than just picking up and leaving?" I wanted to tell him about Sammy, but there wasn't enough time. I hadn't even had enough time to truly process the fact that I was a mother for myself just yet.

King ran his thumb over the back of my neck. "You should know by now I'm not a man who takes no for an answer, Pup. This isn't a negotiation. When all this shit is over I'm taking you home. With me. If you want to fight it, fight me? Go right on ahead, because honestly, I'm getting hard just thinking about you handcuffed to my bed again." His words vibrated against my throat as he spoke them right into the sensitive place behind my ear.

"Are you on that damn houseboat, child?!" Nadine called out from the dock. Between the tree branches, I saw Nadine. She was standing on the dock with my shorts in her hand. "That thing is ten seconds from rotting into the water. It's not safe."

"Go," King whispered. "I love you." He took a deep breath

and disappeared under the water, barely making a ripple in the surface. The hammering of my heart the only real reminder that he was ever really there. I stepped out from behind the trees and Nadine's head snapped toward me.

Nadine pushed out a hip and stuck her hand on it. "Girl, I've been looking for you everywhere! What the hell are you doing in there? I came to check on you, and you were gone. You scared the bejesus out of me!"

"Sorry. I couldn't sleep and decided to go for a swim," I lied.

"During the storm?" Nadine asked skeptically.

"It wasn't storming when I came out here."

Seeming to accept my answer Nadine tossed me my shorts. I shimmied back into them before emerging back onto the little beach.

Nadine guided me back up to the house by my elbow like I was an elderly person who'd wondered off. "Not feeling like you're home just yet?"

I shook my head.

Nadine patted my hand. "You know, those waters are pretty dark at night and there are things lurking in there that most sane people would be very afraid of."

I tried to contain to contain my smile.

If you only knew…

Chapter Six

DOE

I WAS ABOUT to get back in bed when the light from the phone I'd plugged in earlier illuminated the room, casting a glow on the ceiling. I unplugged it and crawled onto my stomach over the comforter, resting it on the pillow. The message on the screen indicated it was fully charged.

I slid the home screen open, but another message appeared asking for a password. I looked around the room and the first thing my eyes landed on was one of the sketches of Sammy hanging from the corkboard.

S-A-M-M-Y, I typed.

The screen unlocked. The home screen was wallpapered with a picture of Sammy, who was sitting in a high chair, smiling from ear to ear, blue frosting all over his face. I smiled at the smashed cake between his fingers. A candle sat in the middle of the annihilated desert in front of him. "Ray obviously needs a course in creating better passwords," I muttered.

I clicked on the camera icon and started scrolling through the pictures. Most were of Tanner and Samuel. One was a selfie of all three of us in a park that we must have taken several times because there were several varying versions of the same picture. We were all smiling.

We looked happy.

I don't know how the pictures made me feel other than confused. I was about to turn the phone off and finally get some rest when something in the background of one of the pictures caught my eye.

Not something.

Someone.

Lingering on a park bench not far from where we were taking our group selfie, sat a girl about my age with bright red hair. I blinked several times thinking that I was just seeing things. But I couldn't shake the feeling that I knew the girl. Her eyes had dark circles around them. Her clothes were tattered and torn. I scrolled back through the pictures again and there she was in each and every picture, looking directly at us as we snapped away. In the last picture she was smiling, but it was a sad smile that didn't reach her eyes.

I sucked in a deep breath.

No, no it couldn't be her.

It made no sense.

I raced around the room and searched through the various framed pictures, knocking some over in the process, until I found what I was looking for.

Until I found *her*.

The picture in my hand was taken in one of those old-time photo booths where they make the people in the picture look like they are from the Old West. Tanner and I were both in the picture as well, dressed like a cowgirl and cowboy. Tall hats and boots, bandanas tied around our necks. And there she was between us. Her foot hitched up onto an overturned barrel. Her dress falling off her shoulders, the side split clear up her thigh to her hip. She looked very different than the way she looked in the picture in the park, but there was no mistaking who she was.

Especially since in the Old West picture, she was aiming a fake gun directly at the camera.

I'd seen her do that before.

The gun aimed at me.

Holy. Shit.

And then something happened. Like a plug finally connecting into a working outlet. At first it was just a sputter of light and images. But then it grew into a steady flowing stream that once it got started, developed into full-fledged rapids. The kind where, once you floated into them, there was no getting out. Wave after wave flooded into my mind.

It was the very first.

It wouldn't be the last.

A memory.

★ ★ ★

RAY

"JUST ONE MORE time, Ray. I promise. I won't ask again, but I have nowhere else to go."

It's the third time in a month my best friend has come to my bedroom window in the middle of the night and asked me to sneak her in. It breaks my heart, but this time I've decided I have to tell her no.

"I can't. Not this time...and not anymore. What if my dad catches you? He said he's going to call the cops. Besides, you can't keep climbing up the tree and coming to my window in the middle of the night. What if Sammy was here?"

"Sammy is here?!" she exclaims loudly. She looks past me into my dark room. Sammy is at Tanner's and once again she was listening to every other word I said. "Sammy loves his auntie! Hey Sammy! It's

me! Your auntie is here!"

"SSSHHHHH! No, he's not here, but you're going to wake up the whole house!" I don't want to scold her like she is a toddler. I want to talk to her like we used to. I want to have a regular conversation with her like she is still the girl I bonded with when I was four years old. The girl I went to preschool with, the girl I got my first detention with because we talked too much in class. But that best friend, that girl I've known my whole life, no longer exists, and in her place is a person I don't recognize.

Her once auburn hair is now some strange shade of reddish purple. Her once bright green eyes are glazed over and unfocused. And for someone who used to take ballet very seriously and who moved around with ease and grace, she is now as jittery as if she'd downed several pots of coffee. Her nails look as if she has chewed them down to the cuticles.

"So, you don't want me around your son now?" She crosses her arms over her chest but sways. Reaching out she grabs onto a tree branch for support so she doesn't topple to the ground. Part of me wants to let her in just so she doesn't fall and break her neck.

"No. I don't." Usually I dance around the truth with her and normally I would say something like 'Of course, I want you around him, but...' and make something up. But I'd danced that dance and sang that song for too long and I've been watching my best friend withdraw from me more and more, sinking lower and lower into drugs and sex.

It started out as just another teenage girl rebelling against her strict parents. Our freshman year of high school she'd sneak out in the middle of the night and go to parties the seniors were throwing. She'd get drunk. She'd get high. She'd hook up with boys in our school.

I don't want to cut her out of my life, but I remind myself that this girl isn't the friend I've always known, the one who was more family to me than my drunk of a mother or my controlling father had ever been. But nothing I'd done has worked. She'd been to rehab three times already. During the third time, she didn't even bother completing her ninety-day stint, and on the day she turned eighteen, she'd signed herself out and walked out.

That's when her parents cut her off for good. That's also when she started disappearing. I wouldn't hear from her for weeks at a time. Then months. Sometimes I thought she was dead and then she'd appear out of nowhere, looking thinner and thinner. Her clothes shabbier. Her hair more brittle. Her skin covered with pock marks and scratches. Dirt caked under her nails. She'd confess to me that she'd been living on the streets. By the time she disappeared again with whatever money I could scrounge up, she'd just appear again at another time, even worse off than before.

"Fine, I won't come in," she says, "but I'm starving. Can I have some money? Just enough to last a week or so. Maybe a hundred? For food."

"If you're hungry I can make you some food and bring it out to you, but no more money." I am so close to cracking, but I hold strong.

"But…" Her lower lip starts to tremble. "Skinny will kill me if I don't have money for him. I'm supposed to give him fifty bucks tonight, but I don't have it. I spent it on a cab to come here…to see you." There it is. The guilt. And it works because I am about to tap into the last of the birthday money from the great grandmother I've never met and hand it over to her.

"Who's Skinny and why does he want fifty bucks from you? Is he your dealer or something?"

"No." She looked from side to side as if we were being watched then her eyes darted back to me. "He's my pimp," she whispered.

"Jesus Christ! What the hell have you gotten yourself into now?" I yell. I pause and wait for signs that anyone in the house has woken

up and when I don't hear anything I lower my voice to an angry whisper. "Why on earth do you have a pimp?"

"I don't know." Her voice cracks. "I don't know where I went so wrong, Ray. I don't know when I met him. I don't remember agreeing to do the things I do. But I do them and it's disgusting and I hate it, but he's really going to kill me if I don't bring him some money tonight." Her head shoots up. "And that's very judgey coming from you, Ray, Miss Teen Mom America, herself," she hisses.

Stay strong, Ray. Remember, she's a master manipulator. She needs help, not money. Both her compliments and insults are trying to play on my emotions, I remind myself, remembering what the articles said that I'd Googled over the last several months.

"I talked to your parents today. They said that if you go back to rehab and stay for the six-month program, you can come home when you're done. Why don't you just do that?" I ask her, hoping she'll agree to go back again. But I sense that this time is different than the other times and deep down I know that this time she won't be going back.

"I know, Ray. I just came from my parent's house. And I agreed to go. I'm going. I just have to get Skinny off my back first and they won't give me any money." Just when I'm about to break, she sniffles and I spot a dash of white powder clinging to the inside of one of her nostrils. It reminds me again that every word out of her mouth is her addiction talking, not her. I know she hasn't been home to see her parents. My room looks into their sitting area where both her mom and dad had been watching some documentary all night until they turned off the lights only an hour ago.

"I'm sorry. I just can't," I say, crossing my arms over my chest.

"Fine!" she shouts, slapping her hand against the tree trunk. "But can I at least borrow your flashlight? It's pitch fucking black out here and I can't see shit. I left mine on the fucking houseboat."

I walk over to my closet and pull out an old pink flashlight, the matching one to the package of two that we'd bought at a dollar store when we were in the fifth grade. We had made up our own version of Morse code and spent many nights sending light signals to one another across our yards, to one another's windows. It wasn't until another neighbor called the police and reported a possible prowler when we were forced to stop.

"Here," I say, handing her the flashlight. She takes it and flips on the switch. When it doesn't immediately turn on she pounds on the bottom with her palm until it comes to life. "You have what you want now. I'm leaving, Ray. You won't ever have to deal with me again."

"Wait! You just said you were going to go back into rehab. Why wouldn't I see you again?" I throat tightens. I made a mistake. It doesn't matter what she's done. I can't lose my best friend. She's sick. She needs help.

She needs me.

"Because I told you, if I don't have his money, Skinny is going to kill me." She pulls her dark hoodie from her head and turns the flashlight upwards until her face is illuminated in the yellow glow. I gasp. Dark purple bruises are smattered across her obviously broken nose, both of her eyes are swollen, and one has a halo of yellow around it. The whites of her eyes are blood shot. The corners of her cracked lips are dried with blood. Her jaw is off-center.

She hadn't been lying. Or maybe she had been but someone had obviously beaten her pretty badly. I am about to change my mind and open my mouth to tell her that she can have the money when she holds up her hand. "Never mind, Ray. It was nice knowing ya." She turns off the flashlight and starts making her way down the tree, temporarily disappearing into the black backyard until her shadow emerges under the streetlight on the front walk. She turns and waves. "Bye, Ray," I hear her say quietly, cutting through the silence of the night. There is a finality in her good-bye that makes the hair on the *back of my neck stand on end. She turns to leave but stops again and turns around. "And Ray? Whatever you do, don't trust the tyrant."*

Then I watch as my best friend turns back around again and walks away.

Maybe for the very last time.

I whisper back to her and can only hope that she can still hear me.

"Bye, Nikki."

Chapter Seven

KING

"**W**HAT EXACTLY DID the fucking thing say again?" Bear asked.

"Here," I said, flinging the envelope across the room. It landed on the floor. Bear reached down and unfolded the paper I wish I'd never received. He muttered as he read through the lengthy letter from the state, informing me that since I didn't qualify for guardianship of Max, that they would like to put her up for adoption. They'd already had an interested family reach out to her caseworker.

They'd already taken her from me physically, and now they wanted me to give them permission to give her to another family and strip the King name from her.

It was the last fucking thing I needed.

Bear and I were delirious and running on only a few hours of sleep in a week. We'd spent a shit load of time running offense, actively searching for Eli. We'd been everywhere from Miami to Atlanta, but the guy was like a ghost. Every bit of information we received brought us somewhere he'd just left.

Sometimes we'd missed him by just minutes.

"Says here they can't do shit without you signing off," Bear concluded, flicking the letter with his index finger, tossing it haphazardly onto the coffee table.

"Yeah, but it's also basically saying that if I don't sign off she'll be in fucking foster care until she's eighteen." I twisted the last piece of my tattoo gun in place. "Don't know if I can do that to her, man. When I was a kid, I would've given anything for my mom to actually be a mom. Fuck, I would have given anything just to know who my father was."

"But your mom was a fucking cunt," Bear stated, "and now she's a dead fucking cunt."

"Her being a dead fucking cunt is the reason I don't have my kid," I reminded him, "and maybe she's better off living with normal people who don't have to worry about all this bullshit of killin' or being killed."

Bear rolled his eyes. "Bullshit. Killing motherfuckers is business. Ain't got shit to do with family. What the fuck do they know, anyway? We're lawless, my friend. Civilians can't wrap their little fucking brains around what that means without getting their frilly panties in a fucking twist."

"You do know that in the eyes of the MC I'm a civilian," I countered.

Bear waved me off. "Just to my old man, and what the fuck does he know?"

I paused for a minute, before I shared something with Bear I'd never told anyone else. Even Preppy. "If I ever get the chance to be a real dad to Max...I'm going full civilian."

"Like you had to tell me. I fucking knew that shit. Let me know how your application to fucking DeVry pans out, you fucking pussy," Ghost-Preppy taunted.

"You ain't thinking clearly right now. We'll get Eli all nice and dead first, and then you can think about what a dumb fuck you just sounded like when you informed me that The King of the Causeway is going fucking legit," Bear scoffed.

I'd expected that response from Bear. I knew he wouldn't understand what lengths a person would go to for their kid, for their family. "You know how you would do anything for your brothers in the MC?"

Bear nodded. "For the MC. For you. Yeah, man. Anything. Steal, fight, maim, kill. Shit, I'd take a fucking bullet. I'd go back and take Preppy's fucking bullet right now if I could." I believed him, because Bear's loyalties ran deep.

"Well," I started, "those things are jack shit compared to what you would be willing to do for your own kid."

It was Bear's turn to shake his head. I knew he would never really understand what I'd meant unless he up and had a kid of his own someday, and that thought was laughable at best.

I rubbed my hand across the stubble on my jaw, which over the past week, had turned more beard than stubble. All I really wanted was to drag Pup into my bed and settle my face in between her legs for the foreseeable future.

But I couldn't do that until we ended Eli.

The guy was smart. He liked his revenge slow, sweet, and torturous.

Torture is the word I would use to describe not being able to reach out to Pup. But it was too dangerous. The last guy Eli set his sights on lost his entire family, right down to his second cousins, before Eli finally put an end to the guy's misery of watching everyone he loved die off one by one.

"We'll start back up in the morning," I said. "Put more feelers out there. See if we can get info from someone closer to him or his inner circle. Someone who will know where he is in present tense, not past."

I rubbed my eyes. I was tired, but also restless. My skin was literally itching to move the fuck on past all the fucking problems and move on to the solutions.

Like putting a fucking bullet in Eli.

Ideally I'd like to do it without even stopping the fucking car, and then hightail it back to Pup. Then, we can figure the Max thing out.

Together.

"You got any space left?" I called over to Bear, who was lying face down on the couch. We were in the apartment he'd built for himself in my garage. With no windows and only a single door in and out, it made us feel less like sitting ducks than the main house.

Bear spoke into the cushion, listing the parts of his body that weren't already covered with ink. "Some on my neck, the inside of my right arm, couple of fingers I think...and my dick, but you ain't my type, fucker, so hands off."

"He can't tattoo you're dick, Bear. He doesn't do micro portraits."

I laughed at the sound of Preppy's voice in my head and took another hit of the joint Bear and I'd been passing back and forth. "What's so fucking funny?" he asked, lifting his head from the cushion. His eyes rimmed in red.

"Prep," I said, holding the smoke in my lungs as long as I could, letting it burn in my chest until I had no choice but to blow it out. "This is fucked up, but...I still hear him sometimes."

Bear sat up and took the joint, taking three hits before leaning back on the couch with his arms spread across the back of the cushions. "I know what you mean. Me too. He's always been there to break up all the heavy shit we're all stewing in. Now that he ain't here, it's just all heavy shit...and no Prep."

The plan had been to take a night and get some rest before

going back to it. I'd tossed and turned for hours, knowing that until Pup was back in my bed, I'd never have a good night sleep again.

I'd heard Bear grunting, doing his own tossing and turning. So finally, we'd just quit trying.

For three hours we'd been getting high, and for a while it was almost like old times when me, Bear, and Preppy, had spent many nights the exact same way. Except without Preppy. And just like those times, I'd broken out my tattoo gun.

"You ready to do this?" I asked, holding up the gun, using the foot pedal to make it buzz in the air.

"Fuck, yeah. Ink me, bitch." Bear came over and sat on a stack of tires he used as a makeshift coffee table with his back to me. With his chin on his chest, he reached behind his head, moving aside his hair. He touched his fingers to one of the few unmarked spots of skin on his body. "Right there man."

I went in freehand and forty minutes later Bear had a new tattoo in big bold lettering.

PREP

He didn't even ask to see it before he fell back on the couch. He lit a cigarette and poured out some white powder from a little bag onto the table, cutting it into lines with a razor blade, using a rolled up dollar bill he snorted two lines. Pinching his nostrils together, Bear chuckled. "Remember that time I jumped off the roof of the garage into the bay? Man, that shit was epic"

"I remember," I said, shaking my head when Bear tried handing me the rolled up bill. "Preppy about had a coronary when you threw him in the water. Had his white suspenders dry-cleaned three times that week."

Bear looked as tired as I did but there was more to it than

just a lack of sleep. I'd never seen him look so worn out. "What's got you all inside out? You haven't been right for a while. Even before shit when down with Preppy. What the fuck is up with you?" I asked.

Bear sighed, resting his hand that was holding his cigarette against his temple. "Pops wants to pass me the gavel."

"Hasn't that always been the plan?"

Bear shrugged. "Yeah, when he died or was like ninety. Even then, part of me thought he would be buried with that fucking gavel in his stiff hands. But he wants to pass it to me…now."

"I still don't understand. What's the fucking problem?"

Bear stood up and started to pace back and forth in front of the couch. "To be honest man? I'm just not sure I want it anymore. What made sense when I patched in don't make much sense anymore. Shit's changing. In the club. Out of the club. Things just ain't how I thought they'd be," Bear said, looking absently at the ceiling. He shook his head as if he were clearing the fog away. "Maybe I just need some pussy," he said. "Maybe when all this shit's over, I'll text that British chick Jodi. She fucks like a champ and prefers it in the ass."

"Some random chick ain't gonna fix shit," I said.

"I know, but my cock in her ass will at least make me forget for a while." Bear plopped back down on the couch. He scratched at his arm. I guess I wasn't the only one restless and itching to get this shit over with.

"Mind if I ask you something?" Bear leaned forward, grabbing his smokes from the table. He didn't wait for my answer. "Why is *Doe* the one that's got your fucking guts all torn in pieces, when you used to go through a bitch or two a day? Sometimes at the same fucking time," Bear lamented.

I raised my eyebrows. "We gonna sit around and talk about our fucking feelings now?"

"I mean, she's fucking beautiful, man. And I've called girls hot, sexy, trashy, but in an I'd-still-fuck-your-trailer-park-ass type of way. She's different. A girl like her should be far far away from anyone who even resembles Florida white trash like us."

I unholstered my gun and set it on the table. "You about to say something I'm gonna need this for?" I asked.

But it was what he wasn't saying, which was written all over his blond bearded face, that was really pissing me off.

He wanted to protect Pup.

Because he loved her.

I wanted to empty the chamber of my gun into his fucking chest, but I didn't. Because I understood. 'Cause Pup was everything in one beautiful fucking package, and it wasn't her fault that more than just me saw that. And it wasn't Bear's fault that he'd felt it too. But it would be his fault if he ever acted on it.

If he ever touched her, I could be standing over his dead body, holding the smoking gun, and I still wouldn't feel the least bit guilty, because it would be that motherfucker's own fault if I had to put him down.

Bear knew this.

"Fuck you and your gun," Bear scoffed. "You already know I liked her from the beginning." He ashed his cigarette into an empty beer bottle. "I regret sending her up the stairs to you that night. Not keeping her for myself." There was a lingering sadness in his voice. "And then when you fucked it all up by almost getting your cock wet, I'd never been more fucking pissed than when you showed back up at the dock." Bear took another drag of his cigarette. "Way I see it, you owe me motherfucker."

Bear sending her up to my room that night being the reason I ever set eyes on Pup, was the only reason why my fist hadn't yet connected with his nose.

We needed a change in conversation before I did something

we'd both regret. Me, because he was my friend. Him, 'cause he'd be full of fucking bullets.

"You still haven't answered the question, motherfucker." Bear leaned forward. "Why her?"

I shrugged. "I don't know," I answered honestly. "It's just another fact. Just like the sky is blue. The grass is green." I shrugged. "She's mine. Just is. Just know it."

"You ever think she deserves better than this shit?" Bear waved his hand around the room. "Than you?" I flashed him a questioning look. If I was on edge before this conversation, I was teetering off of it now.

"Not me, motherfucker. Just...better. Than this. Than this life."

"'Course." I lit a cigarette and inhaled, tossing the lighter onto the table. And then I looked up at Bear and smiled.

"But she doesn't have better...she has me."

I'd barely gotten the words out of my mouth when concrete and steel came crashing down around us, flying into the apartment like a tornado was ripping through.

I ducked. Crawling on my stomach, I sought cover behind the coffee table. I coughed as I inhaled one lungful of dust after another. I squinted, looking past the settling debris toward where the crash had sounded.

There was a gaping hole where the wall had stood only seconds before.

The remnants of that wall, a huge pile of toppled concrete block, covered the living room.

And the couch that had been against that wall.

And the person that had been lying on the couch.

Bear.

Chapter Eight

DOE

I T WAS TOO early. Or too late.

Or too, something.

I'd finally had a memory of someone pre-memory loss and it was of someone I knew post memory loss.

Nikki.

My best friend since I was in diapers. Who was also the hooker who'd acted like she was doing me a favor by letting me tag along while we both tried to survive on the streets.

There was no doubt in my mind that it was the connection of my past and present that helped me to remember. It was the only thing that was clear to me. Everything else was like driving a car, with a muddied windshield, trying to look through the smears to see the road.

Why would Nikki, knowing who I was, knowing that we'd been practically sisters, suggest that I sell myself to a biker at King's party in exchange for a warm bed and protection?

Unable to sleep and with way too many questions running through my mind, I'd come out to the front porch and had been sitting there staring at the framed picture of Nikki ever since.

King hadn't been the only one lying to me all that time. "Why didn't you tell me who you were? Who I was?" I asked her picture, running my fingers over the silver frame.

"Hey Ray, long time! What's crack-a-lacking? How's it going? How was your trip? How's the tyrant doing these days?" I looked down to where a postman stood on the bottom step. It was light out, but I didn't even remember the sun rising. He wore dark blue shorts with matching knee sox. His smile was one of those ginormous ones that said he was either one of those truly happy people, highly medicated, or completely insane.

"Hey..." I sat up from the porch swing, squinting in an effort to read his name tag, "...Barry? He's fine...I guess?" I was a horrible liar, but at the same time, I couldn't bring myself to tell him that not only did I not remember him but that I hadn't seen my father since he dumped me off the previous day with no word on when he'd be coming back.

I didn't want to offend his smile.

Barry didn't say another word, but he didn't need to. His furrowed brows and wrinkled nose spoke volumes for him. He set the mail on the ledge and without another word, he slinked backward, before turning around and walking away as if he'd just fed an angry pit bull and was trying not to get bitten.

But I was angry. Confusion is a bitch. It leads to questions, which only lead to more questions, which leads to being frustrated, which leads to being pissed off.

"He wants to see you in his office," Nadine said. "Your mother is there, too. They're waiting for you."

"Really?" I stood from the swing, automatically smoothing down my hair and adjusting my shorts, pulling on them so they would appear longer.

Which was odd, because I didn't care what they thought of me, but the motion to make sure I was presentable was automatic. I'd seen the same Town Car that had taken me from King's pull up that morning, but I didn't have any sort of urge to rush up to the senator and welcome him home either. He may not have been the one who had ordered for King to be killed, but there was something way too coincidental about the entire situation that was keeping me on edge with my guard up and locked firmly in place.

"Is my mother feeling any better?" I asked as I followed Nadine to the study. The house wasn't large by any means. The glass doors of my father's study could be seen from any point in the great room and kitchen and it was a straight shot from the front door. There was no need for her to show me where it was. But then I realized that Nadine was just trying to be mindful of my memory loss.

"Thank you," I said. Nadine nodded and with a tight smile, before going back to her work in the kitchen.

And then it happened again. For the second time in less than twelve hours. This time the sputtering was only for an instant. The images coming in faster, clearer.

Another memory.

★　★　★

RAY

15 YEARS OLD

MY FATHER'S OFFICE is his temple, a virtual shrine to himself and all of his political idols. American flags hung on the walls in frames, photos of himself shaking hands with men with fake bright white teeth, and even faker smiles. Men who he saw as more than mere mortals.

Men who he aspired to be like.

The gods of the Republican Party.

In his quest to become them, my father had long ago chosen poli-

tics over family. Except, of course, when the bill or law he was pushing involved family values of some sort. Then, we were at the forefront, paraded around and used as examples everything a good conservative Christian family should be.

A cross hung behind his desk, next to the American flag.

It's complete bullshit.

HE is complete bullshit.

He's never stepped foot inside of a church for reasons other than having to do with politics, but he tells people he's a Protestant.

What he is, is a fucking liar.

Everything about him, everything about his office, screamed formality and bullshit.

Which was why I chose this very room as the place I was going to tell him the news, and during his regular business hours, in hopes that he would curb his temper while on his sacred holy ground.

I dress for the occasion like I am going for an interview. Matching yellow jacket and pencil skirt, straight out of the Jackie Kennedy handbook. I've been hiding the bump for months now under baggy clothes, but the suit accentuates my rounded belly. I am six months along and there is no more hiding.

I spy my father through the glass French doors, with his back to me, leaning against one of the green chairs in front of his desk. I take a deep breath and push on the handle. "Dad, can we talk?" The word 'dad' feels funny to say. I haven't called him it in years. The use of the word is strategic on my part, starting the conversation with a reminder of who he is to me.

Something I think he often forgot.

He hasn't been any sort of father to me in years.

He isn't a dad at all.

He spins around when he hears me come in, revealing that he isn't alone. Tanner is sitting in one of the big green chairs in front of my father's desk, smiling a little too brightly for my liking. Some-

thing is up. "What's going on?" I ask, taking tentative steps further into the room.

The senator speaks first, "Tanner told me your news," he says, straightening his jacket, yanking at the bottom hem. He looks down to where my hands rest against my rounded belly. He looks disturbed, as if someone has just told him his numbers are down in the polls, not that his fifteen-year-old daughter is pregnant.

"He did?" I am going to kill him.

"Yes," he says, rounding his desk and taking a seat in his high-backed burgundy chair, which is more of a throne than office chair. His lips set in a straight line. "And as much as I don't want to, I'm going to have to bring someone else in on this."

Who could he be bringing in? Oh. Shit.

My mother.

I hadn't even really thought about telling her. To me, my mother is a non-issue. I rarely see her and when I do, it is at a function where she pretends to be the PTA-type mom, then when the lights go out in the ballroom, the switch on being 'mom' is turned off and she goes back to ignoring me like always.

I don't even hear my parents speak to one another anymore unless they are bickering about something. And it's always something to do with my father's campaign. They stopped arguing about their relationship years ago.

It's hard to argue over something you don't care about.

"Okay," I say meekly, preparing myself for the shit storm I am about to receive. And although I am shrinking into the seat next to Tanner, I'm oddly looking forward to what is about to take place. I wring my hands. Tanner doesn't seem affected. He sits casually with his ankle crossed over his knee.

My father stands up, looking impatient. "I will be back in a moment," he announces and leaves the room.

I snap my head to Tanner. "What exactly did you tell him?" I *whisper.*

He whispers back, "The truth."

I punch him in the shoulder. "Why the hell did you do that? I was going to tell him. That's what we'd agreed!"

"Yeah, but I thought about it and I decided it was better if it came from me because he can't get pissed at me."

"That wasn't your decision to make, Tanner. You can't just decide all the rules all the time on your own, you know." I cross my arms over my chest. "And why can't he get mad at you?"

"He can get mad, he just can't kick my ass or anything. Because if he does, he knows that all it would take would be me telling my dad how mean the good senator was to me. And just like that, his number one campaign supporter would bring the money train to a screeching halt," Tanner says proudly. He winks at me.

He's got a point.

I'm still pissed though. "I'm glad you're sitting over there all smug and cocky while I'm literally shaking in my boots," I say.

My father comes back into the room, his cell phone in his hand. He takes his seat and sets down his phone on the desk.

Maybe his plan was to call my mother? I knew she wasn't home, but had no idea where she disappeared to this time. I can just imagine what she'll have to say about this.

Her questions to me are always about what I've gotten myself into or contain some other snide remark suggesting I am anything other than the perfect obedient daughter that I am.

Or was.

"Ramie Elizabeth…" the senator starts. That's what he always calls me when I haven't lived up to his impossible standards. Then he adds an accusatory third-person statement to the end of it.

Ramie Elizabeth decided to quit piano without telling me.

Ramie Elizabeth seems to think her little drawings are more important than a real education at a real school.

Ramie Elizabeth has been hanging around with that horrible Nicole Arnold girl again.

In an odd way I am really happy to be able to give him something worthy of his disappointment. Everything else has been a mild annoyance. A fire drill leading to this very moment. He will be able to put his making-me-feel-like-a-failure skills to good use today.

Because today the fire is real.

"...you're pregnant," my father says, like he was the one telling me the news.

I flinch because hearing the words out loud somehow makes it even more real. Like now that he knows, I am even more pregnant than I was when I came through the door.

"They don't teach you kids about condoms in that private school of yours?" the senator asks me. I see the regret cross his face the second the question leaves his lips, because he already knows the answer.

Tanner sees the same thing I do and he answers for me. "No sir. They don't," he says with a huge smile. And I know why he is smiling. My father has campaigned against teaching contraception in our local school district. His plan for teaching sex-ed had been an abstinence only course called, well, Abstinence Only.

"Wipe that ridiculous smile off your face," my father says to Tanner, leaning across the desk. "I'll have Nadine call a private doctor. Of course I can't stand behind a termination, but as of right now the law is on your side, and it's still your decision to make, until the Republicans change things, that is." It isn't a statement about my options, it is a suggestion. An order.

"No!" I say, standing up. I press my suit against my very rounded belly so he can be face to face with what it was he was suggesting I do. "It's too late for that," I say, "and even if it weren't, I wouldn't just call a doctor and get rid of it." I stare him down.

"What do you mean it's too late?" my father asks cautiously.

"She's already six months along," Tanner says, trying to deflect

some of his bitterness away from me.

Thankfully it works because the senator moves on to a new plan. I'm still waiting for him to call my mother.

"We need to sort this out, figure out how we are going to approach this mess," my father says. "There is a lot to consider in matters like these." And he's right. We have to talk about what I am going to do about school. Who would be taking me to my doctor's appointments, and lots of other details. I intertwine my fingers and take a deep breath.

"Look," I start, but my father holds up a hand to silence me and reaches for his desk phone, dragging it from the corner to the center. He grabs his cell phone and scrolls through. Finding what he's looking for he pushes the speakerphone button on the desk phone and references his cell as he dials.

"This is Mags," a woman's voice announces.

"It's Price," my father starts. "We have a situation here. We're going to need to work out a strategy, backlash, and then we need to talk approval rating. Maybe take a poll."

Mags. I know that name.

The man in front of me, my father, the one bent over the desk phone, doesn't care one bit that his teenaged daughter is pregnant. He doesn't care that I will miss school. He doesn't care that I don't know the first thing about taking care of a baby, or that my entire world is about to change in the most drastic way imaginable. No.

This phone call is like tossing a bucket of ice over my head and dragging me back to the reality that is the senator.

Because his phone call was to the one and only Mags Allbright.

Public relations extraordinaire.

I am not his daughter.

*I am a **situation**.*

That was officially the last day I called him Dad. From that day on I called him by one name and one name only.

The senator.

My father sat behind his desk looking very much like he did the day I told him I was pregnant, except maybe a little worse for wear. There were circles around his eyes, his hair was noticeably grayer, his complexion now slightly yellowed. I sat down in the same green chair I'd sat in three years before.

"You're not going to say hello?" a voice asked from the corner. I turned my head to see my mother sitting with perfect posture, her legs crossed at the ankles, in a high-backed chair.

"Hello," I said. My mother sat forward, bracing herself on the armrest. She picked up a glass tumbler that was filled with some sort of dark liquor and stood. She set the glass down on the senator's desk, the liquid splashing over the side. "Are you feeling better now that you're back from…the spa?" I asked.

"I'm fine, dear. So glad to have you home," she said robotically. "I'm assuming you don't remember me either."

I shook my head and then remembered the picture frame I was still clutching in my hands. "I remember her, though." I turned over the frame in my hand and pointed to Nikki.

"You remember Nicole?" my father asked, sounding very surprised.

I nodded. "Just one memory. She'd come to my window, asked me for help. Money." My eyes welled up with tears, but I fought them back. "I told her no."

The senator sighed. "I'd forbidden you from seeing her after she went to rehab the first time, but you didn't listen. You never did when it came to that girl."

"Apparently one time I did because I remember sending her away from my window."

"And you should be glad you did," my mother chimed in, "because she's—"

"Margot," the senator warned.

"She's what?" I asked. I already knew the answer, but a part of me needed to hear it out loud.

"She's dead," my mother finished, with a shrug of her shoulder. "That poison she was shooting into herself finally killed her. They found her in a dirty motel on the side of the highway." There was no reverence in my mother's voice; her nose was turned up as if she smelled something foul in the air. "She had a purse full of condoms and drugs. She'd turned to selling herself to support her habit."

I stood from my chair, almost knocking it backward. "So, just because you buy shit with a fancy label and pour it into crystal, you think it makes you somehow different?" I pointed to the drink in her hand. "Nikki shot her shit into a vein, you're mainlining yours down your throat." I shook my head in disbelief. "You ignorant bitch! She was an addict, just like you're obviously an addict. The only difference between the two of you is that she didn't try and make it look pretty."

"Get. Out," my mother said, her hand visibly shaking. She threw the glass against the wall and it shattered against a picture of George W. Bush.

"Both of you. Stop. Margot, the car is waiting. Go. I'll join you shortly." My mother leered at me as she did what she was told, leaving the room in a huff. The front door slamming shut a few seconds later.

My father didn't address my mother's behavior. "We have to leave for an event in Myrtle Beach. In the meantime, there is a specialist coming to see you. He's an expert on brain trauma and memory loss. He works mostly with veterans at the VA, but has agreed to come work with you. Try and behave while we're gone and…your mother…she's…fragile these days. Go easy on her."

He stood up and buttoned his jacket. He opened his desk drawer and retrieved a gaudy bright gold watch with a red diamond encrusted bezel. "We'll be back Thursday," he clipped, and left the room.

Suddenly my fear of being alone made no sense at all. Because I'd much rather be alone than spend another minute with my parents.

I vowed right then and there to be the mother to Sammy, that according to my memories, my mother never was to me.

I wanted Sammy to grow up feeling loved and knowing that I'd always be there for him, no matter what. The last thing in the world I ever wanted was for him to grow up and hate his own mother.

Like I hated mine.

Chapter Nine

KING

W HEN THE DEBRIS settled in the room, I crawled on my stomach, stealing a glance out from behind the coffee table where I'd ducked for cover. The couch where Bear had been sitting could no longer be seen in the rubble.

And neither could Bear.

There was a commotion of voices. Commands were barked. It sounded as if the orders were being spoken into a canyon, and all I could make out were the echoes of their voices.

Pain, dull and pulsing, radiated from my head. Blood dripped into my eyes. My vision blurred, I squinted. Two men carrying AKs clamored over the remains of the wall and entered the apartment. They were fixated on something hanging from the pile of debris on the couch and that's when I finally caught a glimpse of Bear.

Or at least, part of Bear.

His leg hung at an awkward angle, dangling over a large piece of concrete. His jeans ripped. His calf dripping blood.

Something moved outside and my attention snapped back to the hole in the wall. There was a large truck just beyond the wreckage; it was still running, the headlights on and shining directly into the apartment. Attached to the grill was some sort of ramming device.

Leaning up against the truck, was Eli.

He spotted me and smiled, tipping his hat to me like he was greeting an old friend.

A crunching noise sounded from behind me. I turned my head to find one of Eli's men standing over me, pointing his AK in my face. "You gonna die today," the man said. Scars covered one side of his jaw, a shitty thin lined prison tat covered his neck. A toothpick hung from his lip, moving up and down when he spoke.

"After you, motherfucker," I growled, rolling over to my side, taking out his leg. I threw him off balance and he fell sideways. I grabbed the gun I kept hidden behind my belt buckle, and before he could lift his gun again, I'd already aimed and fired, sending him to the place in hell reserved for pieces of shit like him.

And me.

I ran over to where Bear was pinned beneath the rubble. Shots rang out, the table exploded, shards of the glass top rose off the table like someone had just canon-balled into a pool of water, then crashed back down, sending bits and pieces of shrapnel soaring through the air, stabbing into the skin on my neck and chest like a million tiny knives, not much bigger than a grain of sand.

A bullet whizzed by my head and lodged into the wall behind me, narrowly missing my forehead by less than an inch.

I stood straight and aimed my gun toward the snarling man who wore a look of disappointment on his face, pissed that he'd missed his intended target.

Me.

I took more time to aim than was safe, standing out in the open with no cover, but my little back up gun only had one bullet left and I needed to make it count. I squeezed the trigger and the man's eyes went wide as the bullet pierced his throat. He choked and gurgled on his own blood as he crumpled to the floor.

I tossed the gun and started clearing the rubble off of the couch. After what seemed like forever, but was probably only a few seconds, I cleared a block that revealed Bear's face and neck. I leaned down and put my ear to his chest.

Still breathing.

I had to move quickly. Eli was standing just outside and God only knew what that crazy motherfucker might be armed with.

I reached behind Bear and tried to wrestle a gun from one of his holsters under his cut. I had no doubt it was fully loaded. Bear was always prepared. I hadn't successfully freed the gun when seven more men came bursting through the hole in the wall. All armed. All guns aimed at me.

I froze.

The front door opened and another four men came barging through, followed by Eli. "I know I made my own entrance, but I had to use the front door, you see. It's more civilized that way," Eli said, pushing his dark sunglasses back up the bridge of his nose. He looked around the room and turned up his nose. "And Lord knows someone has to remain civilized in this godforsaken shit town."

I wouldn't blame any man for giving up if they were in the same situation I was in. Unarmed, facing a firing squad.

I wasn't just any man.

I had things to live for. People to live for.

My girls. Bear. Grace.

My family.

"King of the Causeway," Eli sang, reading it off of a street sign on the wall Preppy had made for me when we'd first moved in. "They worship you here." It was a statement, not a question. He blew out a long sigh. "It's too bad, you know. We could have done some business together, you and I."

He sounded just like Isaac before the shit when down with Preppy. "But now? Now that you killed Isaac without so much as a thought of the repercussions...well, I don't do business with stupid men, *King*." He stressed my name as if it were a ridiculous thing to say.

I cracked my knuckles and hissed through my teeth. "You best be careful about who you call stupid, motherfucker," I spat. "Isaac came at me and my people *after* I'd already offered to cut him in on our business. If you want to call someone stupid, it should be him," I chuckled. "Oh wait, you can't...'cause I made the fucker's head explode." Maybe I was the stupid one after all, because I knew that taunting Eli wasn't the brightest thing to do, but I needed to let that motherfucker know that he wasn't dealing with someone who was just going to roll over and die.

That wasn't a fucking option. So while Eli spoke, I formed a plan.

"That wasn't your fucking call to make!" Eli said, his pale face turning red. He took off his dark sunglasses. His right eye was missing, nothing but a gaping hole in its place. "I decide who lives and dies in this state. Not you! Not anyone! Me! That is my call!"

I spotted my other gun, the one I had threatened Bear with earlier on the ground only a few feet away. "Isaac made it my call when he aimed his fucking guns at me and my boys and raped..." I was about to say *my woman*, but quickly corrected, "...some biker bitch who didn't like what he was offering."

"I don't care if he raped your fucking cunt mother!" Eli

seethed. "And what you did was stupid, because it's going to cost you...your life." He nodded to his boys who began to descend upon me. Leaning back against the wall, I found what I was looking for and clicked the switch with my shoulder.

The old garage door on the side of the room, the one Bear had covered with a huge Beach Bastards flag screamed to life, shrieking and scraping, dragging metal against rusted metal as it struggled to open for the first time in years, sending the furniture and a glass cabinet, which had been leaning up against it, tumbling over. Glass crashed. Wood snapped.

It was just the distraction I needed.

Just enough time for me to grab the gun off the floor and dart toward Bear. I pulled and pulled but he was stuck under the concrete. A bullet grazed my shoulder, leaving a burnt trail of flesh across my skin. I dove through the hole in the wall, managing to get off a few shots of my own in the process. Sending at least two more of Eli's men to hell in the process. Bullets chipped away at the concrete all around me. I slid down the side of the garage and made my way into the thick brush that lined the yard. I hid between a patch of cypress knee roots.

"Find him or you all die!" Eli screamed, still inside the garage, his hands on the wall over the hole. Heavy footsteps jogged passed me in both directions. Some going the way of the road, others the way of the path.

I wasn't going either of those ways. As soon as the footsteps passed, I ran through the brush, expertly avoiding collision as I skillfully navigated the woods I'd been familiar with most of my life. Even when Preppy and I hadn't lived in the stilt home, we'd camped in the woods surrounding it.

I ducked under the mangroves and eased my way into the water. I held my breath, sinking down as deep as I could before pushing off the bank and swimming across the small lake to the other side. I emerged, only up to my nose, before lifting myself onto the shore.

I looked across the lake, watching the men run back and forth to Eli. Most likely delivering the news that they couldn't find me. He shook his fists in the air and let out a frustrated roar. Two of the men ran back into the garage and emerged a few minutes later. One was walking backward while the other was hobbling forward behind him. They were struggling to carry something as they made their way to the fire pit in the center of the yard.

Eli followed behind him, seeming calmer than just moments before. He pulled out a cigar and lit it with a match. The smoke shrouded his face in white. He tossed the match into the fire pit and after stoking the embers with a long stick, it came roaring to life and I was able to see what they'd been carrying.

Bear.

He was laid out on the ledge of the brick pit, his one hand dangling just above the red embers.

Eli looked out across the lake, and even though I knew he couldn't see me, he somehow knew I was watching him because he tipped his hat and smiled.

It was a challenge.

I was the rabbit he wanted to scare out of the hole.

Bear was the smoke bomb he was going to use to do it.

His plan just might work too, because there was no fucking way I wasn't going to go back to save Bear.

At the very least, I was going to die trying.

Chapter Ten

DOE

I FELT LIKE I was walking around wearing Kevlar to protect myself from the parents who genuinely didn't give a shit about me, and from the questions that sat on my brain unanswered like a fucking aneurysm about to burst, and from Tanner. Who, when looking back, I felt shitty about how we left things. I truly felt like he could be a good friend. But instead of being sympathetic to what he was feeling, I threw it in his face and yelled at him.

I was alone.

Utterly fucking alone, and for some reason, that made me spitting fucking mad. I was either a raging bitch or so numb to everything I was practically a mute.

And I'd pushed Tanner away.

Which in turn meant I'd pushed Sammy away.

And that was the opposite of what I wanted.

I'd been just about to go see Tanner, but going to him and forcing him to talk to me before he was ready might be like kicking him while he was down. So I decided to wait for him to come talk to me when he was ready.

If he was ever ready.

At least with the arrival of the specialist I had a temporary distraction to occupy some of my time.

The specialist had showed up and grilled me for an hour. Dr. Royster, a man old enough to be my grandfather's grandfather, didn't ask me anything about how I was feeling. He'd cut right to the chase and asked me what I remembered. I told him about Nikki. "No two brain injuries are alike." Dr. Royster had said. "Especially those that affect memory." In the end, he told me that I should seek help from someone who knew me. Someone I'd spent the most time with who could walk me through my life and hopefully evoke some sort of mental exorcism.

After the specialist left I found Nadine in the kitchen. "How did it go?" she asked, spraying cleaner onto the countertops and wiping it off with a rag.

"Basically, if he were giving me my chances to live, I've got a 50/50 shot," I said, taking a seat on one of the barstools. The cleaner smelled like a nauseating combination of vinegar and bleach. "He also wants me to have someone walk me through my life. Places I went, things I liked." I leaned forward and bit my bottom lip, "What do you say?"

Nadine smiled. "Baby girl, I'd love to help you, but I don't think walking you through how I make breakfast and watching me fold laundry is really what he had in mind. If you want to talk to the person who knew you best, you would need to talk to…" She paused and folded the rag, placing it over the faucet of the sink, setting her hands flat on the counter. She looked out the window like she was reflecting on something.

"Nikki?" I offered.

"Who told you about her?" Nadine asked, refocusing on me.

I shrugged. "I think my mother mentioned something about her being my best friend and a *bad influence*."

"She was much more than that," Nadine said. "She was like a sister to you. The two of you did everything together."

"Including run away?" I asked. "Right?"

Nadine looked away thoughtfully and turned back to me. "Gone after her? Maybe. But never run away. You wouldn't leave Samuel and Tanner. You wouldn't leave me. That I know." She tapped me on the tip of the nose. "Tanner, he's the guy you want to talk to. Besides Nikki, you two were tighter than the lid on a jar of pickles."

"I might have messed that up. He came to talk to me and he got mad. Instead of being understanding, I kind of yelled at him." Nadine shook her head and offered a small smile.

"Girl, there ain't nothing that boy wouldn't forgive you for. Go find him. I'm sure he'll help." Nadine shooed me off the barstool. "Now get girl, I gotta mop these floors. Whoever decided that dark wood was a good look was the devil himself 'cause I'm having a hell of a time trying to keep them clean."

Tanner only lived a block or two over. Nadine pointed me in the right direction. But just like I knew where the boathouse was, my feet knew the way to Tanner's.

A large woman with chubby cheeks and bright red lipstick answered the door and informed me that I'd just missed Tanner.

Feeling defeated, I made my way back to the house, but I wasn't ready to go back inside. I made my way out back to the abandoned houseboat. I carried my shoes as my feet sunk into the soft sand. I'd just rounded the mangroves when I spotted Tanner, sitting on the edge of the pier with his feet hanging off the edge of the dock. He was wearing a plain white T-shirt and blue basketball shorts. He appeared to be lost in concentration, focusing on his flip-flops that dangled off of his toes.

"Hey," I said as I approached him. "Where's Sammy?"

He looked up and shielded his eyes from the sun. "Hey. He's with my parents at the club. Grandparent/grandkid square dance." He laughed, but it fell flat, his smile never reaching his eyes.

"This seat taken?" I asked.

"All yours," Tanner said softly, scooting to the side to make room for me.

I sat down next to him and looked off over the water, unsure of what to say, nervously fidgeting with my hands in my lap. Thankfully, Tanner spoke first. "This was kind of our place, you know. We spent hours here fishing off the back of the boat or watching the storms roll through. When your dad told you it was a safety hazard and wanted to have it hauled away, you cried for a week."

"He doesn't seem like the kind of person who wouldn't do something just because it upset me."

"Oh, he's not." Tanner agreed.

"Then why is it still here?"

Tanner smiled. "The senator doesn't see emotion, he sees reason, and more than that, he sees legalities." He laughed and his bright brown eyes lit up. "I wish you could remember the look on his face when you handed him the survey you printed out online. When you pointed out that the houseboat wasn't on his property, so technically wasn't his to remove, I thought he was going to pass out. Then when you informed him that you'd filed documents to declare it a historical landmark...I think it was the only time I'd ever seen him actually laugh. He looked almost...proud."

"So the houseboat stayed," I said.

"Yeah, he had the walls reinforced with steel piping so it wouldn't fall down around us, but it stayed." He turned to face me, lifting his foot up onto the dock, resting his chin on his knee. "Because of you."

"Then I guess he can't be all bad."

Although I'd yet to see it.

"Listen," I started. "I wanted to say that I'm—"

"No, Ray. I'm the one who's sorry. I yelled at you." Tanner shook his head. "I've never yelled at you before. I was so mad at myself when I left your house. I should have been sympathetic. You needed a friend and instead I unloaded all my bullshit on you."

"No, I'm sorry. This has to be difficult on you. My attitude and being so defensive hasn't been helping any."

"Well, then I guess it's settled," Tanner said. "We're both sorry."

"That we are," I admitted.

"So where should we go first?" Tanner asked, standing up from the dock and reaching out a hand.

"Huh?"

"I came to see you and ran into Nadine, she said you need a memory exorcist." He pointed at himself with his thumbs. "I'm your guy."

"You don't have to do this." I took his hand and he helped me up. Now it was my turn to shield my eyes from the sun as I looked up at him.

"I know exactly where we should go first," he said. When I started to pull away he looked down at where his hand still held mine. "Sorry," he said, letting go. "I can't promise things like that won't keep happening. It really is just a habit. But I promise I'll be more understanding when you pull away."

"Maybe this isn't—" I started.

"Dress comfortably. Meet you out front in twenty minutes!" Tanner said, turning and jogging back down the dock. I didn't feel threatened by Tanner's affections. In fact, a part of me liked it when he grabbed my hand. Not because I liked him that way, but because it felt nice to know that while I was gone and worried that no one had missed me, that I didn't have anyone who cared, that Tanner was here all along, missing me.

With our son.

Chapter Eleven

DOE

EVERYTHING IN RAY'S closet, *my* closet, was light in color. Beyond the slitted bi-fold doors was a sea of white, yellow, and pink. Mostly sundresses, Jackie-O looking skirt-suits, and blouses that button up to the neck. It wasn't that anything was ugly. On the contrary, it was really beautiful. A little conservative, but beautiful. But I wished for the clothes I'd left back at King's. Black tank tops, snug fit jeans, and flip-flops.

All were chosen and bought for me, courtesy of Preppy.

Which was another reason I probably loved them so much.

I ran my hands over the different fabrics in the closet and wondered how in the span of a few months, my taste could change so drastically. Or maybe I always liked my comfy clothes, but just hadn't been able to speak my mind.

Maybe when I lost my memory, I grew a pair of balls.

After a little further searching, I had found a few things I felt comfortable in, and after a quick shower, I put on a pair of black Converse sneakers, a black V-neck, and a pair of ripped jean shorts. I met Tanner out in front of the house as he'd instructed. He pulled up in a newer model shiny black truck with bright chrome accents. Something had been done to it to make it a lot taller than most trucks on the road, which got me to thinking about another black truck. More of a farm style truck from the sixties or seventies, and the man who looked so good driving it. "Mommy!" Sammy shouted from the backseat, bringing me back to the present, and my heart did a little skip.

"Let's go make some memories!" Tanner said, rounding the truck to open the door for me.

During the entire half of an hour ride, Sammy babbled end-lessly. I was impressed with Tanner's patience, especially when Sammy let out a high-pitched screech that could only be de-scribed as a pterodactyl scream and Tanner only laughed and shrugged his shoulders. "He does that when he's frustrated." Tanner pursed his lips. "And when he's happy, and when he's upset, and when...he does it all the time," he admitted. We turned off on an exit marked Indian Reservation. We crossed under a sign made out of bent branches that announced that the place was called ALLIGATOR FUN LAND. Sammy squealed with delight when Tanner took him out of his car seat and the second his little feet hit the ground he raced through the gates in front of us.

We chased Sammy from exhibit to exhibit. The entire time, Tanner talked me through what we'd done there before. What I'd said. What I had thought about the flamingos or the turtles. Anything to connect the past to the present and trigger a memory. Most of the time, I just smiled and nodded as I watched the little boy of energy that was my son run circles around us.

For lunch we ate hot dogs from a cart and brought them into the little arena to watch the alligator feeding.

Sammy crawled up on my lap. "Mommy, look!" he cried out, pointing to where a man dressed in a safari type outfit, khaki shorts, and a matching short-sleeved collared shirt, had entered the gate housing a small dark pond. "Where the gators?"

he asked, chewing on his fist as he spoke, spreading the mustard from his hot dog up into his nose. Tanner reached out and wiped his face with a napkin.

"You gotta watch the pond buddy," Tanner said, pointing to the water. When the trainer tied a piece of red meat to the end of a rope, attached to a long pole, the audience of around twenty people went quiet. He pushed the pole out over the water and shook it so that the rope and the meat dangling from it danced in the air. In less than a second, several alligators rose to the surface in a series of splashing and thrashing, opening their strong jaws and climbing over one another to get to the meat. The largest of them all was the one who was successful, clamping his razor sharp teeth around the meat, snapping the rope, and disappearing back under the water as quickly as he'd appeared. Tanner and Sammy clapped and cheered along with the rest of the audience but the entire thing felt unsettling to me. The trainer was provoking beasts kept in captivity.

It felt *wrong*.

There was enough trouble in the world; there was no need to go looking for it by dangling bait in front of a hungry beast with sharp teeth.

Tanner nudged my elbow. "The feeding show always was your favorite."

Either that has changed or Ray was a really good liar.

I shrugged and looked down to Sammy who was still on my lap, clapping so hard his hands would miss each other every so often and land on his chubby arms. He looked back at me and smiled, mustard crusted around the corners of his mouth. I didn't care if it left me with a bad taste in my mouth, if it made Sammy smile like that, it was alright by me. "Nah, it's great."

On the way back to the car, Sammy walked between us,

grabbing both of our hands. We swung him back and forth as he shrieked in delight, my stomach doing a little flip every time I knew his smile was a result of something I'd done.

We'd done.

"You know, we had our first kiss here. Right in the parking lot. We actually couldn't afford to go inside so we set a blanket on the grass by the fence to watch one of the shows until we were told to leave by security," Tanner said, his eyes squinting as a low hanging cloud rolled away from the bright sun.

"We did?" I looked around to the lot crowded with families and searched for something familiar, something that would snap it all in place for me.

But it never came.

When Sammy's little legs got too tired to keep walking, Tanner lifted him and carried him on his shoulders as we made our way through the parking lot. When Tanner's hand sought mine out, I could already see where the truck was parked. The happiness radiating off of the boys was infectious as they listed all their favorite parts of the day. I didn't want to ruin the amazing day we'd had by pulling away and again reminding Tanner that the girl he loved wasn't his anymore. So for the twenty or so feet to the truck, I let Tanner hold my hand.

And for all twenty or so feet, I thought about King.

After we'd left, I was surprised when instead of taking me back to my house, Tanner passed it, and instead pulled into the driveway of his parents flamingo pink house.

"What are we doing?" I asked, as Tanner continued down the long winding driveway to the back of the house.

"I live in the pool house out back," Tanner explained.

"No, I mean why didn't you drop me off?"

"I figured you might want to give Sammy a bath, read him a

bedtime story, help me put him to bed," Tanner said, parking the truck right outside a smaller but still bright pink version of the main house. The windows of the truck were only slightly lower than the roof of the pool house.

The truth was that I wanted to do all of that and more. I didn't even have to think hard on it to know that what I really wanted was to keep Sammy with me. Have him sleep in his room down the hall from me, have me be the one who he wakes up to in the morning, and who rocks him to sleep at night.

But I wasn't going to push anything. I was still the girl with the brain injury. Of course no one would trust him with me full-time when I don't even remember being a mother in the first place. But I didn't have to remember being Sammy's mom to actually be his mom.

Because he remembered me. And looking in the rearview mirror, into Sammy's identical eyes, I knew that nothing else mattered but being everything to that boy that he wanted me to be.

That I wanted me to be.

"Yessssssssssss," Sammy agreed from his car seat. "Storrrr-ryyyy."

"I guess I'm giving a bath and reading a bedtime story then." It's not like I could argue with that level of enthusiasm even if I wanted to.

I didn't want to.

"It's nice to see you smile." Tanner said, coming around and opening the passenger side.

Inside the pool house was more like a large hotel room; the bed and living room were one in the same. A small portion of the main room had been walled off to make a makeshift room for Sammy.

Tanner ran the bath water and, at first, I stood there in the center of the bathroom, feeling useless and uncomfortable, not knowing what to do with my hands. But when Sammy threw a washcloth and it smacked against my face, I pulled it off and went over to the tub. The second I kneeled down beside him, it all fell into place. I washed his hair and soaped him up as if I'd done it a thousand times before.

Because I have done it a thousand times before.

When bath time was over, I dressed Sammy in the PJs Tanner had laid out and he clamored up onto my lap as I read to him from *Larry the Leopard Learns His Spots* by Dr. Nellenbach. When he drifted off to sleep, his head on my shoulder, I walked him over to the other side of the room and set him in his bed, which was low to the ground, and had a guardrail along the side so he wouldn't fall to the floor during the night. I was just about to leave when Sammy's little voice pulled me back into the room. "Mommy?" he asked.

"I'm here," I said, kneeling beside his bed.

"Mommy, sunshine song?" Sammy asked, talking with his thumb in his mouth. He yawned. "Sunshine song when I go na-night."

I opened my mouth to tell him that I didn't know what song he was talking about, but the words of the song came out instead. As I softly sang to him, Sammy closed his eyes and hummed along.

You are my sunshine, my only sunshine
you make me happy when skies are gray
you'll never know dear, how much I love you,
please don't take my sunshine away.

When the song was over Sammy opened his eyes. "Mommy,

snuggles with me?" Sammy lifted his little blanket.

It was an offer I couldn't refuse. I sat on his mattress and lifted him into my arms. I sat back against the headboard and cradled him under my chin, setting his blanket down over both of us.

And for a long time, I just sat there, breathing in his hair. Absorbing the feel of his soft chubby fingers absently playing with mine. A peacefulness I hadn't known since I left King's washed over me. The way I felt about Sammy was the most overwhelming sensation I'd ever experienced. Like every single part of me belonged to him. Like the very reason I was ever put on the earth was to be his mother.

"Mommy," Sammy said, snuggling into my chest, "I wuv you much."

I covered my mouth with my hand to muffle the sound of the sob that came out of nowhere. I brushed his curls from his eyes and leaned over to kiss him on his head. "I love you too, baby. So much," I told him.

And I did.

My brain may have forgotten him, but my heart hadn't.

I stayed there for a long time with my son wrapped in my arms. Long after his breathing became even and I knew he'd long been asleep.

I was careful not to wake him when I wiggled out from underneath him. When my feet hit the floor, Sammy stirred and I stilled until he rolled over onto his stomach with his hands above his head.

Deep in sleep.

I kept my eyes on Sammy as I tip-toed out of the room, running right into Tanner who was standing in the doorway. "Have you been here the whole time?" I whispered.

"Yeah," Tanner admitted, stepping aside to let me pass. He shut the door. "I couldn't take my eyes off you guys. Reading stories, bath time, it's something I never thought I'd see again."

"It was...amazing," I admitted.

Tanner grinned and plopped down on the couch. "His room in your house is bigger, but I built this for when he stays with me. Although, I admit, sometimes my mom is the bath giver." He patted the couch cushion next to him. "My mom and dad have been spoiling him rotten these past few months."

"Two rooms in two houses," I said, still standing.

"He was usually only here with me a couple of nights a week." Tanner said, again patting on the cushion, motioning for me to take a seat. I sat, but on the opposite end of the couch, up against the armrest.

"I don't bite, Ray," Tanner said with a laugh.

I tried to relax, but I needed to say something and I didn't know how he was going to take it. "I don't want to push things, Tanner. And I know that I don't really remember him as my son. But I feel him. He's a part of me. I know it." I paused. After starting with all the reasons why he should be reluctant to allow what I was about to ask, I was hesitant to continue.

I closed my eyes. Took a deep breath, and blurted it out. "I want Sammy with me as much as possible. I think he wants to be with me too." I turned my head away and braced myself for the rejection.

Tanner scoffed. "You're his mom, Ray. You don't need my permission to spend time with him." He stretched his arm over the back of the couch. "Let's take it slow. Sammy can start spending more time with you, but I think it would be better if it was gradual. It was a hard adjustment for him to be without you, I don't want to push him into anything too quickly."

I felt my face light up. It felt good to smile again. "Thank you, I really mean it. That would be great." I sighed in relief. "Can I ask you something else?"

"Absolutely anything," Tanner said, and I could tell from the way his eyes shone when he spoke that he really meant it.

"If we were together, then why didn't we live together? With Sammy? This two houses less than a mile apart thing kind of seems a bit strange. Don't you think?"

"I know it's not common these days, but after we had Sammy, we decided we wanted to do things the right way and wait until after graduation, like how we'd originally planned." Tanner laughed and scrunched his nose. "Actually, you decided that we were going to wait. I'm not going to lie, I did try to talk you into it a few thousand times or so. So that was it. We were going to move in together after the..." he trailed off and slapped himself on the thigh. "Nothing, I shouldn't have said anything. Just forget it."

"No, tell me. You promised to help me, to walk me through my life, right?" I reminded him.

Tanner stood and walked over to the kitchen. He opened one of the drawers and pulled something out of it. Holding whatever it was in one hand and covering it with the other, he walked back over to me and sat back down on the couch, this time with his thigh pressing up against mine.

Tanner took his one hand away, revealing a small black box in his palm. "We weren't going to move in together until after..."

Sheer panic. It's what I felt as he opened the hinged top of the box, revealing a thin gold band topped with a tiny round diamond.

The few other memories I recalled had kind of flowed into

my mind. This one came crashing in like an out of control bus.

★ ★ ★

RAY

15 YEARS OLD

TANNER IS SICK. Really sick. Sicker then he's letting on. It breaks my heart to see the dark circles under his eyes. The cheeriness of his bright pink Polo doing nothing to brighten the mood of what I know he is just about to tell me.

When he goes to sit at the edge of my bed, he winces when he connects with my soft mattress. He is in pain, has been for a long time. But no matter how many times I ask him if he's okay, he brushes it off and tells me he's fine. He can't brush it off anymore. He was about to come clean and I don't know if my heart can handle it.

"So, you know I've been sick for a while," he starts, reaching for my hand and intertwining his fingers with mine. Holding hands came naturally to us. We've been doing it since we were five. He is my best friend. Him and Nikki. Always have been. We used to act out getting married in the houseboat when we were younger. Upon Tanners insistence, Nikki was always the reverend and Tanner and I were always the bride and groom.

"You're so bossy. You're always telling us what to do. It's not fair." Nikki used to tell him. "Why don't I ever get to be the bride Mr. Bossy-Pants?" She'd whine.

"Cause Nikki," Tanner would answer. "Me and Ray really are gonna get married someday."

Tanner has always been so certain of our future together. It's his certainty that keeps me from telling that I think of him as just a friend. But that's also a lie in a way, because I may not love him the way a wife would love her husband, or the way a girlfriend loves her boyfriend, but Tanner and I are so close that he IS so much more to me than just a friend.

And I do love him.

He's my family.

He is my world.

Him and Nikki both are.

I always thought that maybe I would grow to feel the same way about him that I know he feels about he. We have time. We're still so young.

We have our whole lives ahead of us...

Recently, all talks of Tanners future stopped.

"Yes, of course I know you're sick, but you're getting treatments, right? You're getting better." I know it before the words cross my mouth that it isn't the truth, and somewhere in my mind, I am hoping he would continue the lie he'd been reciting over the last few months. That it is getting better. That it is going to be okay.

I search his eyes for any sign that he is about to tell me that he's made a miraculous recovery but the hope in his eyes is dying right before me. "Ray, I stopped responding to treatment."

I feel like someone is punching me in the gut.

No, in the heart.

"But there is something else they can do, right? Some other treatment? Here," I say, grabbing my laptop off my night stand, opening it up. "Let's Google what else there is to try. Maybe something Eastern or holistic." My fingers flew across the keyboard as I tried to find something that I knew didn't exist. Tanner might be done lying to me but I'm not done lying to myself.

"Ray," Tanner says softly, shutting my laptop and tipping my chin up so that our eyes meet. "There is nothing else. Trust me, they've tried everything." Tanner has been in and out of the hospital too many times to count since he got sick. At one point, he was away

more than he was home because his parents were flying him around the country from specialist to specialist. "But we have time. There is nothing else they can do for me, but what I have is slow growing. I'm not going to see graduation, but they think I have six months, maybe a year. Possibly more."

Six months. A year. One more birthday with Tanner, one more Christmas. We are fifteen. Life isn't supposed to end at fifteen. Life should just be beginning. There are so many things Tanner wasn't going to get to experience. Prom. Graduation. Having kids.

We have the rest of our lives...

I just always thought the rest of our lives would be longer than six months. A year. "That's no time at all," I admit, hot tears form in my eyes and spill out onto my cheeks. Tanner leans over and wipes a tear away. His chestnut brown eyes may have lost hope but there is still life in them. There would be no brown-eyed curly haired kids with his eyes calling him Daddy.

"I think I'm going to be sick," I say, leaping from the bed. I barely make it to the bathroom before emptying the contents of my stomach into the toilet until I am heaving and nothing else comes up.

I make a promise right then and there, leaning over that toilet bowl, that I am going to make the best of the time we have left. To do everything I could to make sure that when Tanner goes out, he would go out having experienced everything he could before his time was up. I flush the toilet and brush my teeth. When I go back out into my room, Tanner is leaning up against my headboard staring out the window. Clouds are rolling over the sun, casting an eerie shadow over his body. "How are you feeling right now?" I ask, making my way over to him. "Physically."

"They gave me some meds this morning. I was hurting for a bit, but now I'm actually feeling pretty good. If they didn't just tell me that I was going to be worm food in a year I would probably be *feeling great." He flashes me a small smile and I wince at his words, knowing full well that they are partial, if not all lies, but my resolve to give him everything and more in the time I still have him is strong and keeps me focused on the beautiful curly-haired boy on my bed. "Are you okay?" he asks me. I let out a laugh.*

"Are you really asking me if I'm okay?" I snort.

Tanner, finding the humor in his question, laughs too. "Yeah, I guess I am." Throughout the years it's been that smile of his that's taken me out of every dark place I've ever been in, and although my family situation is far from ideal, Tanner always makes me feel like as long as I have his smile, I am the luckiest girl in the world.

"Can I try something?" I ask. He looks at me and raises a brow.

"Sure, what's up?"

I don't answer, instead I pull my t-shirt over my head and unclasp my bra. "What are you doing?" he whispers, his eyes wide as he stares at my bare breasts for the first time.

"Just tell me if I hurt you," I say, pushing my jean shorts down until I am only in my cotton panties.

"Ray, you don't have to do this. I don't want you to have sex with me because you feel sorry for me. I don't want pity sex from you."

"Pity sex?" I bark loud enough for other people in the house to hear. "Pity sex?" I repeat in a whisper. "Tanner Redmond, this isn't pity sex. This is just making the most out of life." I straddle him and look for signs of him being in pain. There aren't any. I grab his wrists and place the palm of his hands on my breasts.

"I don't want to do it this way, Ray," Tanner says, although something stiffening in his jeans tells me otherwise. He must read my face. "No, I want to. Of course I fucking want to." Tanner never cursed, but there was excitement in his voice. "Roll over." He pushes me off of him until I am flat on my back. He stands up and removes his shirt. His once muscled and tanned body has been replaced with

pale skin over protruding bones. He is still beautiful to me.

He would always be beautiful to me.

I lift my hips and pull off my panties. His boxers tent as he gazes down at me. "Under the covers," he says. I shift and raise up my comforter and sheet, scooting underneath. He pushes down his boxers and I lift up the covers so he can join me. I spread my legs and he settles himself on top of me, his arousal pressed up against my stomach.

For the first time in our lives we are skin to skin.

"Are you nervous?" Tanner asks. He could probably feel my heart pounding like a hammer and fluttering at break neck speeds in my chest. Because I feel his and it is doing the exact same thing.

"No," I lie.

"Me either," he lies.

Tanner kisses me and after a few minutes, he positions himself with his hand and slowly enters me. It hurts at first. Just a little pinch of pain, but then it's gone. It doesn't feel good, it's uncomfortable at best, but it feels good to be sharing this with him.

It is over in just a few minutes. He collapses on top of me and kisses my neck. "I love you, Ray. I love you so much it hurts."

And it did hurt.

So much.

"Holy Shit!"

I clasped my hands over my mouth in surprise.

"What? Did you remember something?" Tanner asked eagerly, searching my eyes for his answer.

I nodded slowly, unable to explain to him what it was I just experienced.

Tanner shook my shoulders like he was trying to shake my answer from me. "Ray! What did you remember? What is it? Tell me!"

"I just remembered…"

"What? What did you just remember?"

"I just remembered—that I love you."

Chapter Twelve

KING

I HEARD BEAR before I saw him. His muffled scream ripped through the air, the breeze carrying it over the lake and right to my face as if he were standing there screaming at me.

I'd raided one of Preppy's storage houses in the woods and found exactly what I'd needed.

"Zombie apocalypse supply center," Preppy corrected.

I'd even found a charged burner in the shed, but when I'd called the MC and asked for Bear's old man, the kid who answered told me Chop wasn't taking calls. When I dialed Chop's cell, it went to right to voicemail. I called every single member of Bear's MC whose number I had memorized, but as soon as they heard it was me calling, they'd all hung up without even letting me explain that Bear was in trouble.

I left voicemails. I sent texts.

Nothing.

The Beach Bastards MC, with the exception of Bear, were working their way up to the top of my list of motherfuckers who needed to be taught a lesson in manners.

In respect.

In fucking *brotherhood.*

"We don't need those motherfuckers, Boss Man," Preppy chimed in. *"We got this shit. Well, we'd have this shit if I could*

hold my gun, or had a body, or was fucking alive. Then we would
sooooo totally have this shit."

"But you had to go and fucking die," I snapped, angry that
Preppy wasn't there with me, and angry with myself for talking
out loud to my dead best friend, and angry that I was angry at
him for being fucking dead for Christ's sake.

I loaded everything into a duffel bag that I rolled in a tarp. I
carried it above my head as I waded back through the water,
staying close to the edge so that I wouldn't be spotted because
even though it was dark out, the center of the open bay always
looked as it were lit up, reflecting the light of the moon and
stars.

I made my way back into the woods. I could see the light
from the fire pit was almost as tall as the house. Bear's scream
once again tore through the air. When I finally had eyes on him,
I found that what they were doing to him, was actually much,
much worse than what I'd imagined.

Bear was tied up in sections. One rope kept his arms tucked
into his sides. One kept his hands tied behind his back. One was
tied around his head, tucked into his open mouth like a gag.
Bear was biting down on it so hard his teeth were almost meeting in the middle of the thick rope. Tears of pain ran down the
side of his face. He was on his stomach, laid out across several
chairs. His pants pulled down around his ankles, his ass high up
in the air. Eli's men stood behind him and prodded at him with
some sort of broken off handle. They laughed every time Bear
screamed. One held Bear's ass cheeks open as another forcefully
rammed the object in and out of him.

Eli sat nearby in one of the folding chairs surrounding the pit
that was usually occupied by bikers when I'd had parties. He was
resting his head back against his interlocked hands. His legs were

stretched out and resting on the ledge of the fire pit.

Eli was as if he was watching an opera, beholding something beautiful and wondrous, his eyes wide, as he intently watched the brutality taking place in front of him. I cracked my knuckles. As the assault continued, another guy, one with bright orange hair, found his amusement by sprinkling the glowing embers of the fire onto Bear's backside.

A bold motherfucker, with a thick black swastika tattoo on his shaved head, pulled his cock from his pants and stepped up to Bear, whose head was now hanging down off the chair, his chin almost touching the grass. The man pulled the rope from Bear's mouth and yanked on his hair, lifting his head up. The man grabbed the base of his cock and rubbed the tip of it across Bear's lips. Bear must have lost consciousness because he didn't even move. It wasn't until the motherfucker forcefully shoved his cock into Bear's mouth when I knew that Bear was not only conscious, but he was ready for a fucking fight. His eyes sprang open and the guy jumped back from Bear, holding onto his crotch and screaming, trying to hold back the blood that was pouring out between his fingers.

Bear spat out what was left of the man's cock and smiled from ear to ear, blood dripping down his face, coating his teeth.

And he laughed.

It was now or never.

I unholstered my gun and pulled a grenade from the duffel bag. I took a deep breath and cleared my mind of everything except what I was about to do.

Crouching down as close as I could to the ground, I snaked my way over to the fire pit. I pulled the pin from the grenade with my teeth and tossed it into the fire.

One second.

Two seconds.

Three seconds.

BOOM

The fire pit exploded into a blinding wall of white light. An image of Pup sleeping peacefully in my bed, her limbs tangled with mine, flashed in my mind as I ran toward the chaos.

Toward Bear.

And directly toward the possibility, that come morning, I'd be in a place reserved just for me.

In hell.

Chapter Thirteen

DOE

I T HAD BEEN three weeks without a single word from King. I was starting to give up hope that he would ever come back for me.

Tanner's mission to help me remember my life continued, fueled by the revelation that I remembered loving him when we were kids. I tried to explain to him that it was a memory, not a current feeling, but I knew that Tanner still looked at it as a step in putting back together what we'd had in the past.

"How are the meetings going with the specialist?" the senator asked, slicing into his rare steak, blood gushed from the meat, flooding the plate with red. He rubbed the piece on his fork through it before pulling it off the fork with his teeth.

It was the first time I was sitting down to an actual meal with my father, my mother once again at the 'spa' or wherever she claimed to be. But despite my angry brain telling me that I shouldn't be nervous, I was still wiping my damp palms on my jeans every few minutes. Sammy was napping on the couch just a few feet from the round dining room table where we sat.

"Okay, I guess. I don't really know how those things are supposed to go, though." In actuality, the specialist barely asked me any questions and on two occasions, he'd nodded off during our session.

"Good. I want you to continue your visits with him. We have some functions coming up at which I'd like you to be present. There is a charity event for the campaign in a few weeks. We are hosting it in the Redmond's backyard, Tanner's parents' place," the senator said, making the event sound more like a business meeting rather than a party.

I scrunched my nose and poked at my dinner with my fork. "I don't know if that's such a great idea. I assume I'm supposed to know who these people are. Won't it be obvious when they start talking to me and I look at them like they have thirty heads?" I asked.

"Ray, you've never liked what I do for a living. You've never really acclimated to being the daughter of a senator," my father said, sitting forward in his chair. "It wouldn't be unusual for you not to know who these people are."

"Ray, it could help with your memory. You should come," Tanner gently chimed in. Trying to regain my memory would be the only reason I'd agree to play the part of 'dutiful daughter.'

"Will my mother be there?" I asked.

The senator kept his eyes on his plate. "Yes, she attends all the campaign functions. It's part of our…agreement."

I snorted. "She attends all the functions, yet she's somehow forgotten to attend her own life," I muttered.

The senator sighed. "Your mother…she blames me for…well, everything," the senator said. "It's hard for her to be around for too long. She gets restless." And for a mere flash of a second, I felt almost bad for him. For one tenth of a millisecond, I thought I saw a tiny glimpse of a man who wasn't a senator at all, but a frustrated husband with an unhappy wife.

He almost seemed…human.

Again his eyes focused on me and he continued. "You see,

Ray, when you were pregnant with Samuel, we took every precaution possible not to alert the media of your 'condition.' And back then, I didn't carry the weight that I do now, so it was easier to keep things hidden. But now that you're back, from Paris for the summer, as I have led them to believe, it will be good for you to show yourself. They've spotted Samuel, and multiple outlets have contacted my office inquiring about who he is. Some reporter from the Times even went as far as to look up his birth certificate. So now it seems as if we have a situation on our hands which requires a...delicate touch."

He wiped his mouth with his linen napkin and set it down in the middle of his empty plate. "And, of course you don't remember, but we've had in-depth conversations about what was best for our family. And for your new family." The senator gestured to Tanner and then toward the couch. "Now is a better time than any. You don't need to make a big spectacle about it, just a courthouse visit. Something on paper to make the media see this union and Samuel as legitimate. You don't have to live together, not if you aren't ready. It's just the documentation we need now to deter any campaign supporters from deflecting."

"You want us...to get married?" I asked. My hand curled tightly around the napkin in my lap. Tanner's hand reached under the table and covered mine.

The senator cleared his throat. "If you don't, there is a big possibility that I lose the election, because my campaign is heavily based on conservative family values. Over the years, I've spent a great deal of time garnering support because of those values I stand by. If you don't make this little family of yours something legitimate, I run the risk of looking like a fraud and letting down all the people whose asses I have been kissing since day one. This could snowball into the fastest decent into political nothingness this state has ever seen."

"I don't understand how my decisions would affect your campaign. It's not your life. It's mine," I argued.

"No, of course you don't understand," the senator said, pinching the bridge of his nose. "But understand this, even if my campaign survives the teen pregnancy scandal, it would never survive a torrid affair with a convicted felon ten years your senior. I wouldn't survive until the end of my term, never mind the end of the election." He folded his hands over his plate. "But if you do this, if you marry Tanner, then they won't have a need to look any deeper and hopefully the name Brantley King will never be part of the equation.

This is where the senator and I disagreed. I wanted nothing more than for Brantley King to be a part of my equation.

"What about what Tanner wants? You didn't even ask him." I stated.

Tanner remained quiet, pushing around the pasta on his plate.

"Just think about it," the senator said, rising from the table. He nodded and left the room without another word.

Tanner was still holding my hand under the table. I used taking a sip of water as an excuse to pull my hand from his. I shook as I raised the glass to my mouth, the glass clanking against my teeth.

Panic set in suddenly and I dropped the glass I was holding when my chest tightened to the point of constricting my breathing. With my hands clasped around my throat I watched as the glass bounced off the wooden table and crashed on the floor, shattering into a million little sharp pieces, the water running like a river into every nook and seam of the floorboards.

The senator wanted me to marry Tanner in order to help his

campaign and career. Tanner wanted to marry me because he was eager to pick up where we'd left off before I'd lost my memory.

But what did I want?

I wanted Sammy. I wanted King. And I wanted Tanner in my life, but wasn't yet sure of how he would fit.

But none of that mattered. Because if I married Tanner, even on paper, there was no doubt that he wouldn't live long enough to make it to our first anniversary.

With King I was strong, willful, and determined. I liked who I was when I was with him.

But in the house I'd grown up in, surrounded by people I'd known my entire life.

I had no idea who I was.

Chapter Fourteen

DOE

MAYBE IT WAS all the marriage talk. Maybe it was me feeling alone all the time, even though I was surrounded by people. But I was started to fucking lose it.

It had been four weeks with no word. No sign. No nothing from King. And I was wearing a hole in the carpet of my room pacing back and forth until a reckless idea hit me.

King had said it wasn't safe for him to contact me, or for me to contact him. But if I tried to get word to him through Bear's MC, then it wouldn't directly link me to King in the eyes of anyone looking in from the outside.

No sooner did the idea take hold was I running downstairs. I grabbed a set of keys off the rack hanging by the door and sprinted to the garage, hopping into a big beige Lexus that reeked of floral perfume.

A scent I knew that was familiar to me.

A scent I knew I hated.

I put the key in the ignition and turned the engine on. And then I paused.

I don't know how to fucking drive!

I pounded my fist on the steering wheel and then my forehead in frustration. But when I'd just about given up hope, I glanced up from the wheel and saw something leaning on the wall of the garage that I knew instantly I could drive.

By the time I pulled up to the Beach Bastards' clubhouse, my anxiety had me out of breath, but I wasn't the least bit deterred.

I jumped off and let the moped fall to the dirt. I ran up to the gate where a skinny kid was manning the door. His cut read Prospect in huge letters. He didn't have a name patch. "You lost or something?" he asked.

I rested my hands on my knees and held up a finger, still catching my breath. "I need to speak with Bear, if he's here," I huffed, "and if he's not, I just need to talk to someone who can get a message to him, or to King."

"Oh, I remember you. From the party, before all the shit went down. Glad to see you ain't full of bullet holes." He hopped of his stool. "Hang on." He slid the gate open and disappeared behind it.

He was gone for what seemed like an eternity. Although the sun had gone down, the humidity had wrapped me in a pool of water suspended in the air and there wasn't a single spot on my body that wasn't soaking wet. I looked like I'd peddled through a rainstorm, but there wasn't a cloud in the sky.

I waited on the prospect's abandoned stool, kicking the gravel around under my sneakers. When he finally reappeared, he wore an apologetic look on his face. A man with a grey beard, older version of Bear, except slightly shorter and rounder, followed him through the gate. The patch on his cut said President. He lit a cigarette and shoved the lighter into the pocket of his shirt. His face was heavily lined with the signs of age, but there was no mistaking the freckles under his eyes. The same ones Bear had.

"Good, you must be Bear's dad. I need to talk to him...," I hesitated, unsure of Bear's dad's name.

"Chop," the man filled in the blank, pointing to his name patch. "You the one King claimed?"

"Claimed?" I paused, remembering that Bear had used the same term on the dock months before. "Um, yeah. I think so."

"You're the girl they sprayed bullets in my house over," Chop said, shifting the toothpick that hung out of his mouth with his tongue. "'Cause we got our own trouble here without you bringing that shit to my door."

"No, that was Isaac. He cornered us, he tried..." I shook my head. "Please, I just need to speak with Bear, just for a minute—"

"Ain't here." Chop shrugged.

I dropped my shoulders in disappointment. "Then can you please just get a message to him or King for me?" I asked hopefully.

Chop narrowed his gaze at me like I'd just stepped on his foot. He pointed a finger at me accusingly. "Like I told my son a million fucking times, Brantley King was not a member of this MC and therefore was no concern of mine."

Was?

Chop turned around but then he stopped and looked back at me over his shoulder. "King's dead. Him and Bear both." He didn't wait around for my reaction before disappearing back behind the gate.

I dropped to my knees, the gravel slicing into my skin as my world came crashing down around me.

Preppy. Bear.

King.

All dead.

They're. All. Dead.

"Nooooo!!" I wailed.

The prospect lit a cigarette and looked down at me with pity.

He turned away from me, refocusing his eyes on the empty street.

"Sorry, kid."

Chapter Fifteen

DOE

NEVER AGAIN WOULD I be able to look at a bow tie, a motorcycle, or someone with tattoos without struggling for air.

It was only because of Sammy that I didn't wish I was dead too. He was the only reason I was able to swing my legs over in the morning and plant my feet on the floor.

I loved the tattoo on my back more than ever because King had given it to me, and it was something I would carry with me forever. A permanent piece of him.

An idea hit me, and once it took hold there was no letting go, and there wasn't anything I wouldn't do to make it happen. Because for the first time since finding out that King was dead, a little sliver of hope cracked through the cloud of despair.

IT TOOK ME forever to remember where the house was where King had taken me when he'd parked and waited, hoping for just a glimpse of his little girl.

I'd only seen the back of the house then, and with only a vague recollection of where it was; it had taken me the better part of the morning to finally find it.

I reminded myself that foster kids moved around from place

to place all the time. The possibility was high that she wouldn't even still be there.

I had to try anyway.

I waited across the street in a vacant lot, for what seemed like hours, in the blistering heat. When the front door opened, out came a shorthaired woman holding the hands of two little kids about the same age.

Between the picture on King's dresser and the small glimpse of her I'd gotten the only night I'd ever seen her, I recognized her right away.

Max.

The woman maneuvered the children into a waiting minivan. I followed them to a building where other men and women were shuffling their kids in through the door. A wooden sign, barely legible, having been faded by the brutal Florida sun, announced that the place was called Maria's Learning Academy and Day Care Center. The woman who brought Max inside, emerged childfree. I waited until she drove off to make my move.

I tried my best to dewrinkle my knee-length pleated skirt with the palms of my hands, but there was only so much I could do after hours of straddling the moped. I ran my fingers through my hair and took a deep breath.

Bells chimed when I walked through the door. Sounds of laughing and crying children sailed through the air. It smelled like disinfectant and sugar. "Can I help you?" asked a bright-eyed pudgy woman sitting behind a partition.

I plastered on the biggest and brightest smile I could muster. *You can do this.*

"You sure can, ma'am. I'll be taking classes at the university in the fall and I'm looking for a great day-care for my son. I was hoping to tour your facility," I said sweetly.

The woman examined my face like she was waiting for me to tell her the punchline to a joke. "You're just a baby yourself," she quipped. "You ain't old enough to have babies of your own." Her eyes were soft and kind.

"Don't I know it," I agreed. "So how about you show me around a bit?" I pressed.

She shook her head and shuffled around some papers on her desk. "Oh, I'm sorry darlin'. Maria, the director, isn't here and she's the only one authorized to give tours. It's a safety thing and we're all about the safety here." Another worker wearing the same turquois shirt as the receptionist entered the waiting area. She gave a little wave and the woman pushed a button on the wall next to her. A buzzing sound came from above the door that connected the tiny waiting area with the rest of the building. The woman opened the door and passed through and when it closed again, it made a loud clicking sound. "See?" She pointed toward the door. "Safety first."

"Oh." My face fell and my shoulders slumped.

She explained further, "She is usually here around this time, so you can come back tomorrow if you want. But if she doesn't attend the public funding meetings, then we don't get the foster kids, and if we don't get the foster kids, then we have to rely on the families who can afford day-care." She sighed. "Which means I'd be out of a job, 'cause there ain't many of those these days."

My confidence suddenly renewed, I leaned into her window and smiled sweetly. "What's your name?" I asked.

"Name's Audrey, Miss," she answered with her own sweet smile.

"Well, Audrey, if funding is your problem, I happen to know a senator who might be able to help you out…"

Five minutes later, I was following around Audrey as she gave me a personal tour of the day-care center. I wasn't lying about the funding. I would talk to the senator and see if I could help them.

I just didn't know if it would work.

Audrey brought me out into the main room filled with cafeteria-style tables that were low to the ground, with equally tiny chairs surrounding them. "We feed them both breakfast and lunch plus two snacks. The rooms are arranged by age. Babies in one. One-year-olds in another, and so-on..." Audrey kept talking, but when I spotted Max only feet from where I stood, I faked interest in the bulletin board hanging above the table she was sitting at.

"That's our activities board," Audrey said, coming up to stand beside me. "That's the schedule of music time, numbers time..." Her voice faded into the background when another one chimed in.

"You're really pwetty," sang a small sweet voice. I looked down into familiar bright green eyes that literally took my breath away. They were the same color as his, but where King's eyes held the harsh and bitter reality of the life he'd lived, hers were void of any contempt and alive with innocence.

I knelt down next to her. "Thank you. You are too," I said. She giggled, her little tiny square teeth reminded me of Sammy. She chewed on her fingertips.

"I like dis," Max said, reaching out to touch a bracelet I'd put on that morning, in an effort to look more like the Ray Price in the framed pictures in my room.

I pointed to the tiny purple plastic bracelet on her little wrist. "I like yours even better."

Audrey cleared her throat. "I'd like to show you to the playground. It's modernized and we firmly believe in at least thirty minutes of physical activity a day, as long as it's not hotter than the surface of the sun outside."

"I have to go," I told Max, who hung her head in disappointment. "But I'm sure I'll see you again," I whispered. She lifted her head and her father's eyes met mine. It hurt my heart, but I had to rip my gaze from hers so that I wouldn't lose it right there in front of Audrey and the thirty or so toddlers in the room.

I stood to leave, but a tiny hand wrapped around one of my fingers and tugged. "Here," Max whispered. She took off the purple plastic bracelet and put it around my wrist.

My heart exploded in a flurry of warmth.

Love at first sight was not something exclusively reserved for lovers, because that day, I'd truly experienced it. In the span of three minutes, I'd lost my heart all over again.

I didn't want to leave her. I wanted to pick her up and run as fast as I could, out of the buzzing door, and straight to the house on stilts. Her and Sammy both.

First things first, I told myself.

I unclasped the silver and gold roped bracelet from around my wrist. I knelt down again, and with my back to Audrey, I carefully looped the delicate chain around Max's little wrist, twice.

I didn't stay to see her reaction to my gift; afraid that if I spent one more second with her, I wouldn't be able to walk out the door.

I stood and turned back around to Audrey, hoping she wouldn't notice the sudden pain in my voice or the tears in my eyes. "Now show me this wonderful playground," I said with a sniffle.

Audrey continued her tour, and as I followed her, I felt the gaze of a pair of beautiful green eyes on my back, as I walked out the door and into the blinding light of day.

Chapter Sixteen

DOE

WHEN I TOLD my father that King was dead, his only concern was how the hell he'd gotten out of prison in the first place. I didn't have the time or energy to explain what had really happened, because what I really wanted was his help. "I want to adopt King's daughter," I told him, standing in front of his desk while he clicked away on his computer.

The senator rolled his eyes. "You're a teenager with no source of income. The court isn't exactly going to look upon you favorably for an adoption," he'd told me, clicking away at the keyboard on his computer.

"You said you know the judge. You can put a word in," I stated.

"Yes, that I can do. But that's just a recommendation, Ramie. Even with a favor from the judge you're still going to have to follow proper procedure. Being a single woman is not looked upon as being a favorable applicant."

"Then I'll fix that."

"IT WILL INCREASE my chances of being able to adopt her," I finished. I was sitting on Tanner's couch in the pool house while Sammy watched TV, wrapped up in his favorite blanket on the floor. Every so often he would look back at me, and after seeing that I was still there, he'd smile and turn back to Elmo.

"Okay," Tanner agreed, way too quickly.

I shook my head. "No, Tanner. It's not that easy. You have to take time to think about it. Just because it wouldn't be a traditional marriage, on paper only, doesn't mean it wouldn't affect your life in some ways. You have to consider all that before you make a decision. Come to think of it, there really is no upside in all this for you. You'd have to be crazy to agree to it."

Tanner wagged his index finger in the air. "And this is why you were never on the debate team, Ray," Tanner said. "You're arguing the wrong side," he added.

"I'm serious," I said. "This is serious."

Tanner smiled. "I know. And I know it doesn't mean much, but I really am sorry about King." It was the first time Tanner had said his name.

"Thanks. I want to do this for him, but for me too. Maybe it's selfish, but I want to keep a piece of him close to me."

"And see, that right there is the very reason I accept your proposal," Tanner said, "because I want to keep you close to me."

"But it won't be—"

Tanner raised a hand to stop me. "You don't have to keep saying it, I totally get it. But I have terms."

"What terms?" I asked.

Tanner crossed his ankle over his knee. "I will accept your proposal and agree to marry you on the condition that you have to try. Not at first, I know you're still grieving, but eventually I want you to try and make what we have a real marriage. We'll make an effort together. For us. For Sammy." He reached out and grabbed my hand. "I promise, if you try and if after a year you still feel nothing for me, then I will back away as far as you want me to go."

"I...," I started to argue. But then Sammy turned around and smiled up at me. I had been willing to whore myself out to a biker in exchange for protection, why was I so unwilling to give a little part of myself for the only family I had left?

"Okay," I agreed. "But I need time, Tanner. I mean it. I don't know when I'll be ready," I said.

Tanner kissed the back of my hand and went back over to the kitchen where he retrieved the ring box he'd showed me the day he took me and Sammy to the alligator park. "I guess this is yours again, then." He didn't try and get down on one knee. He didn't try to put it on my finger for me. He just tossed me the box.

And it was the best thing he could have done, because just then, I had real hope that he really did understand why I was doing this. And because he understood how important getting Max was to me, I could try and understand how giving our marriage a real shot in the future was important to him.

I opened the box and stared down at the little diamond, "I guess it is."

Chapter Seventeen

DOE

THE MORNING OF the party I went to the courthouse with Tanner and picked up the application to start the process to become Max's adopted mother.

It was also the morning I became Mrs. Tanner Redmond.

And while I was dying inside, it was the thought of being there for Sammy and Max that kept me breathing. They were the ones propelling me forward, moving my feet, one in front of the other.

King was willing to do whatever it took to get his daughter back. He proved that when he was willing to let me go. Now it was my turn to do this for him.

Choosing something to wear to a wedding where I'd be the reluctant bride was a daunting task. I didn't want to pretend the marriage was something it wasn't. I skipped over the rows of knee-length sundresses, pausing for a moment at a white one with a halter top, but it was too 'wedding,' and this wasn't a wedding.

It was just paperwork.

Business.

Family business.

I finally decided to pass on the dresses altogether and instead chose a pair of dark jeans and a fitted black V-neck.

I was doing this for King. I wasn't ready to be a show pony led around by her halter. King would have liked my choice of outfit. And the senator may have succeeded in containing me, but I was never going to be tamed.

I wasn't about to wear white and pretend to be an angel, when I'd lived and fallen in love with the devil.

There was a wild part of me that flourished when I was with King. I liked who I was with him. I *knew* who I was with him. That part, the part that couldn't be controlled, belonged to King, and no matter where I was or where he was or what either of us were doing, no one could ever take that from me.

At the courthouse I fully expected to sign some papers. Signature and stampings. That was it. But when Tanner and I had finished signing the license and the woman behind the desk handed us our IDs, she stood and slid her chair back against the linoleum floor. To my great surprise, and horror, she started to speak. "Do you Tanner Redmond take—"

"Wait," I said. "I thought we could just do the paperwork."

The woman looked down at me through her thick glasses in a manner that made me feel like I was nine years old. "Miss, the ceremony is less than a minute long, and in the state of Florida, a ceremony needs to be performed to make the marriage legal, and since you checked the box that you'd like to file the license today…shall I continue?"

"Yeah," I said.

Tanner grabbed my hand and squeezed it. I was tired of him needing to feel like he had to reassure me. I didn't want reassurance; I wanted to stop having to go through things that required it. I nodded and the woman started back up. She was right, the ceremony was short. Just under a minute.

"Do you take Tanner to be your lawfully wedded husband...?" They weren't romantic words, but nonetheless they were promises. Promises spoken out loud in front of the clerk and whatever God might be up there listening. I robotically recited my vows, lying to Tanner with each false promise I spoke. In order to push down the need to flee, and make it through without running screaming down the courthouse steps, I imagined playing with King's daughter. Pushing her on a swing set. Building her a treehouse. Running through the sprinklers with her. Then the picture shifted, and I was exactly where I was standing, in the courthouse reciting vows, but only it wasn't Tanner I was making promises to. It was King. And they weren't lies at all, they were real. My heart soared and I smiled, happily imagining that I was promising to love King in sickness and in health, in good times and in bad, until the end of our days.

When the officiant said, "You may kiss the bride," I'd gone as far as leaning in, before I came back down from my daydream, turning my head at the very last second, so that Tanner only caught the edge of my mouth. When he pulled back, despite my obvious aversion to his kiss, he was smiling as if I really was his wife.

Then it hit me.

I really was.

I must have looked like I was about to have the stroke I was almost positive was about to happen, because the officiant kept asking me if I was okay. "Mrs. Redmond, are you alright?" I nodded and smiled the best I could manage. Tanner paid the forty-two dollar fee for the license and filing. I didn't speak again. I couldn't. Because if I'd answered her question, if I'd opened my mouth to speak at all, I was afraid the truth would have come tumbling out of my mouth. So, I kept quiet and Tanner and I walked in silence from the courthouse and remained silent during the entire drive home. I didn't even say good-bye when he'd dropped me off at my house.

I didn't speak again until I was alone on my bed in a room I didn't remember, in a life I didn't want, in a family that was built on a foundation of lies. I rolled over and pressed my face into the pillow.

And just like millions of other brides before me, I cried on my wedding day.

Chapter Eighteen

DOE

'D THROWN UP three times that morning and was still queasy, threatening to expel whatever contents remained in my stomach, if any. I had no doubt that what I was experiencing was a full body rejection of my current circumstances.

The party, or fundraiser, was being held at Tanner's family's backyard, and it was the last place I wanted to be.

The senator was in his element, shaking hands and recalling the names and occupations of each and every guest at the party as if he were a best friend to every person in attendance. The Olympic-sized pool had been covered with plexiglas to create the illusion of walking on water.

How appropriate, I thought as I saw my father cross over the pool.

My mother held court by the bar with several women wearing varying shades of the same style sundress and the same chunky jewelry and French twist hairstyle. They weren't doing half as good of a job pretending to be sober as she was. And as my father was, acting every bit the practiced and perfected politician. I was learning that my mother was every bit as equally practiced in the art of public intoxication.

FLASH: My ninth birthday. My mother stumbling into the backyard wearing a low-cut tight blue dress and gold heels. She has a glass of wine in one hand and knocks over a table full of my birthday gifts in front of my friends from school. Nadine cuts my cake and my mother tells everyone that we shouldn't eat cake at all because it is high in calories and will make our asses fat and men don't like fat asses. Her wine sloshes over her glass, and the magician Nadine hired has to grab her by the elbow to save her from crashing into the pool, when her heel catches on the pavement.

Miraculously, she manages to catch her falling wine glass. "I saved it!" she shouts, holding it up to our little group like it's a trophy. "Totally saved it," she says again, before walking back into the house without another word.

I guess she wasn't always that good.

It was too hot for the white cardigan I was wearing, but I was playing by my father's rules tonight which meant covering up any signs that I wasn't the picture-perfect daughter of the picture-perfect senator. Several people came up to me to welcome me home and shake my hand. I smiled politely and asked them how their summer was and what their plans were for the fall. The senator had told me a secret of his, which was when you don't remember the person, name or face, ask them about themselves.

"Ramie! So good to see you!" A short plump man wearing an off white linen suit stepped into my line of view. He grabbed a glass of champagne off the tray of a passing waiter and handed it to me. "How was Paris?" he asked.

"Parisian?" I said. His laugh came out in one big burst, like a shot through a cannon.

"I see you gained a sense of humor in France. Hard to do. The French aren't exactly known for their humor," he said. "Are you still considering art school? Francine said your drawings are quite impressive. How long has it been since you've seen her?"

Crap.

My father came over and stood by my side. With a smile still on his face, he waved to the passers-by who called out greetings while he returned them with his own. In a stealth-like move, he took the champagne glass out of my hand and held it in his, as if the drink were his own.

Shit. Drinking age. Not allowed. I mentally chastised myself. "George, my friend, how have you been? Ramie was just saying how she and Francine needed to catch up. And art school is so far away in Rhode Island. I think now that she has a family of her own, she'll be sticking close to home."

"Ah, then you will be joining your father on the campaign trail?" he asked me.

"We haven't really talked about it yet," I answered as sweetly as I could manage.

"Well, I think you should consider it. Seeing this man behind a podium is a wondrous thing to behold," George said, holding up his glass to my father.

"Ah, you are too kind George. Let's have lunch this week, if you're up for it."

"Always am," George said. "Ah, I see Nathan over there. He owes me twenty pounds of stone crab claws for losing our bet on the Rays game. Oops..." He said covering his mouth. "I shouldn't tell our future president about my betting habits should I?"

"I'm a politician George, not the police. And Nathan's stone crabs are the best, so I can't fault you for that wager."

"I look forward to hearing you speak," George said. "Lovely to see you again, Ramie. I will tell Francine to give you a call."

"That would be great," I said. When George was out of ear-shot, my father, with his smile still plastered on his face, leaned in so only I could hear him.

"Champagne?" he asked through his teeth.

"He handed it to me. I wasn't thinking," I said apologetically. "I'm trying here, so cut me some slack. I did what you asked of me. Besides, I have a kid and technically a husband, and I can't have a glass of champagne? Maybe you need to add that to your political platform."

"Yeah, and then I'll make sure to go ahead and legalize prostitution and call the cartels to see if maybe they want to set up some coke shops. Like a 7-11 for illegal drugs."

"Holy shit. If you weren't such a prick, you'd actually be kind of funny," I said. A loud cackling ripped through the air and the senator's eyes darted over to where my mother and the other women, who looked like Stepford wives but drank like members of the Beach Bastards, were reaching their limits. "And if you're really dead set on the booze thing, maybe you should think about reinstating prohibition."

"Noted," he said, making his way over to my mother. I watched as he used the same technique to take away her drink as he did with me. My mother shot him a glare when no one else was looking, and at one point, pinched his arm behind his back far enough to where I saw him visibly wince.

One thing was for sure, this life was turning me into a raging bitch.

"Champagne, ma'am?" A familiar voice asked from behind me. I turned around and found myself eye level with a black dress shirt and a school bus yellow bow tie with pink stripes. I looked to the tray he was holding and I could've sworn that I saw colorful tattoos peeking out on the upturned wrist holding the tray of champagne flutes.

I sucked in a breath.

Preppy?

My hands trembled.

Just as I was about to look up at the waiter's face, the screeching feedback from the microphone came blaring over the speakers. I covered my ears and turned around to where my father had made his way up to the makeshift stage set up on the side of Tanner's pool house.

The senator was tapping on the microphone and gesturing for someone off stage to come make the adjustment when I spun back around to the waiter, but he was already gone. And when I looked around for him, I found several of the same dark shirts and yellow bow ties, all holding trays with the same champagne flutes, fizzing with pink bubbles.

I'm seeing things. Mind and body are both now rejecting my farce of a life.

"Mommy!" a little voice broke through the crowd. Sammy came crashing against my leg. I smiled and lifted him up and set him on my hip in a move that felt natural to me. Nadine, who had been chasing him around the party-goers, appeared next to me, out of breath.

"Your little one is getting fast," she said, with her hands on her knees. "Don't let those little legs fool ya. He can really move! Either that, or I'm out of shape. Could be both," she huffed. Nadine had traded her usual Polo and khakis for a button down black dress shirt and black pants. Instead of her orthopedic black sneakers, she was wearing a pair of rounded-toe, shiny black ballet flats.

"You look great, Nadine," I said. She returned the compliment with a roll of her eyes.

"I'm just glad I wore black," she said, fanning herself. "Because I'm sweating like we're standing in the middle of Hades with the devil himself."

I thought King was the devil. But I was sure that I was in hell and he was nowhere to be found. I looked up at the stage. And I was pretty sure that the devil voted republican and wore Hugo Boss.

"Mommy, Nay-neene couldn't catch me!" Sammy exclaimed. "I fast! I fast like this!" he said, holding up the red Matchbox Corvette he held in his hands and flying it around in the air.

"Oh yeah? Are you being good for Miss Nadine?" I asked him, ruffling up his perfectly combed hair, his little giggle exposing his bottom row of adorably super tiny teeth.

"Nope," he said, still looking at his car. His natural curls sprang to life. "There, that's better," I said, smushing my nose against his. I was too busy interacting with Sammy when Nadine cleared her throat. When I looked up I noticed that a lot of the crowd had stopped doing what they were doing and were watching me interact with my son.

My father was back on the microphone, sans interference, and the crowd turned from me to him. My mother stood obediently off to his left, next to the long American flag. He started his speech by welcoming the crowd to the event and mentioning the charities that would be benefiting from the silent auction and donations they received during the evening. "What did I miss?" Tanner said, pushing through the crowd to stand next to me and Samuel. "Hey kiddo! High five!" Samuel lifted his palm up and Tanner pressed a high five to his hand. "All right buddy, you're getting good at that."

"Not much. He just started," I said.

The senator paused and looked out over the crowd. He took the cards from the podium and placed them into the pocket of his dress shirt. "I had all these notes prepared. I wanted to talk with you about the agenda of the campaign and about what we hope to achieve over the next few months. But I can't do that right now." The crowd murmured in confusion and a few shouted the "Why not?" the senator was obviously fishing for.

"I've made no secret that family, and traditional American, and Christian values are one of the most important things to me to withhold during this campaign." The crowd applauded and he held up his hand to silence them. "But as you know, family isn't always predictable. It isn't something you can control," he said. "As you all know by now, either through rumor or from reading it in the paper recently, a few years ago, I became a grandfather."

It was the first time I heard him reference Sammy as anything other than my son. Grandfather wasn't exactly the title I would have given him either.

"My daughter, Ramie, and her boyfriend, Tanner, made a decision to enter into a relationship they weren't ready for at the tender age of fifteen. I'm not excusing their actions, nor their behavior, but what some of you don't know is that Tanner was sick…."

"Oh my God, he's telling them everything," I said, covering my mouth in shock. Tanner grabbed my hand and held it in his.

"I'm not surprised," he muttered. "Did you really think he was just going to let them think we were two horny teenagers who had sex under his roof? Too much blame in that. He's going to blame my illness now. This is an art form to him. More so than your sketches are to you. He's creating emotion, opinions. He's telling them what they need to think without coming right out and saying it. It's kind of beautiful if you think about it."

"You don't sound embarrassed," I said. "You sound impressed."

"I'm not embarrassed. He's telling the truth. It's us. Nothing about us would ever bother me, Ray. Besides, it's probably the most honest thing he's said all day," Tanner said, staring at the stage with an interest that made me uncomfortable.

"We thought we were going to lose him," the senator continued. My mother reached out for a handkerchief that one of the guards handed her and dabbed at the corner of her eyes.

"Nice touch, mother," I whispered.

"The doctors all said the same thing...that there was no hope for him. They told his parents, Chuck and Ranae to make their final arrangements." The senator sought them out in the crowd and nodded toward them. "Nice to see you two here," he said with a smile when he found them. "We were all preparing for the death of my daughter's best friend." The crowd gasped. He had them eating out of the palm of his hand, and they were jumping up to eat every morsel he was throwing at them. "It was a strange thing to be thinking about, especially since Margot and I, and I know Tanner's parents as well, always thought that our two crazy kids would grow up to get married and have a family of their own." The senator's eyes went misty. He should win an Emmy. My mother walked up to him and dabbed at his eyes with her handkerchief. No, these two should win an *Oscar*. "Sorry about that," he said sniffling. He paused for a moment before looking out into the crowd. "It's funny how God works. You never know what his plan is going to be. Chuck and Ranae had given up the hope of ever becoming grandparents. Our hearts ached for our daughter and the future that was no longer a possibility for her. On the day that Tanner received the news that his time here on God's great creation of a planet was coming to an end, my daughter and Tanner made a decision that I don't agree with, that I don't support. But in many ways, I see it now as part of the bigger picture; God's great plan that we as his followers don't ever have any hope in understanding. That decision resulted in my daughter and Tanner coming to me and my wife in my home office. They informed me that she was pregnant, and I openly wept. My own daughter. The daughter who I raised to clearly understand the values which the Price Family stood for—and believed in—had come to me and told me that she disobeyed my rules and God's law.

It wasn't until later that night when I woke from a restless night of sleep and it dawned on me. This is God's plan. This was his way of providing Chuck and Ranae with the grandchild they'd given up on having and it gave me new cause. And this cause was to reach out to every specialist and doctor in this great country, and even the world, to see if I could save my daughter's hope for a future, a family, of her own."

Half the crowd was in tears and Tanner leaned into my neck. "This all sounds so much better than 'my daughter had pity sex with her sick boyfriend and they didn't use a condom.'" My father's head snapped up and he shot us a look which I knew was meant for me, as if he'd heard Tanner's remark, although it was impossible.

"With the help of Dr. Reynolds, in Tennessee, we were able to bring Tanner back from the brink." The crowd started to applaud, and again the senator held up his hand. "I am now proud to say that Tanner has been in full remission from his leukemia and continues to show no signs of the cancer that almost took him from us." This time he lets the crowd clap. "Come on up here, you two. Bring Samuel." A hundred pairs of eyes turned to us and we had no choice but to make our way to the stage. Samuel clapped along with the crowd and laughed. I would have given anything to be shrouded in the same beautiful ignorant bliss.

We stood next to my mother who made a show of taking Samuel from my hands and putting him on her hip just as I had him. She turned to the crowd and waved and Samuel mimicked her, which just made them grow more wild. "Now I haven't told you the best part," the senator said, motioning for the crowd to quiet down. He was the maestro and they were his orchestra, playing to every one of his gestures. This was the grand finale, because I knew what was coming, and there was nothing I could do to stop it. "This morning, in a small ceremony, surrounded by only family and their son, my daughter and Tanner Redmond were married." The applause from only a crowd of a hundred or so people, was deafening. The senator shouted into the microphone above the crowd. "So, I would like to take this time to introduce you to the new Mr. & Mrs. Redmond and their beautiful son, my grandson, Samuel. May God bless your union." He came over to me and cupped my face in his palms pulling me in for a hug that made my stomach turn.

"You bastard," I said. "This wasn't supposed to be a public display or a political tool." I was surprised, although I knew I shouldn't have been. The senator cared about the campaign first, campaign funding second, and campaign supporters third.

"It's all a political tool. All of it," the senator said. "You. Me. Tanner. Samuel. Your mother. It's all for the greater good." I honestly think he believed that crap. He released me and pulled Tanner into a hug of his own. Unlike the scowl I was wearing, Tanner was smiling from ear to ear and genuinely looked like he was enjoying himself, accepting the congratulations as if the marriage were real.

I'm so fucking stupid.

Suddenly I was so angry I couldn't breathe. I was angry at myself, at the senator, at King for leaving me, at Tanner for no reasonable explanation.

My hands shook as I saw red.

The senator waved to the crowd. Nadine came to the stage and took Sammy, who was wiggling in my mother's unfamiliar arms, and motioned to me that she was going to take him back to the house. I nodded. Nadine had a great sense of when shit was about to hit the fan and I was glad for it.

Because shit was about to hit the fan.

I stepped up in between where my father and Tanner were waving to the crowd and I added a wave of my own. The senator looked at me suspiciously, and Tanner was still smiling like he'd just won the lottery and was accepting his giant check. "It's hot out here, isn't it?" I said, leaning toward my father who furrowed his brow but then quickly corrected himself when he realized he'd made a negative facial expression in public.

"It's Florida, during the summer. It's always hot," Tanner said before his eyes went wide and the realization set in. "Don't," he warned, but I didn't listen.

"If you want to put me on display, you are going to have to put all of me on display." I made a show of fanning myself and then I unbuttoned my cardigan and took it off. My father didn't find anything unusual about me taking off my cardigan. He was right. It was Florida, during the summer. It was hot. But he didn't know what was underneath the cardigan. He'd yet to see it. I held my sweater in my hands and heard a gasp from behind me that I assumed came from my mother.

"Don't," Tanner repeated, and this time he sounded angry. I spotted a chair and turned to my father. "Can I rest my sweater on that?" I asked him.

"What are you up to, Ramie?" he asked, looking worried.

"Nothing at all, *Daddy*," I said. I turned my back to the crowd and bent over to place my cardigan on the chair.

The tattoo King had given me was on full display for the crowd.

There was nothing anyone could do. My father could rush to cover me up, but that would reveal the fact that he didn't approve. He could address it, but that would make it worse. I turned and shot them both a look that told them that I was not one to be fucked with. With one last wave to the crowd, who was now gossiping amongst themselves in loud whispers like a pack of rabid mean girls, I left the stage.

I walked along the property line to the back of the house, not wanting to deal with any of the party-goers that might have been lingering on the walkway from the back patio to the house.

"What the heck was that?" Tanner asked, jogging to catch up to me as I passed the treehouse oak. "What was that, Ray?" he repeated.

I stopped and turned around to face him. "That was me not being stepped on! You said I could have time. The look on your face in front of those people said you already think this is real. But it's not real Tanner. Not to me. I'm not ready. And I may have loved you once, actually I know I loved you once, but I don't even know if it was romantic love. I love that you are kind to our son and I respect the hell out of you for everything you've been through, and I hate that I've hurt you. But I don't want to be with you like that right now. Not when my heart still belongs elsewhere."

"What do you expect from me, Ray? To be sorry that I'm happy to be your husband? Because I'm not. I'm not sorry I married you, whatever the reason. You are the love of my life for

Christ's sake! Always have been. We were always meant to be together. So, of course I jumped at the chance to announce it to the world, because it was always meant to happen." Tanner's eyes softened and he took a step toward me, folding his hand around my wrist.

"No, Tanner," I said, pulling out of his reach. "Don't."

Tanner ignored me and reached around my neck to pull me toward him. He softly pressed his lips against mine, and I just stood there and let it happen. His lips were soft and warm, his breath cool against my skin. I imagined that Tanner really was the one who I wanted, but instead of recalling feelings for him, King's angry face kept flashing in my mind. Tanner opened his mouth and I reluctantly followed his lead, his tongue dancing on mine. In a way I wished for the memories to come flooding back. For me to feel what it was he wanted me to feel. But as we continued to kiss and his hands slid from my neck to my waist, the only thing I felt…was wrong. Beyond wrong.

I pushed against his chest, but he moaned in to my mouth and held me tighter. I tried again and when he didn't budge I bit down. Instantly he reeled back, holding his hand against his bloodied bottom lip. "You are ruining everything I thought I felt about you. Don't make a mess of what I do remember about us."

"I'm the one making a mess of this?" he laughed. "You ruined everything when you went after Nikki. You couldn't just let her go. I told you a hundred times not to get mixed up in her mess of a life but no, you had to let her drag you down with her. You put her above your family by going after her, by getting hurt, by going away. You are the one who ruined us that night. Not me. I'm trying to save us while you're hell bent on destroying us! So fuck you, Ray! You broke my heart when you left. You smashed it to pieces when you came back. And I don't know who you think you are, but you aren't the Ray I knew. And this person I see before me? I kind of fucking hate her right now," Tanner said. He turned and stormed off into the darkness.

I opened my mouth to call after him but I didn't know what else I could say. He was hurt and I'd done the hurting. I'd done nothing but make one stupid decision after another since I'd been there. It was stupid of me to flaunt the tattoo. I'd acted out of anger. But that didn't give him the right to treat me like I was a commodity that could be bought or traded...or married.

Although that was exactly what I was.

Chapter Nineteen

DOE

I CLOSED THE door to my room and pressed my forehead against it. Devastated didn't begin to cover how I felt. King was dead and I'd lost my only friend because I was stupid enough to think that I could use a marriage certificate as a tool to get what I so desperately wanted.

A family. A real family that I chose, just like I'd chosen King and Preppy.

I let out a frustrated scream and clenched my fists, banging on the door until I was all out of fight. I rubbed my lips to erase the taste of Tanner until they felt raw.

"Take your fucking clothes off," a deep voice growled.

Awareness washed over me like static electricity.

I gasped and turned my tear-stained face from the door. Hundreds of years could pass without me hearing it and I would still know exactly who the voice belonged to.

King emerged from the corner of the room, the shadow falling away from his body like a blanket slowly being tugged off. "You know I don't like to repeat myself, but for you, I'll do it just this once, Pup." He stopped in front of me and peered down, his eyes burning with both lust and anger. "Take your fucking clothes off."

"You're alive," I whisper as my heart hammered in my chest.

Was I imagining this?

"You're about to find out how alive I really am." He stalked toward me. "You and I communicate better when I'm inside you, and there is a lot I've got to say... So instead of the question-and-answer bullshit that will get us a fuck of a lot of nowhere, we're going to do this in a way I already know works."

"I thought you were dead." My chest heaved with fear and desire. My skin prickled, my nipples tightened.

"Were you grieving when that kid had his tongue down your fucking throat?" King reached for my hand, holding up the finger that held Tanner's ring. "Is your grief the reason why you're wearing this?"

I ripped my finger from his grip and placed my hands against his chest. My intention was to push him away, but as soon as I made contact I couldn't let go.

I didn't want to.

I fisted his shirt in my hands. The relief I had felt over him being alive was being replaced by my anger at his accusatory tone. "I thought you were dead," I repeated.

He spoke into my hair, his breath warm against my scalp. "Oh, Pup. I'm pretty sure even death couldn't keep me from you."

I inhaled, taking in the scent of cigarettes and wind. I'd missed the familiarity of his smell almost as much as I'd missed him. "I never thought I would see you again. I went to the MC. Bear's dad is the one who told me you were dead."

King shook his head slowly from side to side. "He'll be dealt with." He narrowed his eyes. "As will you," he said so low and deep, I felt his words to my very core.

"What?"

"Did you really think it would be that easy to get rid of me?

For fuck's sake I remember what it feels like to be inside you. You think I can just forget that? You think I haven't been trying for weeks to convince myself that it's just my cock who misses you? Because I'll tell you, nothing would make me happier than to be able to rid myself of this fucking hurt, right now. Right here." King pounded on his chest with a closed fist. "I sometimes wish I could just forget it all, but I can't. I won't. Because I don't want to ever want to forget you. And I welcome this pain because it reminds me that you were real." I bit my lip so hard I could taste the copper in my mouth.

King spoke while walking toward me, backing me up further into the shadows until my back connected with the dresser. He placed his hands on the wall around me, caging me in, leaning down until we were eye to eye.

"I don't know why you're holding on so tight, Pup, when your body is clearly telling me that you're still mine." King inhaled me, like I did him. Closing his eyes, he rubbed his nose across my jaw line. "Do you love him?" he growled, nipping at my neck with his teeth.

"Yes," I admitted. King pulled back and scowled. I clarified, "It was never a love like he thought it was, like he wanted it to be. I loved him like a best friend, never like the way—" His eyes searched mine, eagerly awaiting the rest of my answer. "Weeks go by without a single word, and you show up out of nowhere, sneak into my room and demand that I take my clothes off on the day I—" I couldn't finish the sentence. I couldn't say the words that I didn't want to be true.

Because King was *alive.*

And I was *married.*

"Got fucking married," King finished for me. His nostrils flared. He turned around with clenched fists like he was looking for something to punch. He placed his hands on his head in frustration. "I watched the entire fucking car crash out there. I know everything."

"Holy shit!" I exclaimed.

King snarled. "You seem to have forgotten who the fuck I am, Pup. So I'm going to remind you." He pressed his hips against mine. "I'm the man who took you against your will and handcuffed you to my fucking bed. I'm the man who wanted you, so I fucking kept you." He cocked an eyebrow. "Do you really think you have a choice when it comes to being mine?"

King lifted me onto the dresser and pushed himself between my legs, forcing my legs apart. He held my wrists behind my back forcing my shoulders backwards and pushing my chest into his. My dress rode up to the tops of my thighs. King pushed a strand of hair behind my ears and leaned in to me, his lips just a breath away from mine. The room was getting hot. I couldn't breathe. I needed...I don't know what I needed. "No more questions."

I opened my mouth to argue. "Stop fucking talking," he snapped.

King lifted me off the dresser and carried me and set me down in front of the full-length mirror that hung on the closet door. He stood behind me. A head taller than me and outweighing me by a hundred pounds, our differences had never been more obvious. His dark jeans and dark tank top were a stark contrast to my little white eyelet sundress. My pale skin next to his tanned. My white hair to his black. It was a sight that made my knees weak. Because although the reflection in the mirror made our differences obvious, it also made me see how well the two fit together.

"You see this?" King said, his arms wrapped around my

waist, speaking to my reflection. "You see how this fucking works? How we fit?" He pushed my cardigan off my shoulders and it fell to the floor. He spun me around and grabbed a hand mirror off the desk and held it in front of me, the same way he did when he was showing a client their new tattoo.

"Do you see this? What does this shit fucking say?" he asked. Pointing to the tattoo he'd given me. The one I just put on full display to spite my father and Tanner.

"It says, I don't want to repeat my innocence, I want the pleasure of losing it all over again. It's an F. Scott Fitzgerald quote," I answered.

"No." He pushed on my head, shifting my perspective to a slightly sideways view. "Tell me again. Look in the crown, in the vines. What the fuck does that shit say?"

"King," I whispered. "It says...King."

Chapter Twenty

KING

"YOU ARE MINE. You always have been," I said unapologetically.

Pup looked in the mirror with wide eyes, still staring at the tattoo bearing my name. "You tattooed your name on me," she said in disbelief.

My gaze met hers in the mirror. "Marked you the first fucking chance I got. My only regret is not making it bigger, because maybe then that kid would've known better than to put his fucking lips on you."

"It's not his fault," she said, glaring daggers at me.

It pissed me off that she was defending the little fuck. He could call himself her husband all he wanted 'cause I found out all I needed to know when her breath quickened at my nearness, when she darted her tongue out and wet her lips in anticipation, the way her nipples hardened against the fabric of the little sexy as fuck conservative dress she was wearing. It wasn't just physical though, because the air around us crackled with our almost palpable connection. I could practically taste it on my tongue.

I wanted to taste *her* on my tongue. I wanted to put my face between her thighs and feel her squirm under my mouth while she scraped the top of my head with her fingernails until she came.

I was so fucking hard, it took every bit of self-control I had not to bend her over the dresser, flip that dress over her ass, and fuck some sense into my girl.

I ran my hand over her mouth and her lips parted. Those beautiful pink lips of hers would've made my cock instantly hard if it wasn't already an iron rod straining against my jeans. "I already wanted to slit the senator's throat for the stunt he pulled with Max, but when I saw him standing up there, wearing his better-than-everyone-suit, and his member-of-the-club ridiculous gold watch, and heard him telling people you'd got fucking married, to someone who isn't me, I wanted to unload my gun into his skull then reload it for the kid.

My words might have been harsh, but they were true.

I took the mirror from Pup and set it down on the dresser. "For a second I thought that maybe I just imagined this thing between us." I untied the halter of her sundress and let it fall to the floor, revealing a matching beige strapless bra and panty set. It was standard everyday stuff, but on my girl, she might as well have been wearing crotchless panties and carrying a whip, because she was the sexiest thing I'd ever fucking seen. My cock was in agony as I swept my gaze over her body.

"It was that look of yours that stopped me," I said.

"What look?" she asked, spinning around to face me.

"The look you get when you're up to no good. And I was right, because you took off your sweater. You showed them your tattoo." I ran my fingertips from the base of her neck to the cheeks of her ass.

"I was showing them I wasn't a monkey and that no matter what I agreed to, I wasn't going to dance for them," she said, unable to contain the thrill of being able to put them in their place.

"You showed them more than that." I said, circling her. Appraising her body that I'd missed so much. Taking her all in. "You showed them you were mine." I stood behind her again and reached between her legs, her panties already soaked. She closed her eyes as I stroked her through the material. "But most importantly," I told her as I rubbed faster and her mouth opened as she lost herself in the pleasure of my touch, "you showed *me* that you were still mine."

I turned her around and crashed my lips to hers. She shuddered under my touch. "Don't be trying to come up with an excuse to argue with me, Pup. The time for excuses is over. I will tell you right fucking now that it doesn't matter what you say. There is nothing you can tell me that changes anything. I claimed you, and I'm not apologizing for shit this time."

"I have to explain—" she started to argue, but I interrupted.

"We can talk later. Do I need to bend you over and fuck you like an animal to remind you whose pussy this is?" I said, biting her earlobe. I roughly flipped her over onto her stomach. I pushed down between her shoulder blades until she was bent over the bed on her elbows. I unclasped her bra and let it fall to the bed. I pulled down her panties with one hand and threw them to the floor. I gazed at the fucking amazing sight that was my girl, naked, bent over for me. I unhooked my belt and took off my jeans while she braced herself on her hands and knees. I crawled over her onto the mattress and took off my tank top so that we were skin to skin. She lifted her head and my lips brushed the back of her ear. "Do you need reminding of who you belong to, Pup?"

"Yes," she breathed. I positioned my cock at her entrance and pushed in hard, past the resistance of her tight pussy. Each centimeter into her heat was an agonizing combination of torture and pleasure.

I paused when I was fully seated inside the fucking greatest pussy ever created. Warm. Wet. Ready. "Tell me you missed me," I said. Doe groaned and pressed her little round ass back against me, trying to get me to move, but I stayed motionless. "No, baby. Not until you tell me what I want to hear."

"I—" I rewarded her attempt with a slow circling of my hips and she moaned into the pillow.

"You what?" I asked, pausing again.

"I missed—" Again I circled my hips, this time adding a single hard thrust. "I missed—"

"Who did you miss?" I asked.

"You. I missed you!" she said.

I lost all control. I reached around her and wrapped one hand around her throat; with the other I anchored myself to the bed. I thrust into her furiously, like the crazed man I was. "I missed you too, baby. So fucking much." Over and over again, I relentlessly pounded into her like I was trying to fuck my way back into her life. "This, me being inside you. It just told me everything I needed to know. I'm not giving up on us. Not now. Not fucking ever."

Pup moaned, her pussy clenching around me, and I had to slow my pace in order not to blow into her right then and there.

A shadow across the open window grabbed my attention and my head snapped up to see a set of eyes watching us from the tree just outside the window. He may have thought he was hidden by branches and leaves, but just like a lion can sniff out nearby males, I knew exactly who it was.

Tanner.

I could have stopped right then. Pulled my cock out of her. Covered us both up. Or at least shut the window for fuck's sake.

I didn't do any of those things.

Leaning down over my girl, I licked her neck as she moaned my name over and over again. Oblivious to our new audience. "Who does this pussy belong to?" I asked, staring straight out the window into the horrified eyes of our uninvited guest.

"You. Always. It's always been you," she breathed. Her pussy clamped around my cock again and I struggled to maintain control. I wasn't done yet. This kid had to know without a doubt that Pup belonged to me.

She is mine.

"I love you, Pup. So much," I told her, thrusting harder and harder. "Do you love me?" I asked, making sure I stroked the sensitive bundle of nerves in the front wall of her pussy that made her scream.

I'd missed her fucking screams.

"Yes. So much. I love you so much!" she said. It started as a whisper, but as her orgasm took hold, it became louder and louder, until she had to shove a pillow in her face to prevent anyone who might be in the house from hearing her.

But someone had heard.

When I felt the tingling sensation begin at the base of my spine, an idea took hold and it was like my baser instincts took over. Once I thought about doing it, I couldn't think of anything else.

I pushed into her twice more then pulled out of her tight heat. I jerked my cock in my hand, making a show of spurting my cum onto her bare back. Doe dropped onto her stomach in exhaustion, but I wasn't quite done. I looked out the window, directly over to where Tanner was unsuccessfully hiding. I ran my hands through the mess I'd just made on her, sliding it around on her back and her ass, marking her as mine. I pulled her up by her hair and stuck two cum covered fingers in her mouth.

She groaned and greedily sucked them clean.

My message was clear.

Tanner stood on the branch, no longer bothering to conceal his presence. For a long moment he continued to stare, until finally he turned and leapt from the tree.

Both Pup and Tanner now knew who she belonged to.

And it sure as fuck wasn't him.

Chapter Twenty-One

DOE

KING FELL ON top of me, pressing me into the mattress as we both caught our breaths. The weight of him over my back was almost crushing, but I didn't want to move. Afraid that if I did, I would wake up and this would have all been a dream.

King sat up and leaned against the headboard pulling me close to him. "Now can I tell you why?" I asked, still catching my breath.

King nodded. "I thought you were dead," I started. "I'd panicked when I hadn't heard from you in a while. I went to Bear's clubhouse hoping they could get a message to you somehow. Bear's dad told me you were dead." King gave me a reassuring squeeze, encouraging me to continue. "And I missed you. I missed you so much." A tear ran down my cheek as I remembered how I first felt when Bear's old man had told me that King was dead. King leaned in and trapped the tear between his lips, catching it before it had a chance to drip from my jaw. "I went to see Max."

King froze.

"What? You saw Max?" he asked in disbelief.

I nodded. "Yes. And she's so beautiful. She has your eyes, your smile. She gave me this." I held up my wrist to show him the plastic purple bracelet, and King ran his fingers over it, as if he were examining the queen's jewels. "I knew right away she needed to be with me. I wanted to adopt her."

"Baby," King said on a strained whisper.

I wiped at another tear spilling down my other cheek. "I wanted to increase my chances of making that happen. The senator said single women looking to adopt are often passed over." I turned to look him in the eye. "I didn't want that to happen. I would've done anything. For her. For you. But to be honest, I was doing it mostly for me, because she's a piece of you, and I wanted that piece with me, always." I laughed. "So I did what I had to do."

"You married Tanner... for me," King said. There was no more anger. No judgment. If anything he sounded in awe of what I'd done. Gently reaching out to cup my face, he leaned forward and pressed a kiss to my lips. Where most of our kisses are full of heat and passion, this one was all tenderness and love. He pulled back slowly, looking me over as if he were searching for something.

"And for me," I reminded him. "I hate to break it to you, but I fell in love with her faster than I fell in love with you."

King laughed. "I love you. I've never said that to anyone but Max before. Since the day you turned up at my party, it's been you." He kissed me again then rested his forehead on mine. "Only you." It was exactly what I'd needed to hear. Warmth spread in my chest and I felt my heart expand as the beautiful man in front of me worshiped me with his eyes.

"I never loved him, just so you know," I said, offering King something I knew he wanted to hear. "I remember him, but it wasn't that kind of love. Not for me, anyway."

"You loved him enough to let him fuck you. To have his kid," King stated. There was no bitterness in his voice, and although it wasn't a question, it seemed like he was waiting for an answer.

"Tanner was sick," I said. "Dying. I thought what I felt for him was real love, but I know now it was just the kind of thing you feel for a close friend. He wasn't going to get to experience graduation, or prom, or—you know, girls. It was my idea." I shook my head. "But, we made Sammy. So, as young and stupid as we were, as I was, I don't regret it. I may not remember my son, but I feel him in here." I placed my hand over my heart.

King chuckled.

As great as it was to hear his laugh, I felt myself getting angry again. "What exactly do you find funny about all this?" I snapped, sitting up and leering at him.

King reached out and dragged me back to him. "Because, Pup. I could feel my blood boiling when I thought you were about to describe fucking another guy. But instead my sweet girl tells me how she gave up her virgin pussy to her dying friend." King nuzzled his nose into my neck. "Sweetest pity-fuck ever," he said, erupting in laughter. I grabbed a pillow and swung it at his head, but he caught it and threw it to the floor, grabbing my hips and settling me on top of him.

"Now tell me where the fuck you were for a whole month," I demanded, feeling free to be pissed at him now that he was alive and well. I crossed my arms over my chest. He pulled my arms away from my body and moved his lips from my ear to my nipples, sending my head rolling backward. I pushed at his head until he fell back against the headboard with a thud.

"Shit with Eli, it's over," he said looking relieved. He rested his hands on my waist. "It wasn't pretty, Pup. He found us first. Shit went down you don't ever need to know about. Shit with Bear."

"What happened to Bear?" I asked, feeling panicked.

King squeezed my hips to grab my attention. "He's alive. Healing. No permanent damage to his body, but after what he went through, I don't expect him to be right in the head, not for a long while. A man can only take so much. Bear took that much and then some. Those fuckers tortured him." King's jaw hardened and his fingers bit painfully into my sides.

My heart ached for Bear, and for King.

"But it's over now," King said, cupping my cheek. "I can't say there wasn't a few minutes where I didn't think I was going to get out of there alive, but I'm here now and I'm taking you home."

"What about Sammy?" I asked.

"I can talk to Tanner if you want," King offered. "Explain to him we'll be wanting a trade off with Sammy. However you want it."

He wanted me to bring Sammy home with us too.

I shook my head. "I think it's better if I'm the one to talk to Tanner. I've screwed this all up. I'm the one who needs to fix it."

King nodded. "Good. I'll be here tomorrow night with the van. Get your shit together. Get Sammy's shit together. If Tanner won't see reason, let me know."

King reached down to his jeans and pulled out a phone. "Here. This is yours. My number is the only one programmed in. Any problems, you call me. You want me here before tomorrow night? I'm here."

"As simple as that?" I asked, feeling like I'd just been given a second chance at life. And in a way I had. Because King was alive and I was still his.

"Nope. Not that simple. You tell him you want an annulment and you want that shit yesterday. He so much as squawks at it, you tell him to come fucking see me." King pressed his lips to mine and inhaled deeply. "In this world, there is very little I believe in, Pup. But I believe we belong together."

"You don't believe in God?" I asked.

"No, Pup. The only thing I have faith in, is you."

King slipped out sometime after I fell asleep in his arms. When the morning light flooded my room, I rolled over to avoid its rays. When I finally opened my eyes, I saw something on the nightstand that made my heart flutter and soar. My smile was nothing short of ridiculously huge. I loved it immediately. It was just like the one he'd left for Grace on her hallway table all those months ago.

On my nightstand, on top of the phone that King had given me, was a tiny white ceramic rabbit.

Chapter Twenty-Two

DOE

THE MORNING AFTER King left I felt both elated and utterly miserable.

I had King back. He was alive and I was so grateful to whatever universal being was responsible for keeping him safe. But at the same time, I'd led Tanner on. Not just by the big fat obvious mistake of marrying him, but while he was on his quest to help me remember, occasionally I'd let him sit too close to me on the couch. I'd let him hold my hand.

It was my fault. Everything with Tanner had been my fault, and for the second time in several months I was going to hurt him all over again.

I had to go talk to him and I hoped he would somehow understand. I took a quick shower and threw on a pair of running shorts. I grabbed a soft cotton tank top from the drawer and pulled it on. I cried out when the fabric rubbed against my nipples, feeling much more like they'd been scraped with a cheese grater than covered in soft cotton.

Why the fuck would my nipples...

I sprinted over to the desk calendar and spent an embarrassing amount of time doing the math, but with my hands shaking and my head spinning, even the simplest of calculations didn't compute.

I pushed the calculator away and pulled out a piece of paper. Maybe a word problem would help make it clearer.

Throwing up frequently

+

No period this month, or maybe even last month

+

Cheese grater nipples

+

Sex with King in the water by the boathouse

+

No protection of any kind

=

HOLY. FUCKING. SHIT.

Chapter Twenty-Three

DOE

I FOUND TANNER sitting on the roof of the houseboat. "You know, I'm beginning to think it was you who made the senator keep this rust bucket," I said. "You're always out here."

Tanner turned around. There was an obvious sadness in his eyes, but there was something else too. Something I couldn't quite pin point. "Sammy wanted to come see you, but by the time he got here he was tired so Nadine offered to put him down for a nap. I figured you'd make your way out here sooner or later." Tanner sighed. "This place is probably my favorite place in the world, you know. The three of us spent all of our time out here when we were kids."

The only thing I could do for him was listen because over the past few months he'd done his share of listening to me.

"I want to apologize, about the party. It wasn't right. I wasn't right." He set his hands on top of his head and blew out a breath. "I shouldn't have gone along with the senator and his speech, especially when I knew your heart wasn't in it." He looked up to the sky and closed his eyes, as if he were gathering his thoughts. He turned back to where I stood on the dock. "I just wanted it to be true. I got carried away. I'm sorry, Ray."

"You don't have to apologize. I feel like we're always apologizing to one another," I said.

"Probably because we are." He hopped down from the roof onto the dock. He stood in front of me with his hands in the front pockets of his jeans. "I know why you're here."

"You do?"

"You're leaving," Tanner said, shifting his weight from one foot to the other.

"Yeah, I am," I answered. "It's never felt right for me here and the more I remember, the more I know the right decision is for me to go."

"He's alive. You're going back to him," Tanner said. It wasn't a question. It was a statement.

"How did you know?" I asked.

"I saw him last night."

I bit my lower lip. "Yes, I'm going back to him."

Tanner shook his head and rested his forehead on his palm. "I guess this changes everything."

"If I've learned anything over the last six months, it's that family can mean so many different things. Just because we aren't together, doesn't mean we can't be a family, Tanner. Family is what you make it, what you want it to be."

"That's not true, because I want it to be you," he said, reaching out for my hand and lifting it in his as if he were studying it. As if he wanted to look anywhere but in my eyes.

"It can be me. I'll still be in your life. Just not the way you're thinking I should be," I reminded him.

"Can I assume that he's coming to pick you two up?" Tanner asked. "Unless you've magically learned how to drive recently."

"You should have told me that earlier. I tried to drive my mother's car and only got the engine turned on before I realized that's about all I knew how to do." I looked at him quizzically. "You're taking this awfully well, Tanner."

He pulled me in for a hug and rested his chin on the top of my head, pressing my face into his chest. "I love you, Ray," he said. Tears welled in my eyes. Tanner had been a good friend and I really was going to miss him, but I was ready to stop missing King.

"Here," I said. Pulling his ring off of my finger I pushed it into his hand and closed his fingers around it.

"Fuck," Tanner said, his eyes glassy. "That kind of makes this all real then, huh? You really are leaving?"

"I guess it does," I said.

Tanner opened his fingers and studied the ring before putting it in his pocket. "Can I ask you a favor? One last thing before you go?"

"Sure," I said.

"A kiss."

"Tanner, I can't—" I started to argue.

"Just one more, Ray. One last good-bye. Something to give me some closure." Tanner looked at me with the big chestnut brown eyes I'd remembered from my dream. I knew why they were the only thing that stayed with me. They were so expressive they were practically arguing Tanner's case for him, pleading with me to cut the kid a break and just kiss him already.

"One quick kiss," I agreed, just wanting to get it over with. I could see his heart was breaking and being a spectator in that sport was adding another layer of guilt on top of what I was already feeling. I had the chance to offer him some closure so I took it.

"I never thought we'd have a last kiss," Tanner commented. He took a step forward and cupped my face in his hands.

"You're very persistent. And very bossy."

It's only Tanner. He just wants to say good-bye.

"They don't call me The Tyrant for nothing," Tanner said, leaning in so close, I could feel his cool breath against my cheeks before his lips softly brushed over mine.

Don't trust the tyrant. It was the very last thing Nikki had said to me when she'd come to my window.

And then it happened.

At first it was like lightning bolts going off in my brain. Sparks of light zapping on and off like a fluorescent office light struggling to turn on. Then, it was like my brain was a carnival where someone had located the power cord and plugged it back in, turning the entire carnival on, lights, music, merry-go-round, and all.

My memory.

All of it.

Tanner pulled away as a very clear memory came bounding into my brain.

Of a very different Tanner.

Sammy refused to close his eyes until I read him at least three bedtime stories. He looks up at me with those puffy eyes, rimmed in red, and rubs them with the back of his hand. He is fighting a losing battle with the need for sleep, although he is putting in an admirable effort. After three stories and two songs, my boy has drifted off clutching his favorite blanket, the one with the pattern made entirely of the shadows of different types of motorcycles.

"Sweet dreams," I say, kissing him on the forehead.

After closing his door as softly as I possibly can, I run into Nadine in the hallway. She is carrying a basket of already folded laundry. "Ray, why don't you go see Tanner tonight? I'll keep the baby monitor in my room. You two kids haven't had any time together in a while. Might do you some good to remember that you are actually kids."

"*Are you sure?*" I ask. She is right. I could use some time just being a kid. Between raising Samuel and worrying over Nikki there's little time for much else. And I miss Tanner. We hadn't just hung out in a while.

"*Of course,*" Nadine says. "*Besides, once that boy's asleep I could have Mardi Gras out in the hallway and he wouldn't so much as roll over.*" That is true. He often goes to sleep and wakes up in the same position.

I thank Nadine and change my clothes, taking extra time to make myself look more like a high school girl, and less like a mom who'd spent the afternoon trying to figure out how Samuel got melted crayons in his hair.

Tanner and I have plans this Saturday. He just moved into the pool house of his parents' house. He is going to make me dinner. He promised me all the plans have been made. We haven't had sex since we conceived Samuel. We are too young, and our lives have become so complicated, that we'd agreed to wait. But I am finally ready and Saturday has been chosen as the day.

But on the walk to Tanner's house, I change my mind.

Tonight is as good a night as any.

I call Tanner, but there is no answer. I send him a text, but he doesn't respond. When I get closer to his house I notice the light is on in the pool house. I smile. Maybe he fell asleep studying. I am planning how I could crawl into his bed and snuggle up next to him when I hear a voice.

An angry voice.

"*What the fuck did I tell you about going to her?*" Tanner asks. I've never heard him raise his voice, and at first I don't think it's him. Creeping over to the side of the house, I crouch down by the corner of the window and peer up. Sure enough, the voice is Tanner's. He is pacing back and forth in front of his bed, his fists clenched at his sides.

"You said not to," says a female voice. I recognize that voice right away, even though it is a mere shell of what it used to be.

Nikki

Pushing up onto the tips of my toes I see her sitting on the corner of Tanner's bed with her head in her hands. She looks even worse than she did when she came to see me the week before.

What is she doing at Tanners?

"If you need something, you come to me. But no, you went to her, and I had to hear all about how torn up she is because you turned into a fucking junkie and she can't save you. You know how much I give a shit about you being a junkie? Zero. I give zero fucking shits. But what I do care about is Ray being upset and making me wait another three fucking years to get my fucking dick wet."

"It's not like you've been celibate, asshole," Nikki says, looking up at him through a gap in her greasy bangs.

"No, I've had to settle for fucking your nasty ass!" Tanner shouts, rounding the bed to stand in front of her.

"What do you have for me?" Nikki asks, her hands visibly shaking.

Tanner raises his hand and with a whooshing sound in the air, his hand lands on Nikki's cheek, forcing her to fall back on the bed. "Are you even fucking listening to me?" he seethes.

I have no idea who I am looking at. This isn't the Tanner I know, and he is smacking around a Nikki who I don't know either.

Who the hell are these people, and where are my friends?

Nikki groans but doesn't say a word. "If you do anything to prevent me from being balls deep in Ray Saturday night I'm cutting you the fuck off. Do you hear me?" Tanner crawls up onto the bed and pushes Nikki down, straddling her shoulders. He pulls a small baggie out of his shirt pocket and waves it in the air. Nikki springs to life when she sees it like she was just given an adrenaline shot. She tries to grab it out of his hands, but Tanner pulls it out of reach. "After," he says, putting the baggie back into his pocket.

Tanner leans forward and rests his hands on his headboard as Nikki undoes his belt. I don't want to watch anymore. It's like a horror movie. But I can't peel my eyes away. But when Nikki pulls Tanner's dick out of his pants and wraps her mouth around it, my stomach rolls. I turn to the side and heave into the grass. "What the fuck was that?" Tanner asks. Nikki pulls off of him, but he grabs the back of her head and starts thrusting into her throat. Her eyes water and she gags every time he pushes in. "Did I tell you to fucking stop?"

Silent tears stream down my face as I witness two people who bear no resemblance to the kids I grew up with—the girl I wanted to be my sister, the boy I wanted to marry someday—destroy everything I thought I knew about them. About our friendship.

It was all lies.

All of it.

"This isn't fucking working," Tanner says, pulling out of Nikki's throat and flipping her around, while grabbing something out of his back pocket. "Let's see if that snatch of yours has been completely ruined by now, or if it still feels as tight as it did when you were twelve."

Holy shit.

My entire life is a lie.

This monster is the father of my child.

I can't breathe. My stomach rolls again. Nikki lifts the scrap of fabric that barely covers her ass up to her waist and reveals that she isn't wearing any panties. Tanner rolls on a condom, grabs her hips roughly, and pushes himself inside her. Nikki cries out and fists the sheets in her hands. "I'm going to teach you a fucking lesson, slut. You need your fix? You come here and you're gonna suck my fucking cock for it, take it in the ass like you are now, but you'll get what you want, and I'll get what my future wife thinks she can deny me."

That's it. That is all I can take. Bile rises in my throat. I turn to leave but am suddenly dizzy. I fall onto my knees, my hands landing on the side of the house with a thud. I listen for any commotion, or a sign that they might have heard me, but I don't hear anything. I stand again and struggle to put one foot in front of the other. Each step is a harrowing adventure. The three blocks home seem like an impossible desert crossing. I've only made it a few steps when a voice from behind startles me.

When I turn I lose my footing, falling backwards onto the grass. I look up as Tanner stands over me. "Like what you saw, did you?"

"You're...you're a monster," I say, using my hands and feet to crawl backwards, away from the boy who only minutes before I thought I loved.

"Oh, Ray. You have no fucking idea."

"Are you okay, Ray?" Tanner asked, when I'd pulled back abruptly. I wiped my mouth on the back of my hand.

"No, it's okay," I lied. "I've got to go pack." I nervously twisted the hem of my shirt in my hands. I plastered on a fake smile and took a step back.

"Are you sure you're okay?" Tanner asked, taking another step toward me.

I held up my hand. "Of course. I'm just, you know, overwhelmed," I said as I backed off of the dock. "And I haven't even told the senator yet that I'm leaving, not like he cares."

"He's not home. Nobody is but Nadine," he reminded me.

"So, I should at least call him then, right?" I asked in a much higher pitched tone than I intended.

Why did I have to be such a bad fucking liar?

"Sammy should be up from his nap soon. Go pack, and then I'll drive you guys," Tanner offered.

"No, I mean, you don't have to do that. King's..."

"Oh, come on," Tanner said, continuing to advance toward me. "Besides, you said we're still a family right? No harm in a little car ride together."

Except there was.

I tripped over the spot where the dock met the soft ground, falling backward on my ass. "I'm such a klutz." I was about to stand up, but Tanner startled me by moving quickly to my side, hoisting me off of the sand.

"I've got you," he said, and when I turned toward him and my eyes caught his, I saw a quick flash of the Tanner from my memory. I took a steadying breath.

"Thanks," I said, trying to appear casual by brushing the sand off of my legs. "And yeah. You're right. A ride sounds great. Just let me get cleaned up and get Sammy's stuff together."

Tanner smiled and pushed a strand of hair behind my ear. All the little hairs on my neck stood at attention and not for the same reasons they did with King. There was something cold behind his words. Haunting.

Sinister.

Chapter Twenty-Four

DOE

G ONE WAS THE boy next door. With that last kiss he'd been replaced with the monster from my memory. That kiss brought it all flooding back, and what I saw, shook me to my very bones. "I'll run to my house and grab the truck. I'll meet you out front, on your porch in say, thirty minutes?"

"Thirty minutes. Yes," I nodded. With a little wave I turned and jogged up to the house, practically falling again, this time over the threshold of the back sliding glass door. I flailed my way up the stairs and ran into my room. I ripped open the top dresser drawer I'd hidden the burner phone in that King had given me, tearing it from its hinges, sending socks and the phone sliding across the room. I dove for the phone and hit the speed dial button. It rang several times.

"Come on, pick up," I prayed, nervously tapping my fingers onto the carpet. When there was no answer I shoved the phone in my back pocket. I was going to grab a duffel bag to toss some essentials into, but looking around that room, I realized there was nothing there I needed.

Nothing I wanted. The only essential things to me were Sammy and King. And one of those was sleeping down the hallway. I'd try calling King again after I got Sammy from his room. "Nadine!" I called out down the hall. The only sounds were coming from downstairs, the hum of the refrigerator and the spinning lull from the running dishwasher. "Nadine!" I called again. "I need you to pull your car around. I'll explain when we're on the road, but we have to leave now!"

I opened the door to Sammy's room. I turned the knob as quietly as I could, closing it again behind me with a soft click. I'd hoped Nadine had heard me and was pulling the car around. I tip-toed over to Sammy's crib. Leaning over the railing I expected to see my sleepy man with his hair pointed in a million directions, clutching his favorite motorcycle blanket.

Sammy wasn't in his crib.

It was empty.

The light clicked on and every hair on my neck and arms stood on end.

"It was that fucking weak kiss that gave you away," a voice said, startling me so much I jumped and knocked into a pile of Sammy's toys, which brought to life in a burst of music and flashing lights. "Tanner. I thought you were meeting us out front? Where's Sammy?" I tried to hide the shakiness in my voice. I fell backwards and landed against something soft but unmovable. When I turned around to see what it was, I was eye to eye with a motionless Nadine. Her eyes unfocused and staring straight ahead. Her mouth still opened, as if she'd been surprised.

Dead.

Nadine was dead.

"What the fuck did you do!?" I cried. Tanner stood from where he'd been sitting on the rocking chair I used to rock Samuel to sleep. "Where the fuck is my son!?"

Tanner knelt over me and smiled. But it wasn't the same toothpaste commercial smile I'd seen before. There was no perfect boy next door behind the menacing expression and crazed look in his eyes. "You used to kiss me like I was the most important person in the world," he said as he reached out and ran his thumb over my lips. I jerked my head away, but he grabbed my chin and yanked it back to him. "You used to love me," he spat.

"At some point I probably did." I shook my head. "But I don't remember," I lied.

Tanner reared back, delivering a punishing backhand across my face. "Liar!" It stung so bad, it rattled my cheekbone and I swore I could hear it vibrating in my ear. "There is no 'probably' about it. I know you remember. Do you want to know how I know?"

"Where's Samuel?" I asked again. "Let me up, Tanner!" I tried to stand.

"No!" Tanner shouted, pushing me down on my shoulders, pinning me to the floor. "You will stay right the fuck there while I'm talking to you. I'll ask you again, do you want to know how I know you remember me?" Tanner hissed through gritted teeth.

I slowly nodded, giving in and playing the game of question and answer Tanner was so hell bent on playing.

"Because, Ray, I felt your fear. I felt your lips tremble against mine. And the only reason they would do that...would be if you remembered the last time you saw me."

"You mean the night I caught you fucking Nikki? The night I saw you give her drugs? Hit her? You mean *that* fucking night?" I yelled pushing up on him. All the anger and rage from that night rushing back into me. Tanner pinned my wrists to my side and laughed in my face.

"Yes, that's the night." Tanner reached up to my throat. "But I refer to it as the night I killed you. At least I thought I did."

He squeezed my throat, cutting off my airway, and then the unexpected happened. It started as a flash of white light, followed by small staccato bits of recollection from right before I'd lost my memory:

Tanner standing over me, reigning down blow after blow on my face and body, as Nikki screams for him to stop.

The feeling of being dragged over gritty concrete and hoisted into a pile of trash. The slanted image of the back of Tanner's legs as he casually strolls from of the alley.

The feel of a finger under my nose searching for signs of breath. The sound of Nikki whispering apologies.

The blue and red lights flashing in the distance. Sirens getting louder and louder as they approach.

Nikki apologizing one last time before the feeling of her frail frame curled up against me disappears.

Being loaded up onto a stretcher as people shout orders all around me.

And then a final memory, but this one different, this one was from weeks after I woke up in the hospital. One I was seeing from an entirely new perspective.

I wake up and open my eyes to Nikki standing over me, eyes furrowed in confusion. "Ray?"

"Huh? I'm sorry do I know you?" For a few seconds I thought she was someone from my past, but then her expression turned annoyed, almost cold.

"No, you don't know me…but you're on my fucking bench."

And then it all made sense.

Why Nikki didn't tell me who she was, who I really was.

Why we went to King's party that night. Why she insisted that the solution to all of our problems would be the protection of a biker.

The entire time we'd spent together she hadn't been lying to me.

She was trying to protect me.

The least I could do was fight to protect myself.

I lifted my knee and with all my might I landed a blow right between Tanner's legs. When he reached down to cup his balls I held his head between my hands, and then there was a deafening crack as my head connected with his. Blood, warm and thick, dripped into the corner of my eye. I stood on shaky legs. "You fucking bitch!" Tanner wailed. Holding onto Sammy's crib in order to keep myself upright, I attempted to put one foot in front of the other and I just about made it to the door, but I wasn't fast enough.

Tanner grabbed my ankle, and on the next step, I landed chin first on the carpet. My teeth cutting into my tongue, filling my mouth with the taste of copper.

"I'd rather have you love me, but I'll settle for you being afraid of me." Tanner flipped me over onto my back. My head hit the baseboard and the side of my cheek smacked into the side of Sammy's dresser. I rolled from side to side, trying to clear the ringing from my head.

"You are nothing but a fucking cock tease, Ray. The only time I succeeded in fucking you was when I was a dying fifteen-year-old. I thought that us having a kid would tie us together, bring us closer. I thought at least then you would let me into your fucking pussy on a regular basis. That's why I made sure I put holes in the condom we used that day. Shocked the hell out of me when it actually worked too. And I guess that makes you the lucky one. You were the only one special enough to carry my baby…because I'd made Nikki get ours cut out of her." Tanner had the audacity to wink. "But even then, with my kid in your belly, you wouldn't wear my ring. Wouldn't wear it after either. Said you had plans. Plans you…" Tanner used his fingers to make quotation marks in the air. "Didn't know if they would include me as more than your best friend and the father of your kid," he said, using a high-pitched voice, mockingly swaying his head back and forth, from side to side. "Well, golly-gee Ray, sign me up, that sounds fucking swell."

"Fuck you," I spat. "Get off of me! You're a fucking monster!"

"Now you get it! It's about fucking time, too! Do you even know how exhausting it is pretending to be something I'm not? The fucking all-American kid next door? Your father even liked me, and that asshole doesn't like anyone! He wasn't even fucking pissed when I knocked you up! Do you know how hard that was to fucking pull off?"

"Do your parents know what a fucking freak you are?" I asked, struggling underneath him. I looked around on the ground but there wasn't anything I could use as a weapon.

"You know better than that. They're more oblivious to me than the senator is to you."

Tanner pulled the hem of my tank top up over my breasts and I kicked my feet out to push him off of me but he pushed my knees together and straddled me, paralyzing the use of my legs. "But that's why I had Nikki. She let me fill every fucking hole of hers since we were twelve. And when she started experimenting with drugs it was like winning the lottery, because in exchange for a taste, the bitch would let me do anything. Cut her, burn her, choke her, tie her up until her wrists fucking bled."

Nikki.

I remembered. All the times she'd shown up to my house with marks all over her body. She'd always made excuses. She cut herself on a nail on the houseboat. She walked into a door. She got bucked off of her cousin's horse. Nikki had always been clumsy. She didn't ever have a boyfriend to be suspicious of. And her parents were the modern day Cleavers.

There was nothing to make me question that her excuses were lies, but every single sign that something was very wrong was there.

I'd failed her.

I'd failed her because I was too busy with my perfect little life to even think about the fact that something was far from perfect in hers. I cringed when I thought about all the times I'd bragged about Tanner. About how attentive he was to me. About how great he was with Sammy. She's the only person I could talk to about being nervous to commit my life to someone when I was still just a kid myself.

"You should thank Nikki, really, she was the only reason I let you have your space. The reason why I was the perfect patient boyfriend. She took every single thing I wanted to give to you. But that fucking slut had to go and fuck it all up. When I dragged you into that alley, she had to go call for help." Tanner rolled his eyes. "And when they didn't find your body, and she stopped coming back for dope, I knew you were alive and that cunt was with you. That the two of you were hiding from me." Tanner smiled a vicious and evil smile again, as he clasped his hands around my throat and squeezed, playing yet another round of his sick choking game. "But eventually I caught up to Nikki, in that shitty motel room, and when she wouldn't tell me where you were..." Tanner looked off to the side, lost in a memory. His face reddening. His forehead creasing as he grew angrier. His neck bursting with thick pulsing veins. He refocused his attention on me, tightened his grip around my throat, pressing harder, until I was no longer able to draw in a breath. Tanner pressed his lips against my ear. "...I killed the whore." He released my throat suddenly. I gasped for air as my windpipe opened back up at an agonizingly slow pace as I tried to fill my lungs.

"Fuck. You," I said, as soon as I had enough air to say it. Tanner killed Nikki. She didn't overdose by accident. She didn't overdose on purpose. My father didn't kill her. No, the boy next door killed her.

My boy next door.

"I think I like it when you're afraid of me, makes my fucking dick hard." Tanner grabbed my wrist and pressed my hand to his hardening erection pressing against his shorts. "Maybe I was wrong all this time. Maybe it should have been you instead of Nikki taking it up the ass," Tanner said, grabbing a hold of my breast and digging his nails into the tender flesh. I tried not to react. I tried not to scream. I didn't want to waste my energy on something that wouldn't get me any results.

I learned that from fighting with King.

"You think I'm afraid of you?" I laughed, shaking my head from side to side. "I've known fear, real fear. Shit that would make you piss your fucking khaki shorts. You think you can scare me? Think again. Because I've seen what real fear looks like and I'll tell you something, real fear is much bigger than you, has bright green eyes, and a lot more tattoos."

"You're talking about that fucking felon?" Tanner asked, bitterly. "That motherfucker is going to pay for what he did to me the night of the party."

What did King do to Tanner at the party?

"Oh, he didn't tell you?" he asked. "I came to your window to make yet another fake apology to the almighty Ray Price when I saw you two." My eyes went wide. "That motherfucker knew I was there watching, made a show of fucking you in front of me, making you tell him that you love him." Tanner heaved, as if he were about to throw up, but took a deep breath and continued, "He fucking came all over your back, literally rubbing it in that you were his!" Tanner grabbed the sides of my head and started lifting it up and pounding it back into the carpet, like he was trying to force his point into me. Over and over again until my eyes started to cross and I saw double. Two crazed Tanners were shouting at me, spit flying out of their mouths as they pounded my head into the floor. "But you're not his! You're not fucking his, Ramie! You're not! You're mine!" Tanner roared. Cocking back his fist, his blow landed in the dead center of my stomach.

All the wind left my lungs. A sharp pain tore up my spine. I turned on my side and folded myself in half, hugging my middle. I prayed that he hadn't taken away the life that King and I had made.

"Are you afraid of me now, bitch?"

"Stop! Don't! I'm—" I croaked out, stopping just short of saying the words. Tanner's eyes went wide. His chest heaved up and down. He didn't blink. His mouth opened but no words came out. Then suddenly, it was as if he'd registered what I'd said, because he stood from the floor and kicked the side of the dresser, sending the baby monitor and the contents of Sammy's diaper changing station crashing to the floor around my head.

He crossed back over the room and stood above me, glaring

so hard I could feel the heat of his stare. I flinched when he bent down, but he'd only picked up something from the floor.

The phone King had given me. A wicked smile lit up his face. With a guttural roar, he lifted his boot.

The last thing I saw was the heel.

The last thing I felt was it connecting with my face.

Chapter Twenty-Five

KING

"SO, I'VE DECIDED I'm not going to die," Grace an-nounced, handing me a beer. Ever since I brought her back home from the safe house, I'd noticed a change in her. She was moving with more ease. Her skin had some color back in it, the bags underneath her eyes were gone.

"That's just something you can decide now?" I asked, taking a swig of my beer and setting it back down on the table. Grace reached over and picked up the bottle, setting it onto the coaster she'd set out on the table for me, but I'd forgotten to use.

I'm pretty sure that if you went back to my house and searched top to bottom, you wouldn't find a single coaster.

"Yes. It is." Grace reached out and placed a hand on my forearm. "You have been through so much, my boy. I don't want to put you through anything else. Besides, you kids need me. That much is obvious. So nope, I'm not dying. I'm staying put."

"What does your doctor say about your new life revelation?" I asked, taking another long pull of my beer. With Eli out of the way as a threat, and a date to bring my girl back home, I finally felt like I could let my guard down.

"Oh, what does he know? I'm feeling great and that's what I am going to focus on. Going back to him week after week, wasting hours of my life just to hear him tell me how much of it

I have left? It's absolutely useless. So I've decided I'm not going anywhere, and that's that."

"Honestly," I started, "if anyone can avoid meeting their maker just because they decided to live instead…I believe you can." And it was the truth. Grace wasn't just an old lady with too many ceramic rabbits. She was a force to be reckoned with and if she wanted to use that force to fight the boatman, then who was I to argue? "So, you won't need me to bring you weed anymore?"

"Now I didn't say that," Grace sang. "And I have to be around for a lot longer, especially now that my boy is going to have a kid running around. Grandma Grace has her spoiling hat on, and I'm warning you, once it's on, it's hard to get it back off."

"Kid's got a dad, Grace. I'm just going to be his…" I paused. In my head I'd never put a title on what Doe and I were. She was just mine. So when faced with having to say it out loud, I faltered.

"Step-dad type figure," Grace offered. Her smile turned into a straight line. She picked at the label on her beer, focusing on the neck as she spoke. "I'm sorry about Max. I would have done anything for you, you know that. I would have adopted her myself if they would have let me."

I nodded. Before I'd left Doe last night, I'd told her that I'd signed off on Max's adoption. I could fight it. But Max deserved a good home and not a battle that could keep her in foster care until she was eighteen. I just hoped that one day she would seek me out and let me explain that I did what I did, not because she was a burden, but because of the tremendous amount of love I had for her.

"Or you can be his real step-dad if you decide to marry the girl," Grace said.

"Can't marry her. She's already married," I reminded her.

"Right now she is. But that will all be fixed. And if you're half as smart as I think you are, you'll figure out that being married isn't just fodder for stand-up comics. If you two have even half of what Edmond and I had, you best snatch it up as quickly as you can. Hold on as tight and never ever let go."

"She's a teenager, Grace."

Grace shook her head. "There ain't nothing about that girl that's a teenager except her age. She's lived two lives already. I think you need to make sure that life number three has been worth the trouble."

"That's the plan."

"So when are you going to get her?" Grace asked eagerly.

"Tonight," I said, hiding the smile that threatened to take over my face. I can count the times I'd smiled in the last year and every single fucking one of those smiles were because of my girl.

My phone buzzed in my pocket indicating a text message. I was going to ignore it, but then I remembered I'd given the number to Pup in case she needed me. I pulled it out of my pocket and glanced at the screen. I had a missed call from her. "Fuck," I cursed. I hadn't even felt it vibrate or heard it ring. Pup had also sent a text.

Well, it was from her number.

I clicked on the icon.

What I saw made my heart drop and my blood boil.

There on the screen was a broken, bloodied, and bruised version of my Pup. The hair that fell into her face was streaked with red. She was tied to a chair, her mouth wide open. Her jaw set to one side like it had been punched repeatedly. Her clothes were torn and hanging off her body.

Then I noticed that the picture had a sideways triangle in the middle of it. "What the fuck is it?" I asked out loud. Grace came to stand at my side to see what it was that had me struck completely silent. I pressed the triangle, and the horrible scene I thought was just a picture played out in front of me in video form.

Pup, being hit over and over again in the face with a man's closed fist. She was screaming, crying, begging for the beating to stop. By the time the frame froze again, she was lifeless, but the blows continued. Delivered by a closed fist wearing a gaudy gold watch with a red diamond bezel.

The senator.

Another text came in, the icon appearing over the playing video.

HOUSEBOAT 11pm
ALONE
UNARMED
OR SHE DIES

Chapter Twenty-Six

KING

THE WORST FUCKING feeling in the world is not being able to help the person you love. Hearing her cries of pain and seeing her bleeding and broken was enough to drive any sane man crazy.

And I wasn't exactly sane to begin with.

I thought the senator might have wanted me dead, but I honestly never gave a thought to him hurting his own daughter. I've hurt people. And given the chance to be a father, I would see to it that harm never came to my daughter.

I was hoping the senator operated under an honor amongst thieves set of rules, but apparently I underestimated his determination to ruin lives.

I was going after her and I didn't care if I died. I didn't care if he shot a cannon at my head, but I was going to save Doe. And then, if I was still breathing, I was going to make sure that before I killed the senator, he suffered pain and fear like he never knew existed.

A funny thing happens when you fear for the worst. Some people give in to their panic and freeze when a situation seems dire. Others, stay and fight, even if the situation is hopeless.

The prison psychologist called it fight or flight response.

I'm a motherfucking fighter.

Always have been, from the playground to the prison yard.

The message said to come alone, but that didn't mean I didn't need back up on standby. I looked down at my phone. Eight p.m. I had time and thank fucking God, because I would need every single second of it. I dialed Bear. No answer. I slammed my fist on the steering wheel and rested my forehead against it. Of course not. He'd been even more fucked up in the head since the shit with Eli went down. He was probably fucked up to no end and cock deep in Beach Bastard pussy. I looked up from the wheel and staring me right in the face was a sign for the exit for Coral Pines.

It was a sign, but I took it as a *sign*.

Because there was only one person I knew in Coral Pines and he was exactly who I needed.

I spun the tires in the wet grass. I barreled off the ramp and toward the only person I knew who could help in a moment's notice.

No, the only person who could *kill* in a moment's notice.

JAKE DUNN WAS a killer for hire. Or at least he *was* before getting married and settling down. Only a few people in this world knew that about him. If he didn't have the tattoos and the attitude, at first glance, you would think he's just another clean-cut kid from the beach.

Jake Dunn was the walking, talking equivalent to an angel of death.

And the only reason I even knew about that part of his life was because we had a mutual acquaintance who put us in touch while I was in prison. The Dutchman called Jake, The Moordenaar. The Murderer.

Subtle.

When I pulled up to Jake's little Mayberry house, I didn't even have time to really take in the absurdity of Jake Dunn living in a house with little pink shutters and a swing set in the front yard.

I leapt out of the truck and up the front steps, frantically knocking on the door. "Just a minute!" a woman's voice called out. I knocked louder. "Just a freaking minute!" she yelled again.

The door came flying open and the little red head who appeared was about to say something, like she had assumed she knew who would be on the other end, until she looked up and her mouth closed.

She never expected me. "I assume you're not here to check on the status of your art work," she said flatly, crossing her arms and leaning up against the door jam. She was wearing little jogging shorts and a clingy tank top that made the fact that she wasn't wearing a bra obvious.

"I need Jake," I said. I wanted to throw her aside and barge in to find him, but Abby was the only thing in the world Jake actually cared about, besides his daughter, so the chances of me doing that and still receiving his help, and not end up at the bottom of the swamp, were slim to none.

"Yeah, I assumed as much. He's out back." She looked down at my muddy clothes. "Go around," she said, pointing to the side of the house. I turned around but her words caught me. "You okay?" "No. I'm not okay at all. My girl's in trouble," I said honestly. I didn't have time for mind games. I didn't have time for anything. I only had until 11 p.m. to figure out how I was going to save my girl.

"I'll take you there," Stepping out onto the front porch, Abby closed the screen door behind her and lead me out back to where Jake was sitting on the seawall, a Corona by his side, a cigarette dangling from his lips.

A pink Barbie fishing pole in his hands.

"Babe, I'm getting her a real pole because this cheap piece of shit doesn't even wind properly. I know she likes it because it's pink, but Jesus fucking Christ, this thing couldn't reel in a minnow."

"Jake," she interrupted and he looked up from what he was doing and spotted me approaching. "He needs your help."

Jake took a swig of his beer and set down the pole.

"Press play," I said, tossing him the phone.

Abby went to stand next to him and while they watched, neither of them said a thing. While Abby looked horrified, Jake didn't even react, while hearing it again made another piece of me feel like it died.

"What you need is a soldier. I'm not exactly the soldiering kind," Jake said.

"If I get her back, and the motherfucker is somehow still alive when it's all said and done, you can have him. Do whatever the fuck you want to him as long as the result is the same—him no longer breathing."

Jake wrinkled his nose. "Nah man. Can't take that from you. Revenge shit like this makes your blood boil and your dick hard all at the same time."

Jake tossed me my phone and I scrolled through the pictures, stopping at the one I'd taken just that morning. I'd taken it for my own sick pleasure, not realizing how it could come in handy. I held up the phone, showing him the screen. "You can also have this," I said.

"Jake," Abby said, nudging him with her thigh. Jake's eyes were glued to the screen, his pupils as big as saucers. "Jake," she said again, pushing against him harder.

Jake looked up at her then back to me. "Okay. I'll do it. Especially because my girl is looking at me like I won't get any this century if I don't. And since I'm trying my fucking damnedest to knock her up again..." Jake put a hand on Abby's back and smiled up at her. There was no mistaking the connection between the two of them, and for a guy who took lives for pleasure, there was a reverence in the way he looked at her.

Like he worshipped her.

Jake took his eyes away from his wife, and when he looked back up at me, I swore I saw his eyes turn from blue to black. His voice was even slightly deeper. More even toned. "You got yourself a soldier," he said, blowing smoke out through his nose into the night air like a fire breathing dragon.

"I'll get your jacket," Abby said, jogging back up to the house. Jake followed her with his eyes until she disappeared behind the sliding glass doors.

"Your girl?" Jake asked, handing me back my phone, the video of Doe paused close up on her face. "She anything like that?" He pointed to where Abby had just disappeared behind the sliding glass doors.

"Like what?"

"She better than you, but for some stupid reason doesn't get that?"

"Sounds about right," I said.

Jake tossed his cigarette into a pink bucket marked DADDY PUT YOUR NASTY CIGAMETTES IN HEERE SO YOUS DON'T KILL THE MAN TEES. "Just take my suggestion and when all this shit is over, and she comes out with a heart that still beats, and lungs that still pull air into them, make that shit legal. Marry her. Knock her up. Anything you can do to selfishly tie yourself to her for life."

Abby came back out and handed Jake his leather jacket. "Keys are in the pocket," she said. Jake stepped toward her and grabbed the back of her neck, pressing his forehead against hers. "Check on Gee. Tell her that her daddy won't be gone long." He touched the pendant on some sort of necklace she was wearing, and Abby covered his hand with her own. After a minute, they pulled apart and Jake shrugged on his jacket, leading the way back toward the front of the house.

"I've got my truck," I said as we reached the driveway.

"Message said you best be there by eleven tonight?"

"Yeah."

Jake shook his head. "I'm gonna grab my bike. Ride around for a bit. Clear my mind on the ride."

"I'm gonna head to the clubhouse, see if Bear's around. I can't get him on his damn phone. Meet you at my place in an hour," I said, turning toward my truck.

Jake lit a cigarette. He straddled his bike and turned the key, the engine roaring to life. With a quick tip of his chin to me, he rode off down the shell driveway and onto the road, kicking up white dust into the black night air as he sped down the road.

I looked at my phone.

Nine p.m.

Two hours.

Two hours until I would see my girl again.

Dead or alive.

Chapter Twenty-Seven

KING

I PULLED UP to the clubhouse and the skinny prospect manning the gate, a little shit they called Thor, stood from his ripped bar stool to slide open the gate. I drove in and parked next to Bear's bike, leaving the keys in the ignition and the door wide open. I jumped from the passenger seat and headed to the courtyard.

"King!" Thor called from behind me. When I turned around, the skinny kid from the gate was running toward me. "Stop!" he shouted, coming to a breathless halt in front of me, resting his hands on his knees to catch his breath. He held up his index finger.

"I ain't got time for you to learn how to breathe again, kid. What the fuck do you want?" I asked him harshly.

"I forgot. I ain't supposed to let you in here no more. You can't be here," Thor said.

"Who the fuck told you that?"

"Prez. He said you ain't one of us so you can't be coming round here no more, and I smoked a joint and I got fucked up and I totally fucked up. He's gonna fucking kill me."

"What the fuck does your VP think of that order?" I asked, crossing my arms across my chest. The kid's eyes went wide as I stared him down.

"Don't know, man. He's been holed up in his room, rotating the BBBs in and out. He doesn't come out except to grab another bottle and buy blow from Wolf. Won't talk to no one neither. But seriously, you got to leave. Prez is going to kill me, and worse than that, I'll never get my patch!"

"What are you afraid of more? Him killing you? Or not getting your patch?" "Patch, 'course," Thor scoffed, scrunching his nose.

"Stupid little shit," I muttered, heading toward Bear's room.

"Seriously man, if you don't turn around, I got to shoot you or they'll shoot me."

"So fucking shoot me!" I called back over my shoulder.

"Fuck man!" he groaned. "Just don't be long. And don't let no one see you! *FUCK!*"

The Lynyrd Skynyrd blasting from inside of Bear's room changed to Johnny Cash, and in the millisecond of silence between songs, I heard a slight commotion inside, like furniture scraping against the floor. I pounded my fist on the door. "Bear, get your fucking ass out here." Looking around I didn't spot anyone but a few of the BBBs on the balcony across the courtyard who winked and crooked their fingers at me. I pounded again. When he still didn't come to the door, I walked over to the end of the hall to the old elevator shaft, which no longer housed an elevator, and pulled at the crumbling knee wall in front of it until I found a piece of concrete that was big enough to accomplish what I needed. I walked back over to Bear's room, pulled my arm back, and launched the block through Bear's window.

A woman inside screamed as I stepped through the window, ducking underneath the jagged shards of glass that still clung to the frame. Bear was lying on his bed. Naked except for his cut, a petite Asian girl was straddling him, the source of the scream.

"Get the fuck out," I told her. She hopped off Bear and pulled down the scrap of material that had been bunched up above her tits until it barely covered her ass. She ran passed me, grabbing a pair of seven inch clear platform heels on her way out the door.

"You ain't supposed to be here," Bear said.

"Yeah, Thor told me that right after he let me in."

"Tight fucking ship we're running here." Bear let out a frustrated breath and ran his hand through his messy mane of blond hair. "And I'm supposed to be captain of the SS Fucked Up when shit's sinking faster than the fucking Titanic." An alarm sounded. The sound of muffled voices from the floor below rose up to Bear's room.

"Alarm's sounding," Bear said flatly. "Calvary's a coming." He rolled onto his side and pulled a cigarette from his pack on the nightstand. He lit it and leaned back onto the bed, pulling off a condom and tossing it into the trash.

"Pops said I can't play with you no more," Bear laughed, taking a swig from a bottle of whiskey he picked up off the floor next to the bed.

"I figured that when he didn't answer my calls. When we were in the weeds with Eli." Bear flinched at the mention of his name. "And I don't give a fuck what your old man thinks right now 'cause we got a fuck of a lot of trouble and no fucking time, so cover your fucking cock and get in the truck and I'll fill you in on the way."

"We always got trouble," Bear mumbled. "What the fuck is new about that?" He swung his legs over the side of the bed and rubbed his eyes with the heels of his hands.

"This is what's new, asshole," I said, tossing him the phone.

"You came all the way here, stormed your way in, practically ripped perfectly good Asian pussy off my cock, and more than likely cost Thor his patch, because you wanted to show me your new phone?" Bear asked, slurring his words. He held his cigarette over the floor and ashed it directly onto the carpet. An unused ashtray sat less than two feet away on the small two-person dinette table.

"Press play," I said, losing the bite in my voice. Bear rolled his eyes at me and clicked the screen. The light from the phone flashed on his face as the video played, and although I couldn't see the screen, the reflection on his skin told me what he was seeing. I took a couple of deep breaths to push down the urge to reach out and strangle something, anything, someone.

ANYONE.

As Bear watched the situation unfolding in the palm of his hand, and the reality of what was going on set in, his entire demeanor shifted. He turned rigid, his shoulders stiffened, and his eyes focused. His brows furrowed in confusion at first, but by the time the video was over and the screen went dark his fists were clenched in anger.

"If you care about her half as much as I think you do, then get your ass up, tuck your dick into your pants, and get in the fucking truck." Bear stood from the bed and pulled up his pants. He walked over to the dresser and pushed it off the wall, exposing a hole in the drywall. He reached inside and felt around, producing two pistols, making sure both of them were loaded before placing them in the holsters under his cut. "Let's fucking go," he said, shoving his feet into his boots which had been sitting by the open door of the tiny bathroom. He didn't bother with the laces.

Bear shoved me aside and left the room first, leading the way toward the back staircase, the opposite of how I'd come. The sound of boots coming up the stairs on the other end of the courtyard echoed underneath the flimsy overhangs.

"I guess it doesn't matter what rules I set, boy. You ain't gonna listen to a damn one of them anyway." Chop stood at the bottom of the stairs. "Had high hopes for you. But how the fuck am I supposed to pass the gavel to a VP who doesn't respect his brothers, his president, or the rules we live by?"

"We can argue about all this shit later, Pops," Bear said dismissively. "King's girl is going to get herself dead in about an hour if we don't get to her, so we can have our little heart to heart when I get back from making sure that doesn't happen."

"In trouble again? Girl looked spooked when she came here a few weeks ago, too." Chop said, sucking on his upper teeth.

"She was here?" Bear asked, stepping back up to Chop. Two of his men flanked his sides when they saw me approach, pushing back their cuts to show me a flash of their pistols, reminding me they were armed.

But so the fuck was I.

"Yeah, she was here. Wanted to talk to Bear," chimed Wolf, who was standing beside Chop. His arms decorated with colorful graphic tattoos of Jack the Ripper, along with the hookers he was famous for murdering in varying levels of dismemberment. It was some sick shit to put on your arms for the world to see, but it was great work.

Some of my best.

"Why didn't anyone tell me she came looking for me?" Bear asked, his chest heaving with anger.

"First off, 'cause we were on lockdown while you were out doing fuck knows what with this one." He waved his hand at me. "And 'cause I gave orders. This is still my club," Chop said.

"And the simple truth is that she ain't club business, son. She ain't no one's ole lady, and she ain't coming here to suck anyone's cock. So I sent her packin'."

"Yeah, you also told her I was fucking dead." I said, feeling the rage building.

Chop had the fucking audacity to laugh. "So fucking what? I told her both of you were dead."

"Fuck you!" Bear roared, launching himself at his father. If Pup weren't in immediate danger, I'd of thrown caution to the wind and taken them out. Biker by biker. But this wasn't my fight and even if it were, I didn't have fucking time for it. "That ain't your call to make."

"Yes, it is my call! That's what you don't seem to fucking get! Every decision involving this club is my decision to make! I'm the fucking President, but you don't seem to remember what that title means these days! I want to pass you the fucking gavel but you spit in my face every time you turn it down."

Bear turned down being president?

I grabbed Bear by the shoulders, catching him before he reached Chop. He shook me off but stopped. I looked around to the various bikers standing straight faced, watching our confrontation unfold. "I've known most of you my entire fucking life," I said. "I've known all of you bitches longer than most of you have known each other. I've never asked you for special favors. I've never asked you for anything I've not paid back tenfold. But my girl comes here looking for help, and you turn her the fuck away because Prez here is pissed that I didn't patch in when he wanted me to?" I shook my head and looked at Chop. "If this is how you treat someone you've known for decades then I made the right fucking decision by not patching in. You're mad at me because some blood was spilled on your doorstep? Be mad at me. But it's not your fucking blood that got spilled. It was mine. My friend. My family. So you can take this self-righteous brotherhood and go fuck yourself with it. Because I know what brotherhood is." I took one last glance at the men around me. "When any of you have ever needed something, I've never turned a single one of you motherfuckers away from *my* doorstep. Preppy knew what brotherhood was. Bear knows what brotherhood is. You?" I pointed to Chop. "You don't know shit."

"You better watch your fucking mouth, boy." Chop seethed. He pointed to Bear. "Whatever his girl's got troubling her doesn't concern you, or us for that matter. Neither does he." Chop turned his attention to me. "You had a chance to be a Beach Bastard, boy. Lots of chances. But you didn't want this life. You turned your back on the chance to have the loyalty and protection of this club." He turned back to Bear. "Yet you still give it to him like he walks around wearing a god damned invisible cut!" He looked me up and down like I disgusted him, then turned back to his son. "He don't deserve your loyalty, boy. Your brothers could've been meeting their makers because of him and you either don't fucking get that or you don't fucking care, and honestly, I don't fucking know which one pisses me off more!" Chop stepped up into Bear's face. They were shoulder to shoulder, staring into identical blue eyes as they both puffed out their chests and shifted their weight from side to side.

"Isaac was here because someone in our club let him in. One of our brothers, one of the people I'm supposed to be the most loyal to, made sure that Isaac was in place to take us all out. Not just King or Preppy, but me too. Whoever let him in was one of our own brothers and he didn't give a fuck that the end result was supposed to be a bullet in my motherfucking head." Chop opened his mouth to speak, but Bear wasn't finished. "And don't you dare fucking speak to me about loyalty. Just ask Mom. Oh wait, you can't. She's fucking dead because of you."

"You ungrateful motherfuck—" Chop wrinkled his nose like he was about to breathe fire from his nostrils.

"Are you questioning my fucking loyalty to this club!? I have taken bullets for you. I have killed without question. I've been nothing but in, a hundred and fifty percent, since the day I put on this cut. It's you who needs a reality check, Pops." Bear took a step back. "Prep, King, they were more family to me growing up than you ever were. And if you really want to talk loyalty, then let's talk loyalty. Because if Prep were still here, I would take that bullet for him. I would gladly give my life for his. And now King's girl is in trouble, might already be dead, and I would step into her place in a heartbeat so that he wouldn't have to live without his girl."

Chop took another step forward, his forehead almost touching Bear's. "I'm not talking about them. I'm talking about your fucking brothers."

"So the fuck am I, old man," Bear said, sidestepping his father and heading toward the gate. "So the fuck am I." Bear nodded to me. "Let's fucking go."

"It's your decision boy," his dad called out. "But if you leave right now, then you leave your cut here. I fucking mean it."

Without hesitation, Bear shrugged out of his cut and held it up, exposing his bare chest and the double gun holster that his vest had easily hidden. "Fine by me, Pops. 'Cause this thing we have here?" Bear looked around to the balconies which were now full of spectators. "This whole thing is supposed to be about family, but as much as I want that to be true…it isn't. Hasn't been for a real long fucking time."

"The only real family you got is me, boy," Chop hissed, his

face reddening as he focused on the cut in Bear's hand.

"That's where you're wrong, old man. 'Cause whether he wears a fucking cut or not, King is my brother. And if you can't respect my family..." Bear looked up to the biker filled balcony. Then he walked over to a broken plastic chair leaning haphazardly against the chipped stucco. With one last reverent glance down at the scrap of leather that meant everything in his world, he set his cut on the chair. "Then I can't respect yours."

"Let's go, man," I said to Bear. I'd been around the Beach Bastards since I was fifteen. Long enough to know I needed to get Bear the fuck out of there as fast as fucking possible. Not just because time was ticking for Pup, but because I knew that once your prospect time was up and you were patched in as a full member of the Beach Bastards, there was no walking away from your brothers.

There was no abandoning your cut.

You were either buried in it...or buried without it.

And if you were buried without it, your death wasn't from natural causes.

I had to get Bear the fuck out of there before they remembered that.

Chapter Twenty-Eight

KING

A T TEN FIFTY-FIVE p.m., Bear, Jake, and I were on our stomachs underneath the tall roots of the mangroves on the back property line. The houseboat was in our sights.

That's where the senator was torturing my girl.

That's where he was going to die.

"Again, the plan is that you wait ten minutes," I said. "No matter what you hear, no matter what you see, you wait ten minutes. I can't risk Pup being killed because I didn't play by the psycho senator's rules." Jake and Bear both nodded in agreement. "I also need to make sure you two both know how this ends. When you come in, if the choice is between me or her, you chose her. You always choose her."

I will always choose her.

I cracked my knuckles. "I can't do this unless I know in the end, no matter how this fucking shit plays out, that she'll at least make it out whole," I said.

Looking back toward the houseboat, Jake nodded. "Agreed."

"No problem," Bear said. "In the event you don't make it out though, I'll take real good care of your girl for you."

"Jake," I said. "If I don't come out of this, shoot that motherfucker in the head." I stood and started walking toward the houseboat.

"10-4," Jake answered.

"What the fuck?" Bear shoved my shoulder. "You can't say that kind of shit to him, man. He'll take you fucking seriously."

That was fucked up, Boss Man. Jake wouldn't know sarcasm if it bit him on his Dexter ass," Preppy chimed in.

"Good. Cause I wasn't fucking joking," I said.

"It's time," Jake said, checking the clip on his gun.

I visualized Doe in my bed, naked and half covered with a sheet, watching one of the 90's action movies she loved so much, turning back to look at me to make sure I was paying attention to all the parts she deemed very important.

It's that visual and the visual of the senator begging for mercy that I carried with me as I went in blind. I cracked my knuckles again and handed Bear my gun. "Fuck, yeah."

It was finally time to get my girl, once and for all.

No matter what, I wouldn't be leaving without her.

Chapter Twenty-Nine

DOE

I KNEW I was in a dreamlike state and no matter how hard I tried, I couldn't wake from it. I couldn't open my eyes. I tried to move my hands but I couldn't feel them. I felt like I was floating and I no longer had use for things like limbs. For a moment, I thought I heard my father's voice. "Ramie, Ramie wake up," he was saying. But I couldn't talk to him. I floated further away until I could only hear the echoes of his plea. I drifted off further and further until I was no longer floating.

I'm nine years old. It's my birthday. My mom just came out and embarrassed me in front of all my friends. She's drunk again. She just finished telling my friends that no one wants a fat wife so we shouldn't eat my cake. She goes back into the house and Nadine finishes cutting slices that none of my friends touch. The music we had been playing has turned off and although we'd been taking turns selecting songs, nobody chimes in that it was their turn to pick another one.

My father appears at the back sliding glass door. He's wearing a suit. It's the only thing I've seen him wear for as long as I can remember. I don't think he owns anything else. He rarely even takes off his jacket. Once we were at a county fair where he was giving a speech in order to support the Future Farmers of America and his jacket was off. His assistant was holding it folded over her arm as if she were holding the crown of the queen of England. His sleeves were rolled up. The site baffled me so much that when his speech was over I'd asked him if he was sick.

He'd laughed and ruffled my hair until it stuck out in all directions and fell into my face. That morning my mother had insisted on blow drying it perfectly straight, burning my scalp in her quest to make me look every bit the picture-perfect political poster child. "That's better," he said, before being whisked off the stage to the awaiting press.

My father slides the door open to the back yard. In his hand, he's carrying a big bouquet of yellow roses. I think they are for my mother, but most nights they don't even sleep in the same room. And it's been months since either one of them has bothered apologizing to the other after one of their shouting matches. They don't even really fight anymore.

They ignore.

I preferred the fighting. Because at least then they were communicating on some level, even an angry and bitter one.

My father smiles and walks up to me where I'm sitting on the edge of the pool in silence, while Nadine tries to raise the spirits of my classmates and friends. "Happy Birthday, Princess," my father says, handing me the flowers.

"For me?" I ask, pushing my bangs out of my eyes.

"It's your birthday isn't it?"

"Yeah, it is." I sound as defeated as I feel.

"You're nine now, and that's a big birthday. I was thinking of getting you another stuffed animal, but I figured that flowers would be a much more appropriate gift for a young lady like yourself." My father stuck his nose inside the bouquet and inhaled, only to pull away abruptly to close his eyes and cough. I giggled. "People always say these things smell so good. To me they smell just awful." My dad laughed when he saw my smile and handed me the bouquet. "But *nonetheless they are for you, my sweet girl." The green tissue paper is melting underneath my wet hand which isn't big enough to fully circle the stems. The flowers tipped in my hand and my father caught them before they fell into the pool. He held them out to me and I pressed my face into the bouquet and inhaled like he had, but didn't have the same reaction. I decided right then and there that roses were my new favorite smell.*

My new favorite thing ever.

"Why do all the party goers look as if they just played pin the tail on the donkey and the donkey kicked them?" he asks, glancing over at the table where my friends sit in silence. I don't want to tell him that Mom crashed my party in every way, but I don't have to, because the sliding glass door opens and my mother walks out in a black bikini and floppy hat. She's still holding a glass, except this one is full to the brim.

"Margot," my father says in a warning tone.

"What?" she snaps loudly.

My father stands and holds onto my mother's elbow as he guides her back inside. His jaw is tight and I can tell that even though his mouth isn't opening and closing that he is doing that thing where he talks through his teeth because his lips are moving.

"FINE!" Comes a shout from inside the house followed by a crash. A few minutes pass and he hasn't come back outside. I just gave up and was about to just tell my friends they should leave before things get worse when the door opens and my father comes running out of the house. Not in a suit. Not in a jacket. Not in a tie. Nope. My father. Senator to his very core. Was wearing long black swim trunks. And nothing else.

Shirtless.

My. FATHER. Shirtless.

"CANNONBALL!" He shouts as he leaps off the edge of the pool and launches himself into the air, hugging his knees to his chest as he

crashes into the water, sending water splashing over the edge like a tidal wave, completely soaking me and the picnic table where my friends sit in total shock.

Followed by total laughter.

"Now let's see who has the best splash," my father says, coming up for air and shaking the water from his black hair. "Nadine, you and I will be the judges. Winner gets extra cake!"

"Mom said that we shouldn't eat cake. Said it will make us fat."

"Well, your mother can..." He closes his mouth, takes a breath and starts over. "Your mother said that because she doesn't like cake. But that's her loss. Besides, everyone knows the calories from cake don't count on a birthday. It's like, basic science. Right guys?" he asks. My friends cheer and shout. Dad hoists himself up and let his feet dangle, as my friends line up one by one to showcase their best cannonball.

"Ramie, you're first. Now make it a good once. The Price Family is famous worldwide for their cannonball skills so don't let me down!"

I go first and emerge from the water to clapping and cheers. "See? Didn't I tell you guys? It's in her blood!"

After the competition, my father's assistant enters the backyard through the side gate and informs him of an upcoming teleconference that he is almost late for. With another "Happy Birthday" and a kiss on the top of my head, my father wraps a towel around his waist and is gone.

I look over to the picnic table where my friends are happily shoveling cake into their mouths and arguing over who had the better splash. My roses are in the center of the table, an old grey paint bucket serving as a makeshift vase.

It was the best day of my life and although he'd only been part of it for less than an hour, it was the best day with my dad I'd ever spent.

Because that hour wasn't about politics, values, campaigns, my mother, how we looked to the public, agendas…it was just about me and my birthday. "You're dad actually jumped in the pool!" Nikki exclaims, dumping a scoop of ice cream onto her third piece of cake.

"I know." I whisper, still not believing it myself. Unlike the other party-goers, only Nikki and Tanner know that this wasn't normal behavior for my dad.

"I wish my dad was more like yours," said Stephanie, twirling a strand of her curly red hair in her fingers. "Because your dad's the best."

I catch a glimpse from the side of the house of my father emerging from the garage in his standard uniform of suit and tie, but before he gets into the awaiting Town Car, he turns and our eyes meet. He waves and blows me a kiss. I catch it in the air and press it onto my cheek. He flashes me one last smile and wave before ducking into the car.

"Yeah. My dad's the best," I agree. And on that day, in that moment, for the first time in my life, I'd meant it.

"Ramie, wake up. Wake up!" I opened my eyes, but only one cooperated. The other was swollen shut. And although my head was still spinning, my vision finally focused in on my father, who was kneeling over me. I tried to lift my arms, but they wouldn't separate. I gazed down to find them bound together in a weave of elaborate knots.

"Dad?" I asked, still thinking I might be caught up in my memory. But as a drop of sweat beaded from his forehead and dripped onto my arm, I knew it was really him.

"Who the hell did this to you, Ramie?" My father asked with genuine concern in his voice. He jostled my wrists around, trying to untie the impossible looking binding.

I opened my mouth to speak again but my tongue felt heavy

in my mouth, dry and thick. All I could manage was a few groans and grunts. "It's going to be okay. I'm going to get you help."

I needed to warn him. To tell him about Nadine. "Tanner," I croaked. "Tanner."

"Where is Tanner?" my father asked still pulling at the ropes. "He is the one who told me to come out here. He texted me, said there had been some sort of accident. I borrowed my secretary's car and raced over here. And where is Samuel?" I was brought fully back into the present at the mention of my son's name. I sat up and the room spun. "Dad, go find Sammy. Please. Don't bother with me. Just go find my son!" I plead. My words coming out garbled but understandable.

My father gave up on the knots at my wrists and snaked his arm around my shoulders. He lifted me up off the floor. It wasn't until I was upright that I realized we were in the house-boat. "Dad, Sammy...because Tanner...Nadine," I started again, but the series of names in no way formed the warning I was trying to relay.

"What happened to Nadine?" my father asked still working at the ropes.

"She's dead. Tanner—"

"What about me, Ray?" Tanner asked, entering through a large rusted hole in the side of the boat. In his hand was a shiny silver pistol with a long wide barrel and a black handle. "Are you talking about that slut Nadine?"

It was aimed at us.

"What did you do?" my father asked, sounding horrified. His face paled.

"Turns out that bitch was keeping an eye out on your daugh-ter for the fucking pedophile she is so obsessed with." Tanner clucked his tongue. "Nothing to worry about now. Bitch got what was coming to her."

"Son, you don't have to do this—" my father started.

Tanner laughed. "Son?" He waved the gun from side to side. "Ray doesn't want me to be your son anymore."

"Watch your mouth, boy, and lower that pistol. Ray's hurt. I'm taking her to the hospital. You and I can talk when we get back," my father argued, his southern accent coming out in full force, which made me realize that in public he took great steps to hide it, but now, not concerned about preplanned speeches or impressing constituents, his drawl was much heavier and thicker than I remembered. He hadn't lost his accent, he'd just been hiding it. "Step aside, Tanner." My father took a step toward the door and I limped beside him. Tanner aimed his gun at the ceiling above our heads and fired off a shot which tore a skylight sized hole in the roof that rattled the houseboat, echoing in the small space, sending rust raining down around us.

Tanner again took aim at us. "The only thing you're going to do is set her down or you can watch as I kill her first."

My father didn't budge. Instead he pulled me in closer to his side, my head resting on the shoulder of his suit jacket. "There is no need to do this," my father started, his accent filtering out of his voice. His cool and calm political persona taking over. "You have a lot going on for you and a bright future ahead of you. You don't want to throw it all away just because my daughter broke your heart."

"No, not just because she broke my heart, because she's been toying with it since we were fucking kids!" Tanner took a few more steps into the room. He was in the kitchen area and we were facing him with our backs to the sliding glass door. "But she hasn't left me. Not yet. I got to her just in time." Tanner cocked the gun. "Now put her the fuck down, Senator. I won't be repeating myself again." Reluctantly, my father loosened his grip around me and gently set me back onto the floor. "Good, now step aside." My father looked down at me and with a pained expression on his usually unreadable face. He took two steps to the side and raised his hands in the air.

"I can help you, Tanner," the senator offered. "Just like when you were sick and I got you help. I can do that for you again," he said calmly. "I can help you."

Every movement of Tanner's was jittery. With sweat pouring off his forehead, his white Polo shirt was wet and yellowed at the armpits. "You wanna help me? You can get the fuck out of my way," Tanner screamed. "All I need is her!" He pointed his gun toward me and then back to my father.

"How do you want me to do that?" the senator asked.

*A good negotiator asks more questions than he gives answers to...*I remembered my father always saying.

Tanner laughed and licked his bottom lip. Sucking it into his mouth he bit down on it and scrunched up his nose.

"You can fucking die."

Chapter Thirty

KING

T HE FIRST THING I heard was a whimper. A small mewing coming from somewhere in the houseboat.

Pup.

I scanned the room, but I didn't see her, my eyes instead landing on the senator, who was standing between the kitchen and the main room with his back toward me.

I cracked my knuckles. "Where the fuck is she?"

My answer was the resounding explosion of a gunshot that tore through the senator's chest. His back exploded. Pieces of his suit along with flesh and blood splattered warm and wet against my clothes and skin. The senator fell backward onto the floor, his eyes rolled upward into his head as he gurgled and strained to breathe. Blood pooled in his mouth and spilled down the side his cheek.

What the fuck?

I looked up from the dying senator at my feet, to where the shot had come from. Standing in the kitchen—gun now aimed at me—was Tanner. The senator's gold watch on his wrist. "You?"

"You looking at this?" Tanner asked, holding up his wrist and gesturing to the watch. "Nice, right? The senator gave it to me last night after the party. A wedding gift for his new son-in-law." Redness crept from his neck to his face. His eyes darted back to me and he pushed out the gun as he spoke. "But I guess it wasn't as good as the gift you gave, Ray," he spat.

"Where the fuck is she?" I roared. I took a step toward him and he cocked the gun, stopping me in my tracks. "Tell me where she is now and I promise that when I kill you, I'll make it quick."

"Sit fucking down and cuff yourself to the chair, and maybe I'll tell you where she is." He gestured to the single wooden chair in the center of the room.

"Fuck you."

"Let me rephrase. Sit in that fucking chair and cuff yourself to it or I'll shoot her just like I did her daddy. Only I think I'll aim for her fucking head, seeing as that's where all the trouble seems to be coming from," Tanner said, an evil glint in his eye.

I reluctantly did as he asked and sat on the chair. He tossed me a pair of cuffs. "To the chair. Behind your back." I cuffed one hand and then the other, looping the chain through the back of the chair. Tanner circled around me and tightened the cuffs. "You know, I'm kind of glad the asshole I hired to kill you couldn't do the fucking job I paid him to do, because how does the saying go? You want something done right—you have to kill it yourself."

"What's your fucking play here?" I asked.

"This isn't a fucking game, asshole. This is my life. A life that you are trying to take from me. You didn't think I was just going to step aside and let that happen now, did you? She's supposed to be my wife."

"No she fucking isn't," I said, clicking the cuffs in place. It took all the self-control I didn't know I had not to destroy the kid with my bare hands.

"Yes, she fucking is! We said vows goddamn it!" Tanner stomped his foot on the floor and his face turned bright red. "I have her father's fucking blessing!"

He looked around my chair to the senator who lay lifeless on the floor. "Or…should I say, had." Tanner smiled his toothpaste ad manic smile. His eyes were blood shot and rimmed in red.

I pulled on the cuffs, itching to damage him in any way I could but they didn't budge.

"Listen, you fucking amateur, there ain't no way you're getting out of this without feeling blowback from someone. Even if you kill me and her, you don't get out of this clean."

"Me? I'm not getting away with anything. I'm just the son-in-law. I was just as shocked as everyone else to hear about the senator's murder." He exaggerated his surprise with his hand over his mouth. "But I was also so glad to hear that the man who killed him, Brantley King, the criminal with a rap sheet longer than a football field, was also found dead."

"Clever," I said sarcastically.

"Shut your fucking mouth!" he spat, shaking the gun at me.

"Where the fuck is she?" I asked, again.

His smiled returned. Tanner walked over to the closet and opened the door. Out tumbled a mess of white-blonde hair streaked in red. She was tied to a small white patio chair. She crashed onto the floor with a hollow thud. My heart seized when I didn't see her move, but started back up again when a few strands of her hair that had fallen into her face were pushed away when she exhaled.

She was alive.

And so was my resolve to kill this motherfucker.

"If you somehow come out of this alive, I assure you, you won't be that way for long. I may be alone now, but there are people out there. They know where I am," I warned.

"Yes, but who do they think you are meeting?" Tanner laughed. "They think you're meeting the senator, right? So, when I crawl out of here they'll easily believe what I tell them to believe, because it's what YOU had believed. You barged in here. Had a fight with the senator. Guns were fired. People died. That's all she wrote."

He leaned down and pushed the hair out of her face, kissing her on the lips. She stirred and my heart leapt. It was killing me that I couldn't help her. I wanted to carry her out of there and put a bullet in this kid's brain. "What's going...?" she started to ask. Her eyes opened and landed on Tanner. She jumped like she'd been doused with ice water, but bound to her own chair, both legs and wrists, she couldn't get more than an inch or two as she tried desperately to scoot across the floor and away from Tanner. He picked up her overturned chair and set her a few feet in front of me so she was facing me. She was close enough to where if I reached out to her, I could put a hand on her leg. If I had use of my arms.

"*Ssshhhhh* darling," Tanner said, running the barrel of his gun down her cheek. "I'm here. Your husband is here. Everything is going to be okay, now."

"Tanner. No. I have to go. I have to go get..." She stumbled over her words, clearly confused from whatever damage Tanner had inflicted. Tanner grabbed her chin and forced her head up.

"This who you're looking for, dear?" he asked, rubbing his nose against her cheek.

Doe's eyes seemed to finally focus, and when they did and they landed on me, her eyes widened in surprise and she gasped. She struggled against her restraints but it was useless. Surprisingly, Tanner released her bindings.

"Kneel," he hissed.

"Please. Don't do this. Let's talk okay? You and me. Let him go. He has nothing to do with this anyway and we'll go for a walk like we used to do and talk."

"The time for talking is over. I am so fucking tired of all the fucking talking!" he screamed in her face. "KNEEL!" he ordered again. This time she complied, looking straight out at me.

I'm sorry, she mouthed to me.

I wish I could tell her this wasn't her fault. This was my fault. It all was. But I was so fucking tired of blaming myself for everything that happened. So instead I focused on not losing hope. I focused on what it would feel like to squeeze the last breath from Tanner's lungs.

"Don't fucking touch her," I roared.

"Do you think she really wants a white trash piece of shit like you? She's confused. She doesn't know what she wants. The only reason she was even with you was because she had a brain injury." Tanner's eyes glazed over. "She's my *WIFE*. We're finally going to be the family we were always supposed to be..." Tanner trailed off.

I wanted to keep him talking. If I kept him talking, then maybe I could stop him from hurting her long enough for Bear and Jake to show up. "You really think she's gonna want you now after you've shown her that you're a complete psychopath."

"Marriage is all about forgiveness," Tanner said. Then he scoffed. "And refresh my memory, Mr. King, but didn't you go to prison because you killed your own mother?"

I shrugged. "Cunt deserved it."

Tanner tapped on Pup's head, "Well, this cunt deserves this." He reached down to the hem of her tank top and pulled it up over her head until it was wrapped around her arms like another binding. She wasn't wearing a bra. Her bare breasts were exposed to the night air and to Tanner who blew out a whistle. "Almost forgot what great tits you have, wife. It's been so long."

I pulled at the cuffs. They dug into the skin on my wrists until I felt the trickle of warm blood drip from my wounds, down my fingers, and onto the floor.

Tanner rounded Doe and knelt behind her, fumbling with something on the floor I couldn't see. "Now this..." he said, tapping on her tattoo. There was a hissing sound. Like gas being released from a balloon. He lifted what he'd been messing with. A mini blowtorch. "This has got to go." He pressed the flame to her skin. I pulled harder at the cuffs.

The smell of burning flesh filled the air.

And so did her strangled screams.

He might as well have been burning my own fucking skin, because I felt her pain in every muscle of my body. The hurt I felt for her was more hurt than I'd ever felt for myself.

She wasn't just mine.

She was a part of me.

"Does that make you feel like a man, motherfucker?" I shouted above Doe whose screams stopped abruptly. Her eyes rolled back in her head. Tanner turned off the torch and she slumped back on the chair, twitching as if she'd just been electrocuted. Smoke rose off of her burnt skin.

He yanked on her hair and her head fell backwards. Her eyes and lips were partially opened, devoid of the life that was in them just yesterday. Her cheeks were covered in dried blood, and fresh dripping red. He released her hair and her chin fell lifelessly onto her chest. "See? She's just being punished. That's what happens to bad girls. They get punished. And Ray here has been a very, very bad girl."

"What's the fucking point of all this?" I asked.

"The fucking point? The fucking point is the same one you were making to me when you were fucking her on the bed where we made our son!" Tanner screamed. "And now you've tainted her! You've ruined what was mine!" Tanner ran his hand down Doe's hair, petting her. "All will be okay though…" He walked over to the kitchen and opened one of the cabinets, producing a rusted fishing knife. "As soon as I resolve one last problem." Tanner ripped her shorts and panties down her legs. He pushed her knees apart, exposing her pussy.

"What the fuck are you doing?" I growled as Tanner knelt down in front of her and held up his knife.

"Oh, you didn't know? Seems my wife here has gone and gotten herself knocked up again!" He looked back at me over his shoulder. "But I'll fix that as soon as I cut your bastard out of her."

Chapter Thirty-One

DOE

BURNING.

Inside and out I was burning up. Sharp unrelenting pain seared through me and even in my state of partial clarity I could feel the flames traveling deeper through layers of skin, muscle, and bone.

It was a scream that brought me back into consciousness. No, a roar. A guttural roar with such strength behind it, it literally dragged me back from the precipice of the unknown. Through the narrow slit in the one eye that wasn't swollen shut, I saw Tanner leaning over me. But just beyond the blond curls, there was King.

He was sitting in a chair with his hands behind his back, just as I'd seen him before Tanner had taken the torch to my back and shoulder, his bright green eyes the darkest I'd ever seen them.

And then he wasn't.

The muscles in his arms and chest tightened, the chords rippling under his tremendous strength. With the roar that had brought me back to life, he pulled his hands apart with such force that the back of the wooden chair shattered into a million pieces.

It was like I was watching him in slow motion. Angry King

was a beautiful thing to behold. And when I'd told Tanner I'd known true fear, this was the fear I'd been talking about.

Tanner was about to meet him too.

Before King was able to take a single step, a bloody hand came up from the floor and reached for King's belt, pulling a small gun from behind his buckle. Tanner's head snapped back to King. He dropped the rusted knife he'd been holding and reached for his gun. He stood, fumbling with it, unprepared for King to be unrestrained.

Unprepared for my father to still be alive.

And armed.

My father raised himself up onto his knees, aimed the small gun, and fired. "No!" Tanner cried out, taking the bullet in his shoulder.

My dad fell back to the ground with a thud.

"Dad!" I yelled as loud as I could, unsure of whether I'd produced any sound.

And then I was sliding, across the floor. "You want her motherfucker? You come and fucking get her," Tanner seethed. Kicking out his knee, he pushed me through the hole in the side of the boat.

And then I was falling backward into the cold water. Searing pain worse than the burn itself exploded in my shoulder. I opened my mouth to scream.

Water filled my mouth and lungs.

So this is what dying feels like, I thought as I drifted further and further away from my body.

I knew I was dead. I knew it because when I opened my eyes, Preppy was staring down at me with the same ridiculous smile that made me want to become his friend all over again. Colorful tattoos covering most of his exposed skin, light purple shirt, bright pink checkered bow tie, and his favorite white suspenders.

He looked like demonic Easter.

"Babe, I know you just got mangled by that motherfucking psycho, 'cause I watched the entire thing. Total bummer I couldn't cut the kid's fucking cock off for you and make him choke on it. But I just have to tell you before I bust...your tits look fucking fantastic in that tank top."

I chuckled. It was so good to hear Preppy's voice again and his never-ending stream of profanity laced words. At that very moment, I couldn't have been more at peace if he were singing church hymns to me.

"I don't even mind all the blood and gore all over you. I kinda like it actually. Very zombie hot chick. Very fucking nice. Reminds me of this hot-ass U-Porn video I saw. Makes little preppy happy and all fucking twitchy and shit."

"I'm dead, aren't I?" I asked groggily, covering my eyes with my forearm from the bright light. And then it hit me. I sat straight up, sending Preppy falling to the floor on his ass. "Oh my God! I'm dead. What about Sammy? King?" I asked frantically.

"Calm your clit," Preppy said, standing up off the floor and rubbing his ass with his hand. "You're not fucking dead. Not yet. But I tell ya babe, if you go first before my motherfucking muscle bound best friend? Me and you are going to finally have that date." *He nodded and flashed me a wink.*

I wasn't dead. I took a deep breath to calm myself.

"And when we get to have that date I am most definitely going to put the motherfucking tip in," Preppy added, flicking me on the shoulder.

I laughed. "I don't think that will sit well with King."

Preppy shrugged. "Fuck him. I don't give a shit. When he meets us up here, he can kill me all over again if he wants." Preppy planted a peck on my cheek. "'Cause you, my friend, are totally fucking worth dying for all over again."

"I miss you Preppy. I miss you so much. All this stuff has happened and you're not there and sometimes it's all just too much…" I wrapped my arms around Preppy and pulled him close. He nuzzled into my neck, his breath warm against my skin.

"Look around. Open your fucking peepers and take a good look at where we are right now." Without letting go of Preppy I did what he instructed and opened my eyes. I was sitting at the dining room table in King's house. Preppy was crouched on the floor in front of me.

"We…we're home," I gasped. Preppy stood from the floor and pulled me up with him.

"Right. We're home. You don't have to miss me because I'm here. Always with you. Looking out for you. Looking out for Boss Man. Fuck, I'll even look out for Bear as long as he does what he promised he'd do if I ever croaked before him, and erase my motherfucking hard drive like a good little biker boy."

"But you're not here. Not really," I said,

"Fuck yeah, I'm here. I'll always be here. You can't make me leave if you got the priest form the exorcist to come remove me. 'Cause I'm one step above demon…I'm Preppy."

"I'm still going to miss you."

"It's okay to miss me. But you've got so much with King, Bear, the kids. You're going to be so fucking busy, you're not going to have time to miss me. But I tell you what; I'll make sure you know I'm around. Can't find where you put your fucking car keys? That's 'cause Ghost Preppy put them in the freezer. Can't find the remote but the channels keep changing? That's because Ghost Preppy can't remember what channel American Ninja Warrior is on." Preppy wiped a tear from my cheek with his thumb.

"I love you Preppy," I said, pulling him in for another hug. "So much."

"I love you too, babe. As much as a motherfucker can love his best friend's girl, in a friendship kind of way, who he also wouldn't mind fucking." Preppy put his hands on my shoulders. *"Time for you to get back to Boss Man,"* he announced. I nodded. *"And babe?"* Preppy asked.

"Yeah?"

"Be good to him. Be good to his heart. He's the best motherfucker I've ever had the privilege of knowing."

"I will. I promise."

"And don't fucking tell him I said that. Kid's already got a big fucking head."

"So what happens now?" I asked.

"Now?" Preppy asked, lifting my hand he spins me around like a ballerina.

"Now, you fucking live."

Chapter Thirty-Two

KING

I RAN OVER to the hole in the boat. Stepping over Tanner, I dove into the water, barely registering the sting of the bullets as they connected with my arm and hip. The water was dark, but shallow. Pup's white hair floated around the surface, the rest of her was submerged under the murky water.

I lifted her up by the shoulders and cradled her against me as I waded over to the shore, kicking through the water as fast as I could. I set her down on the sand, and although the water had washed away most of the blood, the black and purple bruising around her eye and jaw were much more pronounced. Her face was so swollen, I could barely recognize her. I tipped her head back and opened her mouth. Pinching her nose closed I took a deep breath and then covered her mouth with mine, blowing my air into her lungs with all the force I could manage. Instantly water filled my mouth and I released her, turning her head to the side as she coughed out the rest onto the sand. I breathed out a small sigh of relief.

"Kid running away. He our guy?" Jake asked flatly as he came jogging up the beach with Bear by his side.

"Fuck!" Bear shouted when his eyes landed on Pup. "I told you we shouldn't have waited ten minutes. It was ten fucking minutes too long."

I looked to Jake and tipped my chin. "Get the fucking kid," I growled.

Jake's eyes gleamed with something so dark and so brutal that I wouldn't want to ever find myself on the wrong end of that stare. He turned and disappeared through the trees.

I lifted Pup into my arms, trying to be as careful as I could not to touch the wound on her shoulder. She was breathing but still unconscious. "I'll pull the van around," Bear said. "And I know you're busy saving the girl and all, but do you know you've been hit?"

"I don't give a fuck," I said, fully registering that I'd been shot.

And more than once.

Bear ran off and by the time I made it to the front of the house with Doe, Bear was already there with the van. He opened the back door and jumped in as I reluctantly handed Pup over to him and climbed inside, shutting the doors behind me. Bear set Pup across the back seat and I climbed over, wedging myself between the front and back seats so that I was eye level with Pup.

"The boy!" I shouted, remembering Pup's son just as Bear hopped back in the driver's seat. "We need to find him. He's two or three and he's…" I started to describe him when Bear cut me off.

"You mean this guy?" Bear pointed a tattooed finger to the passenger seat where Pup's kid had gotten up onto his knees and peeked his head over the seat. "I don't think anyone's had the stranger danger talk with him. Because rule number one is that you don't jump into strange unmarked vans with the bad guys," he said, throwing the truck in drive.

"Hi Mommy," the boy said. "You sick?" Sammy asked.

"Mommy just had a fall. She just needs some sleep," I said

softly, trying to quell the panic rising in me with each second that my girl was unconscious.

Sammy smiled, revealing his tiny little teeth. "'Kay," he said, before turning around and plopping back down on the seat.

"Seatbelt kid," Bear ordered. Sammy stretched the belt over his lap, but was lifted off the seat when it sprang back. Bear leaned over and inserted the belt into the buckle for him and took off down the road.

Pup stirred, just a small moan, and her one eye fluttered before opening slightly. "Preppy?" she asked in a whisper, glancing up at the rearview mirror.

"No Pup, Preppy's gone," I said.

"Am I dying?" Pup asked.

"You're very much alive," I whispered, pressing my lips to her forehead.

"No, I'm dying," she argued.

"Why do you say that?" I asked.

"'Cause," she pointed out. "I see Preppy…" she trailed off.

"Stay with me, babe. Stay with me," I told her as we pulled up to the hospital. But it was too late. Her eyes rolled back in her head and she slipped back into unconsciousness.

When Bear pulled in under the emergency overpass, he rushed out to open the door for us. He stayed back with Sammy as I ran through the glass doors. A nurse saw us coming and motioned for us to follow her to a room where they placed Pup on a gurney. "Sir, sir are you family?" another nurse came up to ask me as I watched a guy in a white coat cut off Pup's clothes and push an IV needle into her vein. I didn't know how to respond. Of course she was my family, but how the fuck could I make the nurse understand that?

"She's pregnant. I'm the father," I said.

She pointed a gloved finger to a chair in the corner. "Sit," she ordered. She shouted over to the people in scrubs and informed them of Pup's pregnancy, which erupted into a chorus of voices, all shouting special instructions over one another.

When the nurse noticed I was still standing, she placed a hand on my stomach and pushed me toward the chair. I took a few sidesteps toward it, but still wouldn't sit. When the nurse noticed that her white glove was coated in red, she lifted her other hand and pointed to the bloody palms. "Where is this coming from?" she asked, looking more annoyed than concerned.

"Don't matter," I spat. "Just take care of her." I craned my neck around the nurse who then stood up on the tips of her sneakered toes, waving the bloody glove in my face.

I grunted. I didn't care if I died.

As long as she lived.

The nurse snapped off her gloves and then snapped her fingers in front of my eyes. "I suggest you take a seat on the gurney right there, Mr. *King*. You can still see her from there while I look you over and patch you up.

She finally got my attention. "How do you know my name?" I asked leaning a little too close in an effort to make her back the fuck off but it didn't work. The bitch tossed her hair over her shoulder and took a step toward me, trying to intimidate me with all a hundred and ten pounds of pink scrubs.

"How do you know my name?" I repeated.

She rolled her eyes and bent over at the waist. She lifted the hem on one of the legs of her scrubs, revealing a small daisy tattoo on her ankle. "This, you idiot."

I recognized my work right away.

She released the fabric and shook the material back in place.

Behind her, the chaos continued around Pup. They placed a mask over her face and plugged a tube into one of the beeping and blinking machines surrounding the gurney.

"Staring at her isn't going to make it better. We need to fix you up."

I shook my head.

She walked over to the glass wall on the far side of the room, and out of the corner of my eye, I saw her pull a fresh set of gloves out of a dispenser. When she came back up to me, she was pulling the latex over her fingers.

A guy in a white jacket, with matching colored hair, cut Pup's clothes with a pair of scissors. My fists clenched so hard my knuckles were about to pop out of my skin.

The most annoying nurse in the world remained unfazed, refusing to accept that I was ignoring her. "What's her name?" the nurse asked.

"Doe." I said, then I corrected, "Ray, her name is Ray."

"Doe. Ray," she repeated, her eyebrows questioning the name just as much as her voice did. "Is there a ME in there somewhere? Her family big *Sound of Music* fans or something?"

"Or something," I muttered.

"Tell me Mr. King, how the hell do you plan on taking care of Miss. Doe-Ray when she's better, if you're standing here in my O.R., riddled with bullet holes, letting yourself bleed to death all over my white linoleum?" she argued.

The annoying bitch had a point. If Pup came out of this. *When* she came out of this. She was going to need me more than ever. Reluctantly, I backed up and sat on the gurney as the nurse looked me over.

I tried to concentrate on the words I'd just said a few minutes earlier instead of the things they were doing to her that made me want to slam my fist through the fucking wall.

She's pregnant. I'm the father.

I wished right then and there, with everything I had, to any god from any religion that wanted to listen, that both Pup and the baby were going to be okay.

Our baby.

That my girl was going to be okay. I wished that when this was all over, and she was hopefully stable, that I have the strength left to tear Tanner's fucking head off with my bare hands.

You do not fuck with what's mine.

It was a lesson he was going to find out the very fucking hard way.

Chapter Thirty-Three

KING

STABLE.

It was the word I was waiting for before I could finally let out a long held breath. The nurse who'd finally said it left the room. I sat next to Pup, holding her hand. Making promises to her that I'd never thought I'd utter to anyone. I promised her a home, a life, a family. I promised her a safe place for our kid to grow up. I told her how much I loved her and how much she meant to me.

"Grace is here, in the waiting room," Bear said, coming into the room. He was speaking to me but his eyes never left Pup. He stood over her with his hands in his pockets. "She's watching the kid."

My phone vibrated in my pocket. I pulled it out and was about to hit *ignore* until I saw who it was on the other end. I pressed *talk* and held it to my ear. "Got him," Jake said. "Barn out on 86 passed the We Are God billboard." The line went dead.

"Jake?" Bear asked.

I nodded. "Stay here with her in case she wakes up. I'll be back." I kissed Pup on the forehead, and although they'd given her medications to keep her sedated, I hoped she could somehow still hear me when I said, "I love you, baby."

★ ★ ★

BLOW BY BLOW I reigned down my fury upon the sick fuck who dared lay hands on *my* Pup. His pale white skin swelled and ripped open, spraying red from where my fists connected, over and over again until his features morphed into something unrecognizable.

His deceiving all-American boy bullshit good looks were gone.

The motherfucker now looked like the piece of shit monster he was.

This wasn't a controlled rage. Far from it. This was me unleashing the pent up anger and frustration I'd been feeling ever since that bullshit fake cop tried to take me to ground.

I looked down at my hand, coated in the sticky red, and smiled.

I wanted more.

I *needed* more.

"Stop. Please. I beg you," Tanner moaned, revealing bright white teeth coated in even brighter red blood. He rolled his head from side to side, choking on the blood that had pooled in his throat.

"You started this, motherfucker. You can't reign it in now just because you're fucking pissing yourself. This is on you. You lay your filthy fucking hands on my girl, burn her skin, try to fucking kill her, and I'm supposed to show you mercy?" I shook my head. "You don't fuck with what's mine. Unfortunately for you, you're about to learn that lesson the hard way."

I looked up at Jake, who was standing to the side. His eyes were black and intently focused on Tanner. At first I thought he was almost bored, and waiting for me to end the kid and get it over with, but when I looked closer, I realized his expression was not bored at all.

It was lust.

And not for the boy, but for his blood.

"You can't kill me," Tanner said, gasping for breath.

"I believe I can, and I believe…I will." I ran the barrel of my gun down his nose and pushed it into one of his eye sockets, while he squirmed underneath me. "It's been a long time since I've killed anyone for the pure pleasure of it…too long really," I said whimsically.

"You think Ramie is going to stay with you?" the little twat said. "She's a fucking teenager. She doesn't know what she wants. She could leave you tomorrow when she realizes that you're just a pedophile with nothing to offer her. She'll remember soon that she's better than you, and she'll fucking leave."

"That's where you're fucking wrong," I said. "You obviously don't know me very well because her leaving me isn't an option."

"Then you're just as much of a monster as I am. You and I aren't so different after all," he quipped, his pupils as big as his eye sockets.

"That's where you're wrong," I corrected.

"Neither of us are willing to take no for an answer. Doesn't sound much different to me." His breathing became more and more labored, his words took great effort to choke out. Jake was growing restless, passing his gun from his right to left hand over and over again, his focus on Tanner unwavered.

I chuckled and ran my hand over my head. "Well, for starters, tomorrow I'll be breathing…and you won't be."

Jake nodded and tilted Tanner's head, pressing the heel of his hand against his jaw, he cracked the bones in his neck.

Tanner's eyes darted from me to Jake, his strained voice turned to panic. "Ramie would never forgive you if you killed me. I fucked up, I admit. I totally fucked up, but she still wouldn't want me dead. I'm the father of her son for Christ's sake!"

"Wrong again, shows how much you really don't know her. Not only will she forgive me, but she'll thank me when we're home and she's back in my bed where she belongs." I scratched my head with the barrel of my gun and stood up. "But just in case, you're right, I won't kill you." I holstered my gun in the back of my jeans and Tanner breathed out a sigh of relief.

I turned around, knowing full well what was going to happen next. I'd only taken two steps toward the door when I heard the sound of a single gunshot.

"Jake will."

Chapter Thirty-Four

DOE/RAY

ONE MONTH LATER

SPENT TIME with Nikki's parents as soon as I was able. I needed for them to know that Nikki didn't die alone as a junkie seeking a high, but as a friend, protecting her very best friend, until her very last breath.

We laid Nadine to rest near Nikki, and just like at Preppy's funeral, I gave the eulogy for the woman who was more of a mother to me than anyone else. Looking back at all the times Nadine defended my father, all the times she stood by him when his own wife hadn't, I couldn't help but think that maybe the two of them had more than an employee/employer relationship.

My mother hadn't officially split, but when the word traveled to wherever she had secluded herself about Tanner and Nadine and what had happened that night, she'd just never come back.

Nobody cared.

And in the end, when it really counted, my father turned out to be a real father after all.

We were standing in the bathroom and King was yet again replacing the bandages on my back over my burns. Since it had to be done three times a day, he'd become an expert. King had also been doing research on tattooing over scars and visited the artist who had done some of the work for Jake's wife, who had scars all over her body and tattoos covering a lot of them. He had a sketch ready for me, but I wasn't ready to look at it just yet. I still had to shut my eyes when King changed my bandage, not yet able to come to terms with my ruined skin. But when I was healed, both physically and mentally, I knew King would be able to make something beautiful over something so ugly.

I was in rough shape for a couple of weeks, but I was finally starting to feel like myself again and just in time too, because in less than twenty-four hours, we would become full-time parents.

"I took the last of the boxes down to the Goodwill," King said, pressing his lips into my neck.

It would've taken King only a few hours to clear out Preppy's stuff from the house. But he didn't want to just get rid of his things, or push them aside like it was a job that needed to be done. Bear felt the same way, so the two of them spent two days and nights holed up in Preppy's room, going through his stuff, reminiscing about old times, and drinking their way through a case of tequila, getting high, and doing God only knows what with the whatever they may have found stashed in Preppy's room.

It was done, and Preppy's room had all been cleared out. Just in time too. Because it took a lot of adjusting on all of our parts, but with the help of Tanner's parents, who I had to reassure a million times weren't going to be cut out of Sammy's life, he was finally coming to live with us in the morning. I didn't want to rip him away from them suddenly; it wouldn't be good for anyone. Plus, I'd needed time to heal. The last few weeks had been a transition, not just for Sammy, but for all of us. "I'm so happy he's coming home today, especially now that I'm mobile," I said.

"Some other things come to mind that we can do now that you're mobile. Dirty fucking things," King said, giving my waist a squeeze. My stomach fluttered and I'm not sure if it was his words, or the baby. I clasped my hands over his and looked at King's reflection in the mirror. I couldn't help but think about Max and what could've been.

"I see that look, and know what you're thinking, Pup. But you have to stop focusing on the bad shit. We've done enough of that. Max will have a good family who will take care of her and give her everything she could ever want. Yeah, it fucking sucks, and there isn't a second that goes by that I don't want to be in her life, but she's been through enough shit as it is. She doesn't need to spend the next fifteen years in foster care just because I was too fucking selfish to sign off on her having a real life or because I wanted to fight the system some more and not get anywhere. Besides, when she's older, maybe she'll want to meet me. Meet *us*. And that's the day I'll focus on when shit gets heavy in my head," King said.

"Where did I get such an amazing strong man?" I asked.

"You came to his party one night..." King laughed. "Come on, let's go."

"Where are we going?" I asked.

"You'll see," he said, mischief glinting in his eyes.

King led me through the grass. I had to hop over bricks from the fire pit that had met their end in some sort of explosion. A burnt hole in the center of the yard is all that remained. Whenever I asked about it, King would just shrug and tell me that it wasn't his story to tell.

We passed the dilapidated garage, which was falling over more and more every day. King had plans to tear it down and build a new one. A bigger one with a new tattoo shop and apartment for Bear.

If he wanted it.

King led me over to the dock, the place where he'd first shared with me his deepest secrets all those months ago.

Max. His Mom.

It seemed like a million years ago yet was as clear to me as if it happened that morning. "You know, with all the shit that's happened over the last few months, there were a few times I thought I'd never be standing on this dock with you again," King said.

"Just so we're clear, you're not letting me go this time?" I whispered. King spun me around in his arms. I placed the palms of my hands over his hard chest. The warmth of his skin warmed my hand through his shirt.

King shook his head and tipped my chin up with his fist. "Fuck, no." Slowly, he ran the tips of his fingers down my arms from shoulder to elbow. My skin prickling to life with awareness as his feather light touch traveled up and down the sensitive skin. My lower lip quivered in anticipation. My knees trembled. He grabbed my wrist and pressed my hand against his lips. "You and me…" I felt his smile against the palm of my hand. It was like I'd touched an electric fence. Sparks shot through my hand and up my arm, coursing through my chest before settling between my thighs. "We're a forever kind of thing."

"We are?" I asked, unsure why it came out as a question, because it's something I'd known since the second my eyes had locked with his in his tattoo studio. It was something I'd spent far too much time fighting against.

I was done fighting.

My future was with King.

"Fuck yeah we are," he said, nipping at the delicate flesh of my wrist.

If King were to dip his fingers between my legs he would find out very quickly how much he'd effected me with just a few words. One word, actually.

Forever.

"I'm going to do everything to you *but* let you go," he murmured against my ear. "That's just not an option." He pulled back slightly, holding my head in his hands, his thumbs digging into my temples, and pressed his lips against my forehead. "Never again," he added. Tangling his fingers through my hair, he surprised me when he yanked back on it roughly, forcing my head back suddenly. Anyone else might mistake that gesture as him wanting to inflict pain, but when I looked up into his eyes and witnessed the look of pure satisfaction crossing over his face, I knew exactly what he was doing.

He was making sure I was real.

His smile turned straight. His expression serious. King licked his bottom lip, leaving it glistening under the moonlight.

Pure. Primal. Hunger.

In my life I'd been hungry before to the point where I'd felt like I was on the verge of death. Yet in front of this man, the most brilliantly beautiful and perfect creature that's ever occupied the earth, that hunger seemed like a mere stomach growl compared to the starvation I felt for him.

I wanted to lie in bed naked with him and watch movies on a Sunday. I wanted to help him in his tattoo studio, creating art that would change people's lives.

I wanted to raise our children in the house built on stilts.

King's kisses moved to right underneath my right eye, and for a moment we just stayed there, our cheeks pressed together. I didn't realize how much I missed the feel of his stubble against my face. How much I missed having to crane my neck to look up at him. I missed that he could toss me around like a rag doll, while at the same time worshipping me like I was the most precious object in the world to him.

We stayed there, lingering in the feel of one another, existing in one another's space, breathing each other in.

Until it was no longer enough.

Because with us, it never was.

He was real, and right in front of me. I was like an addict who'd not just fallen off the wagon, but leapt off blindly, while it was still in motion. In that moment, I was willing to do just about anything to feed the insatiable hunger that was erupting inside of me, occupying every sense I had. I wanted to touch him, taste him, smell him, drink him in.

I wanted it all.

We weren't starving for one another.

We were fucking ravenous.

We were still kissing when he reached behind him and yanked his shirt off over his head, but he didn't do it fast enough. I needed to see him. I needed to feel his warmth against me. I needed to taste the sweat on his skin on my tongue. When he was free of his shirt he tossed it onto the dock.

King was even less patient. He didn't remove my shirt entirely, just yanked it down to expose my breasts.

That was exactly how I felt.

Exposed.

Being vulnerable in front of King was a risk I was more than willing to take, because it was well worth the reward. His gaze dropped to my breasts. He growled from deep within his throat, looking down at me with both animalistic need and something that I didn't expect from King.

Appreciation.

"I love your fucking tits," King said, dropping to his knees. He wrapped his full lips around the very tip of my nipple, licking ever so slightly. I moaned at the contact, needing more. So much more. King chuckled. "I got you, baby," he said. Flattening his tongue, he slid it over my stiffened peak in a long lick that made me want to cry out. And then he did it again, at a pace that was so torturously slow, I'd rather him bite me and draw blood than continue the lazy lapping of his ridiculously talented tongue. "So fucking perfect." He released me just long enough to speak the words against the swell of my breasts before he started back up again on the other breast. This time he started off slow but then increased the speed until he was interchanging licks for light sucking, leaving me almost unable to stand on my own. Sensing my imbalance, King held me upright by my waist. I writhed against him, holding on to the top of his head. His short hair bristled against my palms as he brought me to the edge of oblivion.

And then he stopped.

King was still holding onto my waist, but his attention was elsewhere. His gaze firmly fixed on my belly. Tentatively, he reached up and placed his hand flat against the slight roundness of my stomach. "It's so crazy," he whispered. He traced circles around my belly button, pressing a kiss to the skin right below it, inhaling as he made his way back up to my neck, lifting himself off his knees. There was a certain reverence in his eyes, but that didn't dim the fire, if anything it blazed brighter. Hotter. I was almost overwhelmed by the way he was looking at me so when King took a step toward me, I took a hesitant step back. "You running from me, Pup?" he asked with low ferocity in his voice.

"Maybe I am," I teased, turning and bolting up the dock

back toward the house. King caught up to me and spun me around, the barbarity in his gaze forcing me to retreat again until my back pressed up against the wall. He was being rough, but cautious at the same time, taking great care to make sure the burn on my back stayed out of harm's way. It was then I realized I wasn't backed up against a wall. It was a pillar.

The pillar.

The one where King and I had first had sex. Angry, hot, hate filled, love fueled sex.

"There," King said, "much fucking better."

"Reminiscing, are we?" I asked, biting my bottom lip. King reached around to the back of my neck and tipped my head up to him.

"Maybe," he whispered. "And later, when I'm done with you out here, I want to take you upstairs and reminisce some more. Maybe cuff you to my bed." He traced my lower lip with his, and when I made a move for more contact, he pulled back. "Would you like that, Pup? Do you want me to cuff you up so you can't move? Run my tongue between your legs, make you come so hard it fucking hurts? Or should I use a belt again? Wrap it around your neck so I have you right where I want you." He kissed the corner of my mouth, tasting me, teasing me. Making me wild with lust.

Anyone could have walked by us and I wouldn't have paid them any attention. They could fucking watch for all I cared. All I wanted was for him to touch me in a way that didn't leave me throbbing and trying to press my thighs together for relief.

He ran his tongue behind my ear, sucking the sensitive skin into his mouth. I practically launched myself at him, throwing my hands around his neck in an effort to get closer, but again he denied me what I was seeking. What I needed. "Not yet, Pup."

I was going to strangle the asshole.

"Are you trying to piss me off?" I asked. My chest rising and falling with my impatience. I was going to be the first person in history to ever die from lust.

Female blue balls.

"Maybe. But I remember how hot it was to fuck you when you were angry. Right here against the house. I get so fucking hard every time I think about being inside you that first time, all the while you wanted to claw my fucking eyes out. I wanted to make it all okay between us, but at the same time, I wanted to make you even angrier. Make you burn hotter. You were so fucking pissed off, but so fucking beautiful. You burned so hot it was like your pussy was begging for my cock to punish it. Punish you."

"Yes. Punish me," I whispered. "Please. Punish me."

I was past having any shame and had moved onto begging. And then, if he ever did fuck me, afterward, I was going to drown him in the bay.

King grinded his huge erection against my thigh. "You see what you do to me? Do you feel how badly I want you?" All I could do was nod. I wasn't even sure of what he was asking. At that point, the answer to everything was going to be *YES*. "Don't fucking move," he ordered. Inserting two fingers in the waistband of my shorts, he pulled them down my thighs. On his way back up, he pressed his nose between my legs and inhaled deeply, darting his tongue out for a lick.

"Holy shit. You're fucking dripping." He sucked my clit into his mouth.

"I missed the way you taste, Pup. Fucking sweet and innocent. You taste like more." His words vibrating against my core which was so beyond ready for him to put the monster throbbing against my leg to good use. Instead, he stood back up, forcing me harder against the pillar. He reached between us and between my folds, spreading my wetness, pushing his thick middle finger inside of me.

His finger was barely halfway in, but I was already clenching around him. "Your pussy missed me," King said, his voice rough and strained. The confidence he possessed just moments ago, now an obvious struggle, as he attempted to stay in control.

I dropped my head back against the pillar. He pushed all the way in and hooked his finger slightly. When he began to pump I writhed against his hand.

Each and every time he pulled out it felt just as amazing as when he pushed back inside. He started to pump faster, steady at first, then more erratic. More desperate. More like King's only mission in life was to tear an orgasm from my body.

I was lost in the sensation of the in and out.

The push and pull.

The clench and release.

The throb and pulse.

The fucking mind-blowing amazingness of being able to not only see this man again. But to kiss him. Touch him.

Have his baby.

There was a time not that long ago, when I truly thought I'd never see him again. I certainly never thought he'd be finger fucking me back against the pillar where it had all started.

Where we had started. It was in that very spot where I gave myself to him the first time. And it was in that very spot again where I gave myself to him all over again.

Even though in my heart I'd never really stopped being his.

Sensation started building on top of sensation. Pleasure on top of pleasure. I could no longer tell a push-in from a pull-out.

I was so charged up, I felt like I could power an entire city on the energy humming inside me.

The mounting pleasure became almost too much. I desperately needed some sort of release before I fell apart under the pressure.

"Fuck!" I cried out.

"That's the plan, Pup." King removed his fingers and sucked them into his mouth. "Fuck. My tongue is going to be spending a lot of time getting reacquainted with that beautiful pussy of yours, but right now I need to put my cock inside you."

"Yes," I panted.

King made quick work of his belt and jeans. His cock sprang free of its confinement. Without another beat King wrapped his hand around the thick shaft and pushed the head into my folds, soaking it with my wetness, before pushing inside with a long hard thrust that made us both cry out at the same time.

King gripped the back of my thighs, his fingers pressing roughly into my flesh.

And then he kissed me. Hard.

He kissed me as if it were that very kiss sealing our connection. Our fate. Our lives.

Together.

I was close. So close that I was almost afraid of how hard I was going to come. King's breathing changed from steady against my lips to erratic as he hammered into me hard and fast. My nipples grazed his chest with every thrust. My clit rubbed against the base of his cock.

The man who I was once so fearful of, a man who was capable of so much violence, and yet so much love, was struggling for control.

Because of me.

Because he was fucking me.

Because he wanted me.

Forever.

We're a forever kind of thing.

It was my undoing.

The tension that had been building inside of me tightened to the point of pain before it finally broke, sending every single part of my body into spasm after spasm, rolling over me in brutal waves of blinding white-hot pleasure. I cried out, a strangled sounding moan, holding tightly on to King, who when I started to convulse around his cock, released a moan of his own. I rode out my orgasm, writhing against him until he'd wrung out every last bit of pleasure from my weak body.

He followed me over, thrusting with wild abandon until he exploded inside of me, filling me with warmth.

With love.

With him.

KING RESTED HIS forehead against mine as we tried to catch our breaths, but he didn't put me down. My legs still wrapped around his waist.

Our bodies still one, neither of us in a rush to break the connection we'd waited so long for.

"What do you want to be called now?" he asked out of nowhere. "Doe? Ray?"

"Why does that even matter? Because whatever I choose, you'll just call me Pup anyway."

"True, but we need to know what to put on the form." King said, pressing tender soft kisses all over my lips and face, even the tip of my nose and eye lids.

"What form?" I asked.

"It's upstairs on the counter. Grace picked it up earlier for me. We'll have to go and sign it together, but we can fill it out here. I figured since we're changing your last name, you might as well change the first one at the same time. Save some trouble."

"My last name?" I asked. "What form? What thing?"

"Always with the fucking questions, Pup." King teased with fake annoyance.

"The paper you need to fill out when you get hitched. The fucking...marriage paper." King said dismissively, like we'd talked about it a million times before.

I gasped. "Are you proposing?"

He cocked an eyebrow. "Fuck no."

"But you want me to fill out a marriage form..." I started. "Where we..." I pointed between the two of us. "Would be the ones getting married?" King nodded. "To each other," I added.

He smiled against my skin and nodded again, continuing his assault of soft kisses on my shoulder and down my arm.

"You do realize that proposing is asking someone to marry you, and that very much seems like what you are doing here," I argued. King's cock, still deep inside me, started to twitch back to life, growing and stretching me again, when he brushed his lips over my nipples. His smirk turned downright wicked. His bright eyes danced with mischief.

"We," King said. "You and me, are getting married. Seeing as how I love you, and I know you love me, and we're about to have a couple of kids running around the house. But I'm not asking you anything. Asking would give you the impression that you have a say in this. So no, I'm not proposing." He pulled out of me a little and then pushed back in. I groaned.

"You're insane," I said, moving my hips with his, trying to

bring him in deeper.

It was the most unfair one-sided non-proposal ever.

And I wouldn't have changed a thing.

"So I see we really are back to where we started," I offered as King slammed into me and we both had to pause a second to take in the sensation. I tried not to smile. I tried to pretend to be angry at his marriage demand, but I failed miserably.

I think it was the ear-to-ear smile that gave me away.

"Yeah. We're back to where it all started," King said. He cupped my face in my hands and looked deep into my eyes. "And there's no place in the entire fucking world I'd rather be."

King started to move again but this time was different. Slower. Less urgent. He rolled his hips and my mouth hung open as I drank in every lingering sensation of his slow thrusts. He punctuated each one with a slight twist of his hips until we were both seeing stars again.

King didn't tear his eyes from mine when he made me come for the second time. He didn't look away when he found his release deep inside me either. And as my orgasm began to fade, there was only one thought running through my mind.

I felt free.

With King, I was the me I wanted to be. The me I was supposed to be.

And that girl, belonged to King.

Body and soul.

Chapter Thirty-Five

KING

"**B**EAR IS TEACHING him how to snort blow off strippers," I answered sarcastically when Pup asked me where Sammy was. She playfully punched me in the shoulder. "Ouch," I said, holding on to my arm as if she were actually capable of hurting me

Physically that is.

"Okay, maybe the stripper thing was a slight stretch," I admitted. "But I did leave him with Bear. He's showing him his bike. I just wanted to come inside and make sure you were okay. You've been in here a while."

"I've been in here for two freaking seconds. I was just getting Sammy's sippy cup," she said, pushing me toward the door. "Overprotective much?"

"Me?" I asked. "Never."

Over by the lopsided garage, Bear was holding Sammy up on the seat of his bike. Although he couldn't reach, Sammy still held out his little chubby arms toward the handlebars. "Vroooom Vroooom."

"Hey big man, looking good on that bike," I said, scooping him off the seat and flying him around in the air like he was Superman. He giggled and clapped his hands together. It felt right that he was with us full-time. And according to Pup, it's good for kids to have a routine. Whatever that meant.

I flew Sammy right into his mother's arms and planted a kiss on her lips.

"*Eeeeeewwwww,*" Sammy shouted, wiggling in her arms. We both laughed and turned back to Bear. He lit a cigarette and leaned against his bike.

He took a long drag, blowing the smoke out through his nose. Without his cut, wearing just a black T-shirt. The leather and patches were noticeably absent.

He looked empty.

As empty as the vacant look in his eyes. The scars on his cheeks from the night with Eli were still red and visible through his light beard.

"You really leaving?" I asked after noticing that both his saddle-bags had already been packed.

"Yeah, I got all my shit out of the garage. It's in storage for now."

"I told you that you can stay," I said, repeating what I'd told him several times over the last month. "We can make room, move some shit around. We've always got room for you, brother."

Bear shook his head. "After all the fucking shit that went down with Preppy dying, then the club, then the shit with Eli, and then that crazy fucking kid…" He took another long drag on his cigarette. "I just gotta get away, man. Clear my fucking head. Get some fucking air. Figure out what the fuck my next move is."

I shielded my eyes from the sun. "You planning on coming back?"

Bear shrugged. "Don't know that answer just yet." He stubbed out his cigarette and straddled his bike. He started up the engine and it roared to life.

With a single sad salute, Bear took off down the driveway. A cloud of loose sand billowed up behind his bike, following him down the road.

"Bye bye!" Sammy shouted, jumping up and down, waving frantically long after Bear had disappeared.

"I hope he finds what he's looking for," Pup said as she came to stand beside me.

"Me too," I said. Bear's shit with his dad and the MC still hadn't been resolved. I hoped that wherever he was going, the time away would help him get his head on straight so he'd be ready to deal with the shit storm that was undoubtedly coming his way when he returned.

★   ★   ★

DOE

"Look!" Samuel said, pointing to where a beige Lexus with dark tinted windows was coming up the drive.

"Who the fuck is that?" King asked.

I picked up Samuel and shrugged. "No clue." But then I remembered that it looked very much like my mother's Lexus, the one I'd tried to take the night I ran to the MC.

The car pulled to a stop and King protectively stepped out in front of me and Sammy, his body instantly going tight. When the door opened and the driver stepped out, I let out a breath I didn't know I was holding.

It was my father.

"I thought you were still in the hospital," I said, taking a step forward. My father didn't come any closer. He stayed by the car, with the door still open, the car still running, leaning against the frame of the window.

"I signed myself out a few days ago. Tired of nurses trying to wipe my ass when I'm perfectly capable of doing it on my own," he said with a short laugh that made him cough and then wince in pain.

It was the first time in years I'd seen my dad wearing anything other than a suit. He looked older without having it to hide behind. His plain white collared shirt and light denim jeans made him look like any other dad.

"I wanted to come here and say I'm sorry," My dad said, his words directed above my head to King who was standing close behind me. King folded his arms over his chest. After my father tried to rescue me from Tanner, I knew that King wasn't gunning for him like before. He wasn't ever going to like him or trust him, but in time, I think he could work his way up to tolerating him. "To both of you," he said, tears glistening in his eyes. "I let a job I love come before *the* job I love *most*, which was being a father."

I reflected back on my childhood to a time when my father was just a computer programmer who was happy volunteering for the mayor's office, stuffing envelopes on the weekends in our living room. My mother had always been withdrawn, unhappy with the life she chose for herself.

Most of the time it was just dad and me. He folded the flyers and I licked the envelopes. We were an amazing team.

We were happy for a time.

It was only when he started in politics when he started to withdraw from me too, throwing himself into it heart and soul. I made do with being a family of one with the help of my best friends.

Tanner and Nikki.

Looking back on my childhood I still couldn't pinpoint when the switch had been flipped, and the Tanner I knew turned into the monster he became.

Though his poor parents, with the help of a counselor, seem to think it started after his initial leukemia diagnosis. It was common for patients who had come so close to death themselves to develop a sort of morbid curiosity about death. It was also common to develop mood disorders, violent tendencies, and compulsive obsessions.

Tanner developed all those things. To the extreme.

The shock of it all came from how good he was at hiding it.

The leukemia might have been the tipping point, the fork in the road to the land of no return for Tanner, but I knew he'd started abusing Nikki as early as age ten. In hindsight, there were signs. Signs no kid would have ever picked up on.

But that fact didn't change that I did have guilt. So much that it felt like I was carrying a ton of bricks on my back.

Nikki had always been happy and outgoing. She was bossy, confident, and a bit of a tattle-tale. It all changed very slowly. Over the course of eight years, the Nikki I knew slowly slipped away and was replaced by the Nikki who needed drugs to cope with the abuse.

One day Nikki was pointing her finger in Tanner's face, calling him out when he'd obviously cheated in a game of Monopoly by skipping spaces with his little racecar, advancing nine spots instead of the seven he rolled.

The next, Nikki was staring at the board blankly, shrugging her shoulders when I asked her if Tanner was cheating.

And although Tanner turned out to be a monster, I couldn't help but grieve for the boy he used to be. One of my best friends. I still went to his funeral with King by my side. I decided that the Tanner who did all of the horrible things he did, wasn't worth the effort of remembering. And when I thought of my childhood and my best friends, every time evil Tanner started to creep into my mind, I killed him all over again.

When King came back and told me that it was over, it was like a switch had been turned on in my mind, closing off that part of my life. I didn't ask. I didn't want to know. I just wanted to live.

"I don't know about you, but I'm kind of over apologies," I said. My father nodded.

"But I don't think I'll ever be done apologizing," he said, adjusting his glasses.

"Why don't you come in the house? We were about to make some breakfast," I offered. King stiffened by my side and I elbowed him. My father smiled.

"Which brings me to the real reason I'm here," he said, reaching into the car and cutting the engine. He finally shut his door and walked around to the passenger side.

He opened the door. "It's okay, you can come out. You're home now," he said into the car.

Who was he talking to?

And then I had to blink several times to make sure that what was in front of me was really happening. My eyes went wide the second blonde pigtails peeked out from behind the door. When her little Mary-Jane's hit the pavement, my eyes darted to King, and watched as the weight of what was happening came crushing down on him. He dropped to his knees on the gravel, his hands coming up to cover his open mouth.

My father knelt down beside the little girl and pointed to King. "Remember him from the pictures I showed you?" he asked her. The little girl nodded. "And who is that?"

"Daddy." She held the hem of her little white dress in her hands and swayed from side to side.

King let out an audible gasp, tears welled in his eyes.

"Do you want to go give your daddy a hug?" my father asked her. Tentatively the little girl shuffled over to King, looking down at her shoes. When she stopped right in front of King, she looked up.

And she smiled.

"Hi Daddy," she said. King opened his arms and she ran into him, closing her arms around his neck. King's shoulders rose and fell as she buried her head in his neck. He held her tight, his hands on the back of her head.

Looking up at my father in complete disbelief, I found him smiling warmly at Max and King's long awaited reunion.

"Hi, Max. Hi, baby," King said, pulling back so he could get a good look at his little girl, tears on her little red face.

"Why are you crying, princess?" King asked.

"'Cause I happy," she said in between short intakes of breath.

"Me too, baby," he said, pulling her in again for another hug, this time standing up with her in his arms. "Me too."

I hadn't realized I was crying as well until Sammy reached up and wiped a tear off my cheek. "No cry mommy."

"They're happy tears, sweetie. Very happy tears," I told him.

"How?" King asked.

"I called in that favor to the judge. Turns out I could do more than just write a letter of recommendation after all," my father said.

"She's ours?" King asked. I could tell he was waiting for the other shoe to drop. For someone to come and take her or for my father to tell him that this was only a visit.

My father nodded. "You'll have to meet with the counselor,

take some parenting courses, and there will be some home visits. That stuff I couldn't get you out of." He laughed nervously. "But the judge has already signed off. She's all yours."

King stood up and came over to me.

And there we were.

King was holding his daughter in his arms.

I was holding my son in mine.

Our baby growing in my belly.

"Hi," Sammy said to Max.

Max pressed the side of her face into King's chest. "Hiiiii," she sang, between the fingers in her mouth.

"Mommy, are you still making pancakes?" Sammy asked, tugging at the ends of my hair to get my attention. Tears formed in my eyes as I looked around from face to face of my family.

My real family.

The one I was always meant to be with.

I pushed Sammy's hair out of his eyes and planted a kiss on his forehead. I looked over to King who smiled a rare ear to ear smile, his eyes glistening with his own happy tears. King reached out and grabbed my hand.

I gave him a squeeze and smiled.

"Because, Pancakes."

I was finally home.

The End

Epilogue

KING

"I'M GLAD I didn't just kill you the first chance I had. It turns out that keeping you alive has served a greater purpose. So in a way, I'm grateful that you're here right now, still breathing." I leaned over the chair and stared into the motherfucker's black soul.

"You're going to let me go?" Eli asked, his face swollen and bleeding, covered in burns from the fire pit explosion.

"Not a fucking chance, you piece of shit. You're going to die. But not right now and not by my hand. I've got special plans for you."

"Ww-hat are you going to do?" Eli stammered.

"I'm going hand you over to a friend of mine. Who in exchange for a little playtime with you this evening, helped me kill another stupid motherfucker who decided to fuck with the wrong trailer trash." I stood and cracked my knuckles, clearing room for Jake to step up. Eli's eyes went wide.

"I know you!" Eli said. "They call you…The Moordenaar."

"Good," I said, clapping my hands together. "Then you two are already acquainted." I pushed off the wall and headed for the door, leaving Jake staring silently down at Eli, his eyes black, the demon within him ready to do what it does best.

Kill.

"But you just said that I wasn't going to die right now," Eli called frantically to me as I opened the door of the shed.

"You're not," I said. "Jake here has cleared his schedule." I tipped my chin to Jake. "He's got all fucking night."

With miles and miles of nothing but the Everglades in every direction, Jake could make Eli scream as loud as he wanted. Which was exactly what he did because I hadn't walked ten steps before Eli's scream tore through the night. I stopped to light a cigarette and smiled to myself.

I whistled the entire way to my bike.

That night, with my girl tucked in close to me, my hand over her growing belly, Max and Sammy sound asleep in Preppy's old room; I was able to take a very long awaited deep breath.

The sounds of Eli and Tanner begging and screaming for their lives lulled me into a very deep and very happy sleep.

★ ★ ★

DOE

FIVE MONTHS LATER

I WAS SITTING at the kitchen table working on a sketch of a tattoo for one of King's clients, my swollen feet propped up on one of the other chairs, when King came bursting into the kitchen looking frustrated.

"Baby, have you seen my keys? They were on the table and now I can't find them," King said, searching through drawers and cabinets.

I looked up from my sketch. "No, did one of the kids take them?"

"I don't see how they could have, I had them an hour ago

before I dropped them off at Grace's." I rested my hands on my belly, the baby, another little girl, had the hiccups so fierce my stomach jumped every few seconds.

"Did you try—" My thought was interrupted when a burst of sound from the living room caught both our attention. We slowly turned to face the TV, which was changing from channel to channel.

"What the fuck?" King asked. Walking into the living room, he picked up the remote from the side table and started pushing buttons, but the TV kept changing channels at the same pace before finally coming to a stop.

Holy. Fucking. Shit.

American Ninja Warrior.

"Check the freezer," I said.

"Why the fuck—" King started.

"Your keys, they're in the freezer," I said, turning to face King, who looked at me like I was as crazy as I felt. Reluctantly, he walked over to the kitchen and sure enough, he produced his keys from the freezer and dangled them in the air.

"Who the fuck put them in there?" King asked.

"Fuck yeah, I am here. I'll always be here..."

"A friend," I said, wiping a tear from my eye. "My *best* friend."

Bear's story is next

LAWLESS

December 2015

CPSIA information can be obtained at www.ICGtesting.com
Printed in the USA
LVOW10s1628200616

493348LV00002B/364/P